MURDER GETS A LIFE

THE BEELER LARGE PRINT MYSTERY SERIES

Edited by Audrey A. Lesko

Also Available in Beeler Large Print by Anne George

Murder on a Bad Hair Day
Murder on a Girls' Night Out
Murder Makes Waves
Murder Runs in the Family

MURDER GETS A LIFE

A Southern Sisters Mystery

ANNE GEORGE

BEELER LARGE PRINT
Hampton Falls, New Hampshire, 2000

Library of Congress Cataloging-in-Publication Data

George, Anne
  Murder gets a life: a Southern sisters mystery / Anne George
    p. cm—(The Beeler Large Print mystery series)
  ISBN 1-57490-290-3 (alk. paper)
    1. Patricia Anne (Fictitious character)—Fiction. 2. Mary
Alice (Fictitious character)—Fiction 3. Women detectives—
Alabama—Fiction. 4. Sisters—Alabama—Fiction. 5. Alabama—
Fiction. 6. Large type books. I. Title. II. Series.

PS3557.E469 M86 2000
813'.54—dc21   99-058850

Published in Large Print by arrangement with
Avon Books, a division of The Hearst Corporation.

BEELER LARGE PRINT
is published by
Thomas T. Beeler, *Publisher*
Hampton Falls, New Hampshire 03844

Typeset in 16 point Adobe Garamond type.
Printed on acid-free paper, sewn and bound by
Sheridan Books in Chelsea, Michigan.

For the ladies at Lakeshore
who know late fruit is the sweetest

Chapter 1

"BELIEVE ME, PATRICIA ANNE," MY SISTER MARY Alice said, striding into my kitchen and plunking her purse down on the table, "wedding presents aren't going to be any problem. That girl doesn't have even so much as a deviled-egg dish to her name."

"You could give her that one of yours that says *See Rock City*. The one where the eggs are toppling over Ruby Falls."

"Are you crazy? That's an antique. I bought it at the Lookout Mountain gift shop when my senior class went to Washington." Mary Alice pulled out a chair and looked up at me. "What in the world are you doing?"

"What does it look like I'm doing?"

"Breaking your neck."

"That's for sure." I was standing on my kitchen counter painting the cabinets, the problem being that while I am five feet one, the space between the counter and the ceiling is four six, resulting in a Hunchback of Notre Dame stance. I laid my brush across the open can of glossy white enamel, sat down on the counter, and rubbed my stiff shoulders.

"You're too old to do that," Mary Alice said. "You could fall and break your hip. I'm sure you have osteoporosis. You're a prime candidate, you know. Just the other day on *Good Morning America* that lady doctor with the big dimples said if you're skinny, old, and white, watch out."

"I enjoy painting," I said. "Instant gratification. Maybe in five years when I'm as old as you, I'll quit."

Mary Alice narrowed her eyes but decided to let it pass.

1

On her last birthday, she had been sixty-six but had decided to start counting backwards. At last count, she's sixty-four. Big difference. It reminds me of that commercial where they're celebrating Great-grandmama's one-hundredth birthday and one woman whispers cattily to another that Great-grandmama is really a hundred and one.

"As I was saying," she continued, "I don't think that girl's got a pot to pee in."

"I assume 'that girl' is Sunshine Dabbs."

"Well, of course, Mouse. Who else would I be talking about?" Mary Alice got up, opened the refrigerator, and took out a pitcher of tea. "You want some?"

I reached behind me and handed her two glasses.

"She seems very nice, though. Pretty. Sweet."

"Well, of course she is. Ray wouldn't have married her if she weren't."

"I don't want somebody after my baby for his money."

"God forbid a woman should marry for money."

Mary Alice wasn't going to let me get by with this one. "That's tacky, Patricia Anne. I loved them all and you know it!" The "all" she was referring to were her three husbands, all of whom had been twenty-eight years older than she was, incredibly wealthy, each virile enough to impregnate her once and thoughtful enough to die neat deaths, though Roger Crane's demise on a transatlantic flight *had* caused a few problems.

"I know you did," I admitted. Though, as Fred, my husband says, "Money *do* help."

"Then quit being tacky." She put the tea on the table. "Get down off the counter and I'll tell you what I've found out about Sunshine. You got any cookies?"

I slid from the counter and looked in the bread box. "Some of those wafer things."

2

"The ones that have that stuff like lard in the middle? I love the way they coat your tongue."

I handed her the package. "I thought you were on a diet."

"I am. I drank one of those diet milkshakes for lunch. That's why I'm so hungry." She took several cookies and chowed down. "Don't you want one?" I shook my head no. "Lord! Anorexia!"

I didn't bother to answer that. My sister and I are proof of the possibilities that exist in a family's gene pool. Mary Alice is six feet tall, admits to weighing two fifty, and has olive skin. She used to be a brunette, but now that's subject to frequent change. I, on the other hand, am tiny, have fair, freckled skin, and hair that Sister used to call "no color." Now it's mostly gray unless I lose my mind and let Sister talk me into putting something on it which she does occasionally.

"Have you heard from Ray?" I asked.

Sister held up her hand for me to wait a minute, chewed, swallowed, and took a sip of tea before she answered. "Last night. It's true."

"Well, why hadn't he called you sooner? He just let a girl you don't know from Adam's house cat walk right in and announce they're married?"

"He had a group out for a week's dive and I guess it just didn't occur to him that Sunshine would get home that quick. He apologized. I told him it was fine, just startling to have this strange girl show up at my front door saying she was married to my son." Sister bit into another cookie. "He says he'll be home next week."

"Are they going back to Pago Pago?"

"Bora Bora. I have no idea. I hope they'll stay here. They could live in Destin. Don't dive ships go out from Destin?"

I shrugged. Deep-sea diving was not up my alley. When Ray, the youngest of Mary Alice's three children, took off for the South Pacific and bought a dive ship, I was suspicious that his ambition was fueled by the belief that he would be welcomed by exotic, grass-skirted native girls gathered on the beach doing the hula and singing "Happy Talk." But his business venture had been wildly successful. And if the grass-skirted ladies failed to materialize, he hasn't had time to be too disappointed. Young American, Australian, and Japanese women are much into diving. Mary Alice has a whole picture album filled with photos of Captain Ray Crane, a big grin on his face and his arm around a variety of bikini-clad ladies.

And now Sunshine Dabbs from Locust Fork, Alabama, had hooked him.

"Tell me what you've found out about her," I said. "For starters, is that her real name? Sunshine?"

"That's what she said when she showed up on my front steps. Sunshine Dabbs. Ray called her Sunny. Anyway, she's only twenty. So there's eleven years' difference in their ages."

"That's not too bad." I was thinking of my own daughter, Haley, engaged to a man twenty years older.

"No. That's fine. In fact, it's all pretty good." Mary Alice drank some more tea. "Lord, it's hot today!"

"Ninety-five," I agreed. Actually, that's par for the course for Birmingham in August.

"Anyway"—Mary Alice reached for another cookie— "she graduated from Jefferson State Junior College with a degree as a licensed practical nurse and she's supposed to start work at University Hospital in September. But I guess that's changed now, since the wedding."

"What about her family?"

"She's always lived with her grandmother. Her mother

4

travels a lot, some kind of sales job, I think. I don't know about the father. Sunshine just said he's never been there."

"Well, he obviously put in an appearance at one point in time. And if her mother has a good job, what makes you think they don't have a pot? Dive trips to the South Pacific cost a fortune. How did she manage that?"

"Won it on *Wheel of Fortune*. Remember when they were in Atlanta?"

"I'll be damned."

"As for not having a pot, take my word for it, Mouse. You should have seen the car she was driving. Had to roll it down the driveway to make it start." Mary Alice broke open a wafer cookie and licked the filling. "I haven't heard a car backfire like that in a long time. But she's cute as she can be. Little bitty thing. Had her hair back in a French braid. Blonde." Mary Alice put the whole cookie in her mouth and kept talking. "I want y'all to come to supper tomorrow night to meet her. Henry's going to fix the food."

"What time?" I asked. I didn't have to wait to see if Fred had other plans. Henry Lamont, Mary Alice's son-in-law, is the chef at one of Birmingham's most elegant country clubs and my husband is his greatest fan.

"Seven. Or is that too late for Fred?"

"I think he'll be able to make it." I snatched the cookie package from her. "Who all's coming?"

"Henry and Debbie, if she feels like it."

"Bless her heart. I remember what that's like, don't you?"

"Morning sickness? I never had it."

"You did! You stayed upside down in the toilet for months!"

"Well, maybe just a twinge or two." Sister snatched the cookies back and took the last one from the package.

5

"Anyway, I'm delighted that they're pregnant so soon. I wonder if it'll be twins this time. Wouldn't that be something?"

I agreed that it would. Debbie has beautiful two-year-old twins, Fay and May. In her mid-thirties and single, she had heeded her biological clock's tick and visited the University of Alabama sperm bank with spectacular results. Now happily married to Henry Lamont, she's two months pregnant.

"Is she able to work okay?" Debbie is a very successful lawyer.

"Says she has a barf bag. When she pulls it out, the judge calls a quick recess."

"I'll bet he does."

Mary Alice and I grinned at each other. We each have three children, all in their thirties now (Dear God! Sister's Marilyn and Freddie, our oldest, would soon be forty!), but with the exception of my middle child, Alan, who has two teenaged boys, none of the others has been in a hurry to produce grandchildren for us to spoil.

"Is Sunshine's family going to be there tomorrow night?" I asked.

"Not her mother. She's out of town. Meemaw will, though."

"Meemaw?"

"That's what she called her. Her grandmother."

"I'm assuming Meemaw has a name."

Mary Alice frowned. "And I don't know what it is. It was 'Meemaw this' and 'Meemaw that' and I forgot to ask. How do you think I can find out? I hate to introduce her as Meemaw Dabbs. You know? God, I can't believe Ray has done this."

"It wouldn't be Meemaw Dabbs, anyway. Not if she's Sunshine's mother's mother."

6

Mary Alice stirred her tea with her finger. "True."

From outside, I could hear my old Woofer dog barking. It was too hot for him to be getting excited about anything; I needed to go put some ice in his water bowl. But just at that moment, a cloud crossed the sun. A precursor of the usual late afternoon August thunderstorms. I watched Sister stir her tea; my shoulders ached and I was suddenly very sleepy.

"Hey!" she said.

I jumped a mile.

"Locust Fork's in Blount County, isn't it?"

"I don't know. Why?"

"Reckon how many people live there?"

"Not many, I wouldn't think."

"I'll bet I know someone who knows Meemaw's name."

"Who?"

"Sheriff Reuse. I'll bet that martinet knows everybody's dog's name and if they've had their rabies shots."

"Call him," I said. "He'll be thrilled to hear from you." My sister and Sheriff Reuse had met the year before when she had gotten a wild hair and bought a country-western bar named the Skoot 'n' Boot. Nothing but trouble. Suffice it to say she and Sheriff Reuse were not soul mates.

"You're being sarcastic, but I bet he'll be happy to hear from me. That man leads a boring life, Patricia Anne."

"Hmmm." What could I say?

"Where's your phone book?"

I located it under the newspaper that was spread on the kitchen counter and followed her into the den. This I wanted to hear.

I got the one-sided version, of course, but it went something like this:

Mary Alice (butter-melting voice): "Sheriff Reuse? How *are* you? It's so nice to hear your voice. This is Mary Alice

7

Crane." (Pause. Voice still sweet.) "No, everything's fine. No, I haven't invested in any more property up there. I know, though I really don't feel responsible for what happened."

(Long pause. Voice not as sweet.) "What I need to know is if you know a family in Locust Fork by the name of Dabbs." (Pause.) "No, I am not buying their property, I assure you." (Nod.) "Sunshine Dabbs is the child's name. Well, it's Sunshine Crane now. She and my son Ray just got married in Bora Bora." (Pause.) "Bora Bora in the South Pacific." (Another nod.) "Yes. And what I need to know is the grandmother's name. All I know is 'Meemaw' and I'm having a dinner party tomorrow night and it would be embarrassing to have to introduce my new daughter-in-law's grandmother and not know her name." (Pause.) "Yes, my son married Sunshine Dabbs. The dinner is tomorrow night. Of course Meemaw is invited." (Disgusted look at me. Holds the phone away from her ear.) "He's laughing."

"Sheriff Reuse doesn't laugh."

"Well, he's putting on a damn good imitation." She handed the phone to me. The sheriff was either laughing, crying, or choking to death.

"Sheriff Reuse?" I asked. "This is Patricia Anne Hollowell. Is something wrong?"

"Turkett," he gasped finally.

"What?"

"Turkett. Her name is Turkett."

"Like little turkey? Turkett?"

"There *is* a God." The gargling sounds started again and the line went dead.

Mary Alice and I looked at each other.

"What on God's earth do you suppose that was about?" she asked.

8

"I have no idea. He said there was a God and hung up. Oh, and he said her name was Turkett."

"What Turkett?"

"I don't know. He was laughing too hard." I held out the phone. "You want to call him back?"

"Turkett?"

"Like little turkey. And then he said there was a God and hung up."

"Meemaw Turkett?"

"Maybe Sunshine will say her name."

Mary Alice put the phone back on the end table. "Shouldn't have called that fool anyway."

"True." I meant it.

She got up. "Y'all come about seven. Okay?"

"I'm looking forward to it," I said truthfully.

Sister started out the back door. "What are y'all having for supper tonight?"

"Lean Cuisines if Fred doesn't stop by Morrison's Cafeteria."

"The paint smell's too loud in here to eat anyway."

"We'll probably take it to the bedroom. Eat in bed."

"You wish."

I was shutting the door when she turned around. "Turkett? You're sure?"

I nodded.

"Reckon why he was laughing so? There's nothing wrong with that name. Not Smith or Jones, but it's a fine name."

I shrugged. Sheriff Reuse's laugh had been disconcerting to say the least.

From the west came the first rumble of thunder. I waved at Mary Alice and shut the door. Meemaw Turkett? I grabbed the paintbrush and climbed back on the counter. Lord!

9

***

"Looks good, sweetie." My husband Fred came in a while later. He stood back and admired the cabinets. "You've done a lot today."

"It does look good, doesn't it? Clean and fresh. What's in the sack?"

"Sweet and sour shrimp. Egg rolls." He put the food on the kitchen table, came over, and patted me on the behind. "Why don't you call it a day? I'll finish this Saturday."

"Sounds like a good idea." I stretched and rubbed my neck. "How did your day go?"

"Great! It's really working out, Patricia Anne." What Fred has done in the last few weeks is consolidate his fabricating business with a larger corporation based in Atlanta. He built his Metal Fab from scratch and loves it. When I retired from teaching, though, he began to realize that he had a whole company resting on his shoulders and that he wasn't free to take small vacations, let alone do any serious traveling. Now, though he is still president of Metal Fab, many of the everyday problems have been lifted from him.

I reached down and kissed the top of his head. And a nice head of hair it is, too, thank you, ma'am, thick and steely-gray on a good-looking sixty-four-year-old guy.

"Why don't you hop down and go get a warm shower before we eat?" he suggested.

"Sounds great."

"I'll even get in the shower with you. Scrub your back."

"Okay. But only if you're up to doing something kinky afterwards."

"Be still, my heart. What do you have in mind?"

"A good rubdown with Ben-Gay."

"Put the paintbrush in the sink, woman."

Chapter 2

FRED WAS DELIGHTED THAT WE WERE GOING TO A dinner that Henry was cooking. On the way over to Mary Alice's the next night, Henry's culinary talents were much on his mind.

"Maybe he's fixed those little pinwheel sandwiches or some of that paté you put on those Norwegian crackers. Lord, that stuff's good."

"Mary Alice still doesn't know Meemaw Turkett's whole name," I said. "She looked 'Turkett' up in the phone book and there were about five of them. One of them was 'M.M.' She said reckon it could be Mee Maw? I told her that was ridiculous."

But Fred, who had laughed like hell when I first told him about Meemaw and Sister's call to Sheriff Reuse, had other things on his mind. "Maybe he's fixed those little chickens with the glaze and the pecan stuffing. That's one of the best things he does. You know?"

"Rock Cornish hens." I was beginning to feel a little testy here. Granted, Henry Lamont is one of the best chefs in the world but, to listen to Fred, you'd think Henry invented the art of cuisine. One look at Fred and you'll see I've done a pretty good job of feeding him for forty years. Okay, so occasionally I get help from the Piggly Wiggly deli or Morrison's Cafeteria, or Stouffer's. So what? I can whip up a mean meal when I have to.

But it was visions of Henry's cooking that were dancing through my husband's head. "He makes it look good, too," he said. "I like the way he puts the green tails on the chickens."

"Doesn't take much talent to stick a piece of parsley up a chicken's butt."

Fred looked over at me, surprised. "What's the matter,

11

honey?"

"Nothing." Am I going to admit I'm a jealous, spiteful person? But Lord! Forty years of slaving over a hot stove deserves some appreciation.

Fortunately, or unfortunately, Fred didn't catch on. He stopped at a light and said he hoped Henry had made those little lemon pies, the tiny ones that were just two bites and had the crust with something special in it so it didn't taste like paper.

Fred was treading on thin ice. Ice that was getting thinner all the time. It just so happens that I make wonderful crust, thanks to Jiffy pie crust mix. And it doesn't taste like paper.

"What did you say the girl's name is?" Fred's sudden veering from the subject of pie crust caught me by surprise. I had to think for a moment.

"Sunshine Dabbs. Crane now."

"I used to have a Dabbs worked for me years ago. Pretty good old fellow. I wonder if he was her father."

I shrugged. We Southerners do this, try to make connections. It's as inborn as the color of our eyes or our hair. Introduce two Southerners and they never lack for something to talk about. And it's not the weather. It's the search for connections. We do love to connect the dots.

"Mary Alice said the girl's parents are separated," I said. "Actually, what she said was the father's never been there, whatever that means."

"Probably wasn't the guy who worked for me then. I don't think he ever missed work."

He was serious. Lord, you had to love this man.

Mary Alice lives in an English Tudor house on the crest of Red Mountain. It's a beautiful old home with a spectacular view of downtown Birmingham. It was built by Will Alec Sullivan's grandfather who was one of the founders of the steel industry in Birmingham. Will Alec was Sister's first husband, the one without a chin. Even Sister admits he was slightly lantern-jawed, a nice euphemism for not having a chin. He was a nice man, though, rich and generous. When he drove his car into their driveway one afternoon, parked, and died, he left Sister not only the house but shares in a steel mill and insurance enough to choke a horse as Fred put it so aptly. He also left Marilyn, Sister's oldest child, who fortunately is not lantern-jawed but a beautiful woman.

The house, which Mary Alice has always wished looked more like Tara, is impressive, especially at night when its location on the crest of the mountain makes it seem to float, bright lights against the sky. This August evening, however, the rays of the setting sun were still glinting off the cream-colored stucco exterior. We parked beside three other vehicles, a Honda Accord which I recognized as our daughter Haley's car, a Bel Air Chevrolet, and Henry's van.

"Are we late?" Fred asked.

I glanced at my watch. "Not unless Sister changed the time and forgot to tell me. Which is possible. She didn't tell me Haley was coming, either."

"Well, long as Henry's here. Come on, honey." As we walked by the Bel Air, Fred gave its fins an admiring pat. "They shouldn't have quit making these old beauties."

That old beauty, I figured, had used a tank of gas to get into town from Locust Fork. I wondered if it was the one Sister said had backfired.

Haley opened the door for us and explained that she was taking Debbie's place, that Debbie couldn't face food, and Aunt Sister had called her, Haley, and said there was an empty place at the table and she could come over if she wanted to.

"What a gracious invitation," I said.

Haley grinned. "I have no pride. Henry's fixing Rock Cornish hens."

Fred rolled his eyes upward. "Thank you, Lord."

"Y'all come on out to the sunroom. Meemaw and Sunshine are already here," Haley said.

"By any chance do you know Meemaw's name?" I asked.

"She said to call her Meemaw. And Mama, that Sunshine is the cutest thing you ever saw. Her name fits her. Ray did himself proud."

"Where's Mary Alice?"

"Talking to Meemaw."

"Connecting the dots?"

"What?"

"Never mind." I walked back to the sunroom.

It's my favorite room in Sister's house. Light and airy, furnished with white wicker, it has windows on three sides. The west windows provide a view of the setting sun as well as of Vulcan, the giant iron statue that sits atop Red Mountain. Sister has a side view of Vulcan and he looks majestic, holding out his torch like a blessing over Birmingham. We in the valley behind him, however, have a different view, a big bare behind. My neighbor, Mitzi Phizer, swears he's anatomically complete under the apron he wears in front, that all the women in her bridge club know this for sure. I can't imagine how. There's not a member of that bridge club, or anybody else for that matter, who would ever have risked a hip to shinny up for a peek at old Vulcan's equipment.

As I walked into the sunroom, Sunshine Dabbs Crane turned from the window where she was admiring the sunset and smiled. Blonde, tanned, dressed in a pink sundress that emphasized her tiny waist, she was a Barbie

14

doll. And on the sofa sat an ancient Cabbage Patch doll talking to Mary Alice.

Mary Alice introduced me to Sunshine and Meemaw Turkett.

"How do you do, Mrs. Turkett," I said to the Cabbage Patch doll.

"Just call me Meemaw."

I glanced at Sister; she gave a slight shrug. Sunshine came across the room on those Barbie legs that reached to her boobs and took my hand. "Mrs. Hollowell—may I call you Aunt Pat? I've heard so much about you that I feel I know you. You and Mother Crane, too."

Mother Crane. I sneaked a glance at Mary Alice who refused to look at me.

"Don't bet on it." Fred had come in behind me. "Over forty years and they still keep me confused."

Mary Alice beamed, "What a nice thing to say, Fred." She introduced him to Sunshine and Meemaw. I wondered if he thought like I did that they had escaped from the local Toys "R" Us.

"Give me your orders for drinks," Mary Alice said. "Where did Haley go?"

"To check on dinner," Fred answered. "Henry will throw her out in a minute."

"He probably will. He brought a boy who works part-time for him at the club to help him, and it doesn't seem to be working out well." A crash from the kitchen underscored this. "Maybe I'd better go check."

But Haley stuck her head in the door. "It's okay. It was an empty tray."

"Well, bring your father a beer and your mother a Coke." So much for orders. Sister turned to Sunshine and Meemaw. "Would either of you like a refill?"

Sunshine shook her head no; Meemaw held out an

empty glass. "Bourbon. One cube of ice."

Haley grinned. "You got it."

"Nice girl," Meemaw said as Haley left. "How old is she?"

I had to stop and think. "She'll be thirty-five in a couple of weeks."

Meemaw patted the sofa beside her and I accepted the invitation. "She's just a couple of years younger than my Kerrigan then," she said.

"Kerrigan?"

"Sunny's mama."

Whump. Age suddenly hit me over the head like a crowbar. Barbie over there could be my granddaughter? Ancient Meemaw had a child who was in her thirties? Lord, the woman must have made the *Guinness Book of World Records* with that birth.

"Of course Kerrigan got an early start. Just like I did."

An early start? I looked at Mary Alice who smiled back benignly.

Haley came in with the drinks; Henry was with her. "Everything's under control in the kitchen," he assured us, passing around a plate of Norwegian crackers and paté. "Your favorites, Fred." Fred grinned and helped himself liberally.

"How's Debbie tonight?" I asked.

"She's fine, Aunt Pat. Really. Just an unsettled stomach."

Having barely survived the nausea of three pregnancies, I was grateful Debbie wasn't there with a weapon when Henry described her stomach as "just unsettled."

"Well, do we have time before dinner to see the video of the wedding?" Mary Alice asked. "I saw it yesterday, but I can't wait to see it again."

"Sure," Henry said. "Dinner won't be ready for about a

half an hour." He put the plate of hors d'oeuvres on the coffee table where Fred could reach it easily.

"It's ready. I'll just turn it on." Mary Alice reached over and punched the Play button on the VCR. We all settled back.

"It's on the beach," Sunshine explained as the tape began to roll.

A low moan and panting sounds from the VCR. Sister looked puzzled. The screen brightened. A woman's face was visible over a man's shoulder as she writhed. "Yes, yes, yes!" she screamed.

"Shit!" Sunshine lunged for the VCR and hit the Off button. "Damn it, Meemaw," she said, jerking the tape out. "You picked up one of Mama's tapes."

"Looked the same," an unperturbed Meemaw said, sipping her bourbon.

"It did not. It said *Wedding* plain as anything on it."

"Guess it's still on the front seat of the car."

Sunshine turned to Mary Alice who for once in her life seemed speechless. "I'm sorry, Mother Crane. I'll just run out to the car and see if it's out there."

Mary Alice nodded.

"I swear," Meemaw said, "that child expects me to keep up with everything."

Haley was suddenly overcome by a fit of coughing and disappeared into the kitchen with Henry right behind her. Fred reached over, got the plate of hors d'oeuvres, and set it on his lap.

"That was my Kerrigan," Meemaw said. "She's a pretty one, isn't she?"

"What?" I asked.

"On the tape. My Kerrigan."

Mary Alice's power of speech was suddenly restored. "The woman on the tape. That was your daughter?"

17

Meemaw nodded yes. "You can see where Sunshine gets her looks, can't you?"

Mary Alice shook her head. "Wait a minute. I don't think I understand."

"Sunshine's mama's a movie star. I'll bet she didn't tell you that."

If someone had taken a picture of us at that moment, they would have caught me with my hand to my heart, Fred with a Norwegian cracker frozen midway to his mouth, and Mary Alice squeezing her cheeks like a Macaulay Culkin lookalike. The picture would be entitled *Family Learns New In-Law Is Porn Star*.

"I do declare," Mary Alice finally managed to say.

"It does boggle the mind. My own child in the movies." Meemaw drained her glass and set it on the coffee table. Fortunately, Sunshine came in at that moment with the right tape.

"Here we go," she said brightly.

"I'll get Haley and Henry. They won't want to miss this." I hopped up and went to the kitchen where those two were stuffing their faces with hors d'oeuvres and still laughing.

"Are we missing anything?" Haley asked.

"You missed the fact that the woman in that movie was Sunshine's mother, Kerrigan."

Both of their mouths fell open. An unpleasant sight, given the paté.

"Get on back to the sunroom. Sunshine's got the wedding tape now."

"Are you kidding?" Henry asked. "That was Sunshine's mother?"

"If I'm lying, I'm dying. Now get in there."

"Is she teasing us?" I heard Henry ask Haley as I left the kitchen.

"Not with her forehead wrinkled up like that."

Sometimes it's better not to overhear things.

"It's on the beach," Sunshine was explaining again as I entered the sunroom. "A friend of Ray's played the wedding march on a ukelele. He wasn't real close, so you'll have to listen."

Haley and Henry came in and sat down and Sunshine turned on the tape. The video camera scanned a beach that looked like a stage setting for *South Pacific*. A few twangy sounds must have been the wedding march, for suddenly three men attired in white suits appeared from behind a palm tree, walked a short distance toward the water, and turned. Long shadows stretching behind them placed the time as late afternoon.

"My baby has a beard," Mary Alice exclaimed.

I looked closely and realized that the heavily bearded man was indeed my nephew Ray.

"The one in the middle is the preacher," Sunshine explained. "The other guy's name is Buck Owens. You know, like the country singer. He works on Ray's boat."

Buck must have weighed three hundred and fifty pounds. I don't know anything about diving, but Buck looked like he might have trouble getting back to the surface.

"Here I come now," Sunshine said. "Those high-heel shoes were terrible to walk in on that sand." The tinkle of the ukelele got a little louder and Bride Barbie appeared beside the palm tree and slowly began her way across the beach toward the men.

"I love your dress," Haley said.

"Thanks. There's a wonderful bridal shop right there on Bora Bora."

"I thought it was Pago Pago," Fred whispered.

"Shhh." I reached for his hand like I always do at

weddings.

Buck Owens stepped out to meet Sunshine and escort her to the minister and Ray.

"Dearly beloved," the minister began.

"Anybody got a Kleenex?" Meemaw asked.

It was a lovely wedding, very traditional in spite of the setting. By the time it was over, Sister had had to pass around a box of Kleenex, but that was fine. The bride was pleased with our reaction.

"I know Ray and I haven't known each other very long, but we really love each other," she said. Which brought on more tears.

"I'm going to go check on dinner," Henry said. He was going to go call Debbie and we all knew it. It had been only a few months since they had repeated those same vows.

"I'll go help," I said.

My sister is the only person I know who can give a dinner party and not lift a finger. Tiffany, the Magic Maid, cleaned up the house and set the table, Henry did the cooking, Haley served the drinks, and here I was, helping out with last-minute details. The boy Henry had hired would do the serving. When I got to the kitchen, though, he was sitting at the counter with his head in his hands.

"Are you all right?" I asked.

"No ma'am," he said, looking up. "Mr. Lamont never told me this party was for Sunny Dabbs or wild horses couldn't have dragged me here." He reached over, got a paper napkin, and held it against his eyes. He had a crew cut which made his ears appear huge and which gave him a vulnerable little-boy look. Crew cuts always get to me, reminding me of my boys when they were children. I was sure that under that napkin were a few zits.

"You're a friend of Sunny's?" Dumb question.

Just then Henry walked in. "Line's busy." He looked at the boy. "Something wrong, Dwayne?" Dumb question.

"I have to go, Mr. Lamont. I didn't know this party was for Sunny and Meemaw."

"That's a problem for you?" Henry asked.

I swear, all the man would have had to do was look at the boy and see that indeed it was a problem.

Dwayne stood, wiped his eyes again, crumpled the paper napkin, and threw it into the trash compactor. "I'm sorry, Mr. Lamont. You can fire me if you want to." And with that, he walked out and quietly shut the kitchen door.

Henry and I looked at each other. "What was that all about?" he asked.

"My guess is that Sunshine's marriage has broken a heart. Is Dwayne a Jefferson State student?"

Henry nodded yes.

"He didn't hear you and Haley laughing about the tape, did he?"

"No. He was in the basement getting the wine. He was back, though, when you came in and said it was Sunshine's mother."

"Oh, Lord." Guilt.

"He'll be okay."

Henry, usually one of my favorite people, was ticking me off tonight. "Let's get dinner on the table," I said.

Henry glanced through the oven window. "Vulcan's Buns need a few more minutes."

Vulcan's Buns. A Birmingham favorite named, of course, for the southern view. Fred was going to think he had died and gone to heaven.

Mary Alice came in. "Everything okay?"

"Dwayne Parker just left," Henry said. "He said he

21

didn't know this party was for Sunshine. Apparently he's a rejected boyfriend."

"There's probably a lot of those." Sister looked into the oven. "Ummm. Vulcan's Buns."

"I'll need a basket for them. Don't you have one of those silver mesh bread baskets? Seems like I've seen one around here."

"I think I do, but I don't know where it is," Sister said.

I left them and went back into the sunroom. I had seen Dwayne's pitiful little pink scalp through his crew cut and it made me mad the way Henry and Sister both were just brushing him off. The boy was hurting. I looked over at Sunshine who was talking to Haley and wondered what kind of swath she had cut through the male hearts of the Birmingham area. She turned and smiled at me. Probably a damn wide one.

Fred was sitting on the sofa beside Meemaw. He motioned for me to come join them.

"Honey," he said, "Meemaw knows this guy named Gabriel who told her we were having Vulcan's Buns for supper. I hope he's right."

"He is."

"He's always right," Meemaw said. "He's my channeler."

"Well, he's a good one," Fred said.

"The best."

My antennae had shot up. "Did you say a channeler? Like a Shirley MacLaine channeler who guides you, maybe, into strange places?"

"Sunny," Meemaw called, "come here and tell these folks about Gabriel."

Sunshine came over, followed by Haley. "What about him?"

"Just who he is."

"He's Meemaw's channeler. If it hadn't been for Gabriel, I wouldn't have tried out for *Wheel of Fortune* and won the trip to Bora Bora."

"A channeler?" Haley asked.

"You know," Sunshine explained. "A guide. Meemaw first met him in . . . when was it, Meemaw? Nineteen eighty?"

Haley gave me an *Are they serious?* look. I shrugged.

"Nineteen eighty," Meemaw agreed. "New Year's Eve, 1980. A friend of mine, Lessie Greenwood, and I were driving home from bingo. Neither one of us had won a dime in spite of Lessie only lacking I-19 for about ten calls on the cover-up game. Anyway, we were going down the cutoff road that used to lead to the old Locust Fork Bridge when a flying saucer blocked the road a couple of hundred yards in front of us. The saucer wasn't in the road, mind you. It was this diamond-shaped thing up in the air with flames shooting out of it onto the road. *Swoosh, swoosh,* like a bellows. And it started going up in the air and then down almost to the ground. Then it started beeping. Loudest beep I ever heard. Lessie started screeching for me to get the hell out of there. Not that it took much urging. I turned that car around on a dime and got out of there. Called Junior Reuse, the sheriff, soon as we got to Lessie's house. Told him it was a flying saucer about the size of a water tower down on the old cutoff road. All he wanted to know was how much we'd had to drink at bingo." Meemaw sighed. "That Junior. Hadn't got a grain of sense."

"Tell them the important part though, Meemaw," Sunshine urged.

"Well, when I got back to the car, I was shaking like a leaf, and I got in and just was sitting there trying to get up the nerve to drive home when this voice said, 'behold, I bring you tidings of great joy.' "

"Gabriel?" Haley asked.

Sunshine laughed. "Meemaw thought she was pregnant. You know. Like the angel telling Mary about Jesus."

Meemaw grinned. "I did. But it was Gabriel. He took me on the spaceship and showed me around. They were all real polite. Looked like E.T., every one of them. Asked my permission to give me a couple of shots that they said would have some side effects sort of like cortisone. You know, like making my face puffy. But that the medicine would make me able to communicate with them whenever I wanted to."

"Where was the ship from?" Haley asked.

Meemaw pointed to the window. "Out there."

"Meemaw can get hold of Gabriel almost any time she wants to," Sunshine said.

"But wasn't 'Behold, I bring you tidings of great joy' what the angel said to the shepherds?" Fred wanted to know.

"That Gabriel's a hoot," Meemaw said.

Just at that moment, Mary Alice appeared at the door. "Supper's ready," she said brightly. "And guess what? Henry's fixed Vulcans Buns."

Now, I'll have to admit that I usually come out on the short end of this sibling business. Sister has a knack for remembering small humiliations like my water breaking in the A & P when Haley was born. But oh, Lord, Gabriel was going to even up a lot of scores. We had barely taken our seats at the table when I informed Sister that Meemaw had been telling us a fascinating story about her channeler named Gabriel.

Sister's eyebrows went up and she leaned forward. "How interesting."

Meemaw went through the whole story again. The

24

flying saucer, Junior Reuse ("I didn't know he was called Junior," Sister interrupted), the voice in the car.

Henry looked at me questioningly. I smiled and widened my eyes.

"And you can get in touch with Gabriel any time?" Sister asked Meemaw.

"Just about it."

"That's fantastic. When you talk to him next time, will you ask him about Bell South? Ask him if the stock's going up. I'm thinking about buying some more."

"I don't think Gabriel does the stock market," Sunshine said. "Does he, Meemaw?"

"Won't hurt to ask," Meemaw said. "Can I have another one of those rolls?"

"Let me stick them in the microwave a minute so the butter will melt," Sister said. On the way by my chair, she managed to get my hair caught in the wire basket. No way I'll ever win.

Chapter 3

ON AUGUST MORNINGS IN ALABAMA, THE SUN COMES up heavily, almost groaning with the effort. The morning newscasts are filled with warnings to drink lots of liquids, be on the lookout for signs of heatstroke, and check on the elderly.

"I'll call and check on you," Fred said, going out the kitchen door. I threw a spoon at him.

I've lived here all my life, long enough to have a great respect for the heat of August and a greater respect for the inventor of air-conditioning. Also long enough to know that the earlier you can do any outside activities, the better off you are. Consequently, I threw on some old khaki shorts and a tee shirt that Haley had given me which has MY MOTHER IS A TRAVEL AGENT FOR GUILT TRIPS on it (she thought it was funny), and went to collect Woofer for his morning walk.

He was curled up in his igloo doghouse, cool and comfortable. I rattled his leash and said, "Walkeeze" like I had seen some famous British dog trainer do on TV. He looked at me as if I were crazy. Didn't I know there was an inversion, whatever that was? That old dogs and people were dropping like flies in the August heat and pollution?

"Out," I said. "We'll make it a short one this morning."

We circled several blocks sedately. Joggers passed us, sweat bouncing from them in little rainbows as their feet hit the pavement. The way I figured it, Woofer and I were going to have to call 911 for at least two or three of them before we got home. But I was wrong, fortunately.

Actually, I had worked up a pretty good sweat myself as we headed toward home. Mitzi Phizer was getting her morning paper and saw us coming.

"You're crazy," she announced.

Woofer collapsed at my feet and agreed with her. I took the paper away from Mitzi and fanned Woofer and me both.

"Keeps the old joints oiled," I said.

"Long as the old heart keeps clicking. Your face is red as a beet."

"I'm going to hop in a cool shower in about two seconds." I handed the paper back to Mitzi.

"What's Ray's wife like?" she asked, taking on the job of fanning Woofer and me.

"Cute. Looks like a Barbie doll. And I swear, Mitzi, her grandmother looks like a Cabbage Patch doll. Round face and squinty eyes." I grinned. "Sunshine kept calling Mary Alice 'Mother Crane'. All I could think of was Mother

26

Goose. I've got a sneaking idea that's going to come to a screeching halt, though. The Mother Crane bit. Every time she said it, Mary Alice's eyes rolled up a little."

Mitzi laughed. "That little Barbie doll's got a hard row to hoe with Mary Alice as her mother-in-law."

"We'll see. Somehow I got the idea that Sunshine Barbie may not be such a pushover. It may be tit for tat."

"Then poor Ray. Keep me posted."

"I will." I managed to get Woofer into a standing position with a lot of sweet talk and shoving.

"Look at that. That poor dog's a hundred and five and out in this heat."

"He's fine," I said. But when I got home, I let him come in the kitchen to drink a big bowl of water. While I went to shower, he stretched out over the air-conditioning vent. I knew it was totally unsanitary; dog dander drifted through the air like snow. But the paint on the cabinets was dry, and I could always mop and dust.

There were two messages on my answering machine, both of which were expected. Debbie wanted me to call her. What did I think of her new sister-in-law? Was Henry teasing her about the porn movie and the channeler? Call her as soon as I could. She had the cell phone in the bathroom with her. The other message, of course, was from Sister. Call her immediately.

The call to Sister would be shorter, so as soon as I got out of the shower, I dialed her number.

"Where have you been?" she asked without any preamble.

"Out walking Woofer."

"You're crazy. It's a hundred and twenty out there today."

"Feels like it," I agreed.

"I'm going to have lunch at the Starlight Cafe. I

thought you might want to go."

"Where's the Starlight Cafe?"

"It's this nice new restaurant in Blount Springs. I'm surprised you haven't heard of it."

I thought for a minute. It didn't take long to figure out why the Starlight Cafe was her restaurant choice. "How far is Blount Springs from Locust Fork?"

"Just a little ways, now that you mention it. We might even come back that way."

"Do I have a choice?"

"No. I'll pick you up a little after eleven."

"The Starlight Cafe?"

"Dress casually."

My next call was to my niece, Debbie Nachman Lamont, one of my favorite people in the world. She hadn't felt like going to work, she said. Richardena, the nanny, had taken Fay and May to Mothers' Day Out at the church, and she, Debbie, was lying on the bathroom floor on a float from the pool. She wasn't sure, but she might have had a couple of near-death experiences.

"But you weren't sick like this with the twins," I said.

"I know. It's Henry's fault."

No way I was going to touch that. Fortunately, she asked about Sunshine, and I got to relate the events of the night before. The porn movie got what I hoped was a chuckle out of Debbie.

"Sunshine's mother?"

"So help me. Her name's Kerrigan. I like the name, don't you?"

"Just talk, Aunt Pat."

So I told her about Gabriel, the channeler. This time I know I got a chuckle.

"You're kidding!"

"So help me. Your mama asked Meemaw to check with

28

him on Southern Bell stock."

"Was she serious?"

"God knows. Probably figured it wouldn't hurt. Sunshine said Gabriel didn't dabble in the stock market."

"Oh, Lord, Aunt Pat. I wish I hadn't missed it."

"There'll be plenty more family fun for you to get in on. Your mama's informed me that she and I are having lunch at the Starlight Cafe in Blount Springs today. Needless to say, it's a hop, skip, and a jump to the Turketts'. Want to lay bets on where we go snooping after lunch?"

"Aunt Pat, I have to hang up."

The phone went dead. Bless her heart. I got a second cup of coffee and settled down at the kitchen table to read the morning paper while I rubbed Woofer with my bare toes. I was relaxed; I was peaceful; I felt kindly toward the whole world. How was I to know this feeling was to be short-lived? Easy. I've been Mary Alice Tate Sullivan Nachman Crane's sister for over sixty years.

❄ ❄ ❄

Lunch was nice. Sister was right; the Starlight Cafe was charming, an old home that had been converted into a tearoom, all wicker and gingham ruffles. We were seated on a porch that had probably once served a family as a sleeping porch. Now glass-enclosed, it afforded a view of a swift creek coursing around boulders and, beyond that, deep woods.

I sank down in a chair and sighed with pleasure. The waitress brought us glasses of sweetened iced tea along with the menus.

"How do you find these places to eat?" I asked Mary Alice.

"If you and Fred would branch out a little beyond Morrison's Cafeteria, you'd find them, too."

I was too relaxed for any adrenaline to surge. "Morrison's has the best egg custard pie in the world."

"That's true," Sister admitted. "Just the right amount of cinnamon."

I sipped my tea and looked at the menu. I was expecting the usual tearoom fare, chicken salad, soup of the day. Instead, the menu claimed the Starlight Cafe served Funky Monkey, Et Tu, Brute, and Pinkies, along with several other unrecognizable dishes.

"What the hell is this?" Sister asked, squinting at the selections listed on a plastic laminated star.

I shrugged; Sister motioned for the waitress.

Blenda (somewhere there had to be a sister named Glenda) came over grinning. "Isn't that menu just the cutest thing?"

"I don't understand it," Sister said.

Blenda giggled. "You're supposed to guess. I'll give you a hint, though. This is what you'd get if you ordered Pinkies." She curved her little finger around.

"Boiled shrimp," I said.

"Right. You've caught right on."

"Et Tu, Brute is Caesar salad." I was getting into this.

"Don't even guess at Funky Monkey," Sister said.

"Oh, it's just chicken salad," Blenda said. "We sort of cut out a bell-pepper monkey and put it on top of it."

"Can I get a turkey sandwich on white and a cup of the soup of the day, whatever it is?" Sister asked.

"It's angel wings today."

"I'll have an Et Tu, Brute," I said quickly.

Blenda grinned. "Back in a minute."

There were a surprising number of people in the restaurant, or so it seemed to me. It was a weekday, and the Starlight Cafe was out in the woods, not a place where you could walk in off the street and order a BLT to go. It made me think we were going to get some good food.

And we did. The angel wing soup turned out to be a chicken noodle made with shell-shaped noodles which could possibly, with a wild flight of imagination, be called angel wings. "Taste it," Mary Alice said. "Just taste it, Mouse. I don't think even Henry can do this good." I did, and motioned for Blenda so I could order a bowl, too.

Everything else was just as good. We ended up with huge slices of chocolate roulage and coffee.

"Lord!" I sighed with satisfaction and pushed my chair back from the table.

"You're not going to the bathroom, are you?" Sister asked.

"Probably. Why?"

"I knew it. You've switched over from anorexia to bulemia."

"I decided it was more fun."

Mary Alice frowned.

"Oh, for God's sake, Sister. Once and for all, I don't have an eating disorder."

"Well, well." We both looked up into Cabbage Patch eyes. "What a surprise. What brings you into this neck of the woods?"

And Mary Alice without the slightest hesitation or look of guilt said, "Well, hey, Meemaw. We've been to see a friend in Rainbow City. We were on our way home, and Patricia Anne said she'd heard of this great place to eat so we thought we'd try it. Are you here for lunch?" Sister pushed out a chair. "Join us. We've had our lunch, but we might try another piece of roulage."

Meemaw shook her head. "I'm just here to get Sunshine some soup. She's feeling a little poorly today, said she's just craving some of the Starlight's chicken soup."

31

"Oh, do you live near here?" said Miss Innocent with a roulage crumb still on her chin.

"Right down the road. Down in what everybody calls the Compound. The Turkett Compound. Why don't y'all let me get the soup and then follow me home? I know Sunshine would love to see you."

Mary Alice smiled. "How thoughtful. We'd love to."

Fifty, even forty years earlier, I would have had the option of leaping across the table and throttling her. The urge was still there, but gravity had done a number on the old bod. The best I could do was a scowl which she, of course, ignored.

❈ ❈ ❈

"What luck, running into Meemaw like that." We were in Sister's Jaguar following Meemaw's old Chevy down the road. "We couldn't have planned it better." Sister turned on her right-turn signal as Meemaw suddenly took a ninety-degree turn into a thicket. "We'd have had trouble finding this place."

"We don't have any business nosing around," I said.

"Don't be ridiculous. Of course we do. And you heard what Meemaw said about Sunshine craving chicken soup. I'll bet she's pregnant. Ray's daddy got me pregnant on our honeymoon." Sister slowed. "Lord, that's not much of a road, is it?" The Chevy seemed to have disappeared like Brer Rabbit into a briar patch. "Oh, well, maybe it gets better."

It didn't. Fortunately, after a few hundred yards, we came into a clearing and Sister stopped abruptly.

Five large house trailers were pulled into a circle.

"The Blount County Indians must be acting up again," I said, the last effort I made at being humorous that day. I looked over at Sister and she was doing the Macaulay Culkin palms-against-cheeks again.

"Oh, Lord, Mouse. The washing machines are in the yard."

"So is everything else," I said. And it was true. The "everything" ranged from tires to old bicycles. Several dogs untangled themselves from various forms of scrap and eyed us silently.

"Are those pit bulls?" Sister asked.

"I don't know; I don't plan to find out. And where did Meemaw go?"

As if in answer to my question, Meemaw stepped from behind one of the trailers and motioned us to come that way. Sister pulled the car up and let the window down.

"You can park right here." Meemaw pointed to a space between two trailers. "This is Kerrigan's place."

"What about the dogs?" I asked.

"There's sticks all around. If they get too close, just act like you're gonna hit them. I don't think they'll bother you, though." She pointed to her right. "This is my trailer. Won't take but a second for you to get over here, but I'll wait right here for you if you're scared of the dogs." She turned toward the trailer and screamed, "Sunshine! We've got company."

The dogs began to howl.

"Do you see any sticks?" Sister whispered.

"Lots of them."

"Lead the way, Meemaw," she said. And then to me, "Marco!"

"Polo!" I shouted as we dived from the car and scrambled up the trailer steps behind Meemaw.

The door slammed behind us and we were safe. We looked at each other, grinning. And that was how we all ended up on the floor. Meemaw stopped dead still and screamed and Sister and I walked right into her and knocked her down.

33

Later on, the sheriff kept asking Mary Alice and me to tell him exactly what things were like as we walked into the trailer, but all either of us could remember was confusion. It was like one of those pileups you see in football. Take one of the players out and see how much he remembers about the field at that particular time.

Neither Sister nor I knew there were four of us on the floor for a couple of minutes. I thought Meemaw was screaming because Sister had fallen on her, a reasonable conclusion. I don't know what Sister thought, but she figured out before I did when Meemaw's scream changed to "Call 911! Call 911!" She was also the one who helped Meemaw to a sitting position and discovered a man at the bottom of the pile. A man with what appeared to be a very large knife sticking out of his chest. A very dead man.

"Call 911, Mouse," Sister said in a calm voice. Then she stretched out on the floor and closed her eyes.

"Sunny!" Meemaw screamed. "Sunshine!"

"Where's the phone?" I asked.

"Kitchen counter. Sunshine! Where are you?"

"Dead man," I managed to say to the woman who answered the emergency call.

"Your name? Address?"

"I'm Patricia Anne Hollowell, and oh, God. I don't know where I am." I turned around to Meemaw. "Where are we?"

"Primrose Lane. Turkett Compound."

I related the information to the operator who then wanted to know if we needed an ambulance.

"Send everything you've got. It's a dead man with a knife in him."

"And the name of the deceased?"

"Meemaw, who's the man?"

"I don't know who the hell he is. But he's got my goddamn good hog-butchering knife sticking out of him."

"She doesn't know who he is, but he's got her goddamn good hog-butchering knife sticking out of him."

"I'll have someone there in a few minutes," the 911 operator said. "Just hang on, Mrs. Hollowell."

"I will, thank you. And you probably ought to tell the rescue people that they'll need sticks for the dogs. I think they're pit bulls."

"Yes ma'am. Sticks for the dogs."

I turned around and surveyed the scene. Sister and the man were both still lying on the floor, but she had moved over against the sofa. Meemaw was sitting next to her.

"My good hog-butchering knife," Meemaw said again. "And who the hell is he, and where is Sunny? Here's her soup. I didn't even spill any."

"I'll put it in the refrigerator," I said. And I walked around the little man in the dark suit with the hog-butchering knife sticking out of his chest, and got the Styrofoam container of soup from Meemaw.

"Sunny!" she screamed. "I know you're here. Answer me, girl, right this minute or I'll beat your butt."

Sister opened her eyes for a second and then closed them again.

Chapter 4

MARY ALICE AND I HAVE ALWAYS REACTED TO traumatic situations differently. She tends to react physically, sometimes fainting dead away which may or may not have happened on this occasion. I, on the other hand, remove myself mentally from the situation. Sister describes my reaction as taking little trips. And I guess I do. After I put the soup in the refrigerator, I sat at a table that folded down from the wall and on which I assumed Meemaw and Sunshine had been playing checkers on a worn board. Some of the checkers were lost, and they had substituted corn and pebbles. I looked away from the sad unfinished game and thought about the white sale Sears was having and how it was a strange time to have a white sale which should be in January. August was the time for back-to-school sales. But maybe kids going off to school needed towels and things.

"Sunshine?" Meemaw called weakly.

I continued my musing. A couple of down pillows would be nice. They cost an arm and a leg, so you have to get them on sale. It would be a nice surprise for Fred, though. And maybe a new bedspread for the middle bedroom. A flowered one?

Sister sat up. "I have to go to the bathroom."

Meemaw pointed toward what I had assumed was a small pantry. "But maybe Sunshine's in there."

"Open the door, Mouse, and see," Sister said. "You're closer."

My vision of Sears' white sale evaporated. There was no way I was going to open that bathroom door. "You open it."

"I swear," Meemaw said, looking around. "I wasn't gone more than fifteen, maybe twenty minutes." She struggled to her feet and opened the bathroom door. "It's empty."

Sister got up and managed to squeeze in. Years of plane travel helped, I'm sure.

"Maybe Sunshine's asleep," Meemaw said, walking back to the bedroom area. Fat chance anyone could have slept through a murder or through our screaming. I held my breath until she turned around and said, "No, she's not here." One dead body in that trailer was one too many.

I forced myself to look down at the man. He was smaller than average with dark hair and olive skin. He was dressed neatly, though warmly for such a hot day, in a gray suit, white dress shirt, and a red-and-gray-striped tie; polished cordovan shoes splayed outward, showing the tops of black silk socks. There was surprisingly little blood on the white shirt. Apparently the hog-butchering knife had gone straight in and was, in effect, sealing the wound. Or—oh, God—was it possible that the knife had gone all the way through the man's body? That he was impaled to the floor?

That thought did me in. Not even Sears' white sale could save me.

"I've got to get out of here right now," I said, heading for the door.

"Grab a stick," Meemaw said.

"Those dogs better not come near me."

"I'm right behind you," Sister said, stepping out of the bathroom, still pulling up her crumpled white linen slacks.

"See if you see Sunny," Meemaw called as we dived for the car. Not a single dog even looked up.

The car was burning-up hot, but Sister and I both had the shakes so bad, it felt good. We huddled on the warm leather of the front seat, our teeth clicking like castanets.

"Who the hell do you suppose he is?" Sister asked.

"No idea."

"And reckon where Sunny is?"

"No idea." I watched Meemaw leave her trailer and walk to Kerrigan's. "Maybe she's in there, in her mother's trailer."

"Dead."

"Of course not. She heard the dead man, whoever he is, coming in whatever vehicle he came in, and she knew what he was up to, and she had time to hide somewhere."

"Do you really think so?"

"Absolutely. Now if we just knew who he is and how he got here and what he was up to, we'd know where Sunshine is." I was babbling, but it seemed to make Mary Alice feel better.

"Are you sure, Mouse?"

"Of course. Sunshine's fine." In a pig's eye. The girl was kidnapped, murdered, or a murderer. Take your pick.

Meemaw came from Kerrigan's trailer and waddled quickly toward us. For just a second, she reminded me of our grandmother Alice. The housedress, I realized. How long since I'd seen anyone wear a printed housedress with a belt to show where the waist is?

Mary Alice let down the window on my side and Meemaw leaned in, panting. "Everything in there's just torn up! I mean everything. They even broke the Elvis magnets on the refrigerator." Meemaw began to cry and held out her hand. Elvis's head had left the building. The white jumpsuit and blue suede shoes remained.

"Kerrigan just loved these."

"Get in, Meemaw," Sister said. "I'll turn on the air-conditioning."

"I want to find Elvis's head for Kerrigan. It can be glued back on."

"We'll find it after the police come," Sister said. "We really shouldn't compromise the crime scene."

I looked at her and she seemed serious. Compromise the crime scene? We had only stepped, fallen, touched, and peed on every inch of Meemaw's trailer.

Meemaw opened the back door and got in, "Oh, Lord." She began to cry in earnest. "Anybody got a Kleenex? Something awful's happened to my Sunshine. I just know it. And that girl's my heart. Always has been."

Mary Alice fished in her purse and handed Meemaw a

tissue. "Sunshine's all right. I'm sure."

Meemaw looked up. "You haven't seen what they did to Kerrigan's trailer."

"But why would someone come in here and do something like that?" I asked.

Meemaw shrugged and blew her nose. For a few minutes we sat quietly, each lost in our own thoughts. Mary Alice started the motor and turned on the air; the dogs looked up.

"Who lives in the other mobile homes, Meemaw?" I asked finally.

Meemaw sniffed and leaned forward. "The one next to Kerrigan's with the Christmas lights around it belongs to Eddie. He's my oldest, works at the chicken plant in Trussville. The one next to that's Howard's. He's the baby. Does something in Atlanta for the city. I'm not sure what, but the Olympics just about wore him out. And then the last one's Pawpaw's. The one next to mine."

Mary Alice, who had been only half listening, looked up in surprise. "Pawpaw? I thought you were a widow."

"A widow? Lord, no, child. Far from it. Pawpaw and I visit each other real frequently. But he likes his privacy. And he's deaf as a post since that accident he had at NASA ages ago when he was working with Wernher von Braun." She began to cry again. "How am I going to tell him that there's a dead man in my trailer and Sunny's gone? He'll have an attack."

I patted Meemaw's hand. "He has heart trouble?"

"No. He just has these attacks."

"What about Eddie and Howard?" Mary Alice asked. "Do they have wives and children?"

"Several. The manufactured homes are the boys' homes away from home, though."

The sound of a siren coming through the briar patch

was a relief. It was also a signal to the dogs to rise up as one, their hackles rigid. Meemaw got out of the car and picked up a stick.

"I'm gonna get you!" she yelled. The dogs slunk back into their somnolent states. "It's Junior Reuse," she said through Mary Alice's window. "Shit!"

We knew what she was talking about. Sheriff Reuse, while very polite and efficient, is one of the most rigid people God ever put on earth.

"I'll bet he's not sweating," Sister said to me. "You want to lay money on it?"

"I'd lose. We heard him laugh the other day, though."

"Probably choked on something."

The sheriff got out of the patrol car and walked toward us. Meemaw met him, and though we couldn't hear what she was saying, the words were accompanied by gestures, one of which appeared to be the insertion of a hog-butchering knife into a man's chest.

The sheriff listened closely and motioned the man who was with him toward Meemaw's trailer. The man, I noticed, picked up a stick. Sheriff Reuse took Meemaw by the arm and led her toward our car. His khaki shirt was starched and dry.

"Good afternoon, Mrs. Crane, Mrs. Hollowell."

"Sheriff Reuse," Sister said coolly. I nodded.

"Mrs. Turkett needs to sit in your car while I go see what's going on."

"What's going on is a murder and a kidnapping. I told you that," Meemaw said. "Sunshine's gone and we need to be looking for her."

"Yes, ma'am. You just wait here in the cool, and I'll go check."

"Asshole," Meemaw said to the sheriff's back. We watched him go up the trailer steps and disappear.

40

"You got that right," Sister agreed. "And he used to date Patricia Anne's daughter. Hard to believe."

Meemaw looked shocked. "Haley? That precious child who was there last night?"

"She just went out with him a couple of times," I explained. "One time was to a policemen's ball."

"Kerrigan loves policemen's balls." Meemaw leaned over the front seat between Mary Alice and me and began to sob. Tears pinged against maroon leather. Mary Alice pointed toward the glove compartment where I found a small packet of Kleenex. I handed the packet to Meemaw, saving a couple of the tissues to mop the seat with. "Everything's going to be all right," I lied.

The young deputy exited Meemaw's trailer, stick in hand, nodded as he passed us, and then got in the police car. Calling for help, I assumed. Or the coroner. Probably both. In a few minutes he went back to the trailer.

"Why aren't they out looking for Sunny?" Meemaw sobbed.

"I'm sure that's what that young man was doing," Mary Alice said. "Putting out an APB on her."

Meemaw looked up. "An APB on Sunshine?"

"An all-points bulletin." Miss Know-it-all dispensing knowledge.

"Good God, what am I doing in this car?" Meemaw groaned.

The question was never answered because just at that second there was a tap on Mary Alice's window. All three of us screamed at the face that peered in.

My first thought was that it was a bear. Mary Alice told me later that she thought the same thing. There's a sizable black bear population still left in rural Alabama. Occasionally they even get confused and end up in a metropolitan area where they have to be tranquilized and

41

returned to the wild.

But this bear, I realized immediately, was wearing a hat, an old brown felt one with a wide brim. I also realized immediately that, in spite of the overabundance of hair follicles, this was Pawpaw Turkett. Meemaw clued me in on that by shouting for Sister to let down her window, that she had to tell her stud muffin what had happened.

The window came down, and the stud muffin leaned into the car and smiled, actually a very sweet smile, at Mary Alice. "Hey, pretty lady," he said. "What's going on?" That's when Meemaw lunged and grabbed him by his beard, nearly breaking Mary Alice's neck in the swiftness of her reaction. At least that's what Mary Alice claimed later.

Now Pawpaw couldn't come in the window, Meemaw couldn't go out of it, and Mary Alice was caught in between. There was a dead man impaled to the floor of a trailer a few yards away and a police car parked behind us with a blue light flashing that looked for all the world like a beacon for a Kmart special.

And all I had done was accept an invitation to lunch.

Enough. I activated the old schoolteacher voice, the one that skims across ice as authoritatively as any Olympian.

"Quit this right now. Meemaw, get out of the car and tell your husband what's happened."

She didn't get out of the car, but she did let go of Pawpaw's beard and sit back, allowing Sister to scoot over toward me.

"Pawpaw," Meemaw shouted, "Sunshine's been kidnapped and there's a murdered man in my trailer."

Pawpaw leaned forward cautiously, rubbing his chin. "What?" Then, to Sheriff Reuse who walked up and touched his shoulder, "Hey, Junior. What are you doing here?"

"Got a problem, Melvin. There's a man in Meemaw's trailer been stabbed."

"Bad?" Pawpaw asked.

"He's stuck to the linoleum," Meemaw said loudly.

The sheriff gave her a hard look. "He's dead, Melvin."

Pawpaw's hands went to his chest. "Oh, my Lord!"

"He's fixing to have an attack," Mary Alice whispered.

The sheriff must have thought so, too. He opened the back car door and had Pawpaw sit down.

"Who is it?" Pawpaw asked, hands still pressed to his chest.

"Deputy Carter thinks it's Chief Joseph, the Mexican guy who chiefs down at Crystal Caverns weekends. You know him?"

"An Indian chief? I don't know any Indian chiefs."

"He's not a real Indian, Melvin. Just dresses up like one and charges people to pose for pictures with their kids."

Pawpaw took off his old felt hat and rubbed the back of his arm across his forehead. A long Willie Nelson braid hung down his back.

"He told you he doesn't know any Indian chief, Junior." Meemaw jerked on Pawpaw's braid. He turned to look at her. "Sunshine's gone, sweetheart. Our Sunshine's been kidnapped."

"Sunshine?" He turned to the sheriff for confirmation. Sheriff Reuse nodded. Still no attack. "Sunshine's gone?"

"She's fine, Melvin. We'll find her."

Pawpaw seemed to think about this a moment, then announced, "I think I'm going to go take a nap now."

"I'll go with him, bless his heart," Meemaw said.

"Good idea," Sheriff Reuse agreed.

"What about us?" Sister asked him.

"You can go home. I'll be in touch." The sheriff headed back toward Meemaw's trailer while the Turketts climbed

43

out of the backseat of the Jaguar.

"Listen here, missy." Meemaw stuck her head in the window. "I saw the way you were coming on to Pawpaw. I don't care whose mother-in-law you are, the Pope's or Jesus Christ's. You just watch your step."

Sister's mouth fell open. "My God! The nerve of that woman!" she said as Meemaw walked away.

Oh, joy! Oh, celestial choirs! I had lived long enough to see Mary Alice Tate Sullivan Nachman Crane meet her match.

"And what fool kind of policing do you call this?" Sister jerked the car into reverse and backed up, narrowly missing the patrol car. "We fall over a dead body, and does the sheriff ask us a single question?" Sister whirled the car around, again almost hitting the sheriff's car. "No. He just says, 'Go on home, ladies. I'll be in touch.'" We headed down the briar patch trail at a clip guaranteed to test the Jaguar's whole suspension system. "I mean, does he think Sunshine's been kidnapped and should I call Ray?"

"Don't know." Like Brer Rabbit, I know when to lay low.

"That's what I'm talking about, Mouse. The man hasn't got walking-around sense. None of those folks back there do."

What happened next snapped me out of the fugue state I was still halfway caught in. We reached the highway, and Mary Alice dutifully almost stopped at the stop sign. She's explained to a lot of cops that that's what keeps her car's transmission flexible. But just as she started to pull onto the highway, a car that seemed to appear from nowhere careened by, missing us by inches.

We both screamed.

"My God! Where did that come from?" Sister finally

said. "Are you okay, Mouse? You're not having an attack, are you?"

I realized that, like Pawpaw, I had my hands against my chest, holding my heart in.

The events of the day were suddenly clear and overwhelming, and this last fright was the straw that broke the camel's back. I began to cry, groping for one of the tissues that I had mopped Meemaw's tears up with.

"Are you okay? Why are you crying?"

"Because we almost got killed."

Sister reached into her purse. "You need some aspirin."

"No, I don't. I'm tired and I just want to go home." To Fred and Woofer and the big pots of red geraniums on the porch.

Sister turned onto the highway and we started back to Birmingham, down Old Highway 31 that parallels a swift creek, curving gently as the creek bed curves. The woods were green and tranquil.

I wiped my eyes. "I wonder if Chief Joseph was married."

"Probably," Mary Alice said. "His clothes matched."

Made sense to me.

Chapter 5

EVERYTHING SLOWS DOWN IN BIRMINGHAM IN August. The streets are almost deserted; children take longer naps. Dogs dig deep holes in backyards and lie in them, grateful for the dark coolness of damp earth.

This was what Woofer had done. When I went out to check on him, he was snuggled in a hole he had dug under the privet hedge that we planted years ago as a screen between us and a new house that was being built behind us. The newlyweds who moved into that house now have grandchildren, and the hedge long ago outgrew our ability to control it.

I leaned down and patted his head. "Don't you want to go get in your igloo doghouse?" He didn't. Wagged his tail. "You want to come in the cool house?" He didn't. A wide yawn.

"We'll go for a walk after while, then, when it gets cooler."

He couldn't have been less interested. I rubbed my thumbs across his forehead toward his ears in a motion he loves. So much gray. Tears sprang to my eyes again. This would not do. I got up, went into the kitchen that still smelled freshly painted, and made Fred a lemon pie for supper with a four-egg-white meringue. The filling was compliments of Jell-O, Jiffy helped with the crust, but by damn, the meringue was mine. And it looked good.

The phone rang while I was beating the eggs, and I didn't bother to answer it. Let the machine get it; I was beginning to feel better.

I took a warm shower with freesia shower gel and put on green and white seersucker shorts and a white shirt. Definitely feeling better. I settled on the den sofa with a big glass of iced tea and listened to my messages.

"*Mama,*" Haley said. "*Call me as soon as you get in. I've got exciting news. Bye.*"

"*Aunt Pat, sorry about hanging up on you. I'm feeling better and would love to hear how today turned out. Bye.*" Well, I'd have to give myself a couple of hours to make that call to Debbie.

"*The Hannah Home truck will be in your neighborhood picking up discards next Wednesday. If you have anything for us, please call.*"

"*Honey, I may be a few minutes late getting home. Love*"

you."

"*Patricia Anne, Betty Sims here. The monthly AAUW reading group meets this Friday at ten o'clock at the Homewood library. Don't forget.*"

My eyes were beginning to get heavy. I had time for a nap. All we were having for supper was turkey sandwiches made from stress-free turkeys raised in the shade of pecan trees. I had seen the package with that advertisement at the Piggly Wiggly and couldn't resist, though it was walking the line of getting a little too chummy with what I was chewing.

"*Mouse, the police found Sunshine's bloody nightgown. I'm calling Ray.*"

Oh, Lord. I dialed Mary Alice's number and after one ring got the answering machine. I knew from experience that this meant the line was busy. "It's me," I said. "Call me back."

No sooner had I hung up than the phone rang, startling me. "Sister?" I said.

"No, Mama, it's me. Wait until you hear my news."

"I've got to hang up, Haley. Something terrible has happened to Sunshine."

"Sunshine? What's happened?"

"Nobody knows, honey. A man was killed in their trailer, and Sunshine's disappeared. But your Aunt Sister just left a message that they'd found her bloody nightgown."

"God, Mama!"

"I'll call you back as soon as I talk to Sister." I hung up and waited for Sister to call. I was grateful that I was not the one having to break the news to Ray and wondered how long it would take him to get home.

The phone rang almost immediately. "I can't talk but a second," Mary Alice said. "I'm waiting for Ray to call."

"Who called about the bloody nightgown?"

"Meemaw. I was surprised. It doesn't sound good, though, Mouse. She said the sheriff's searching the woods around the trailers. Sounds like he thinks he's going to find a body, doesn't it?"

"What can we do?"

"Nothing right now that I know of. I'll call you if I hear anything."

I hung up the phone and forced myself to relax. I tried closing my eyes and saying my mantra. I tried the old imagining-the-penny-on-the-forehead trick. But it did no good. Images of Chief Joseph's body impaled with a hog-butchering knife kept pushing forward.

"Think it's the Mexican guy who chiefs at Crystal Caverns." I could hear Jed Reuse's voice. *"Dresses up like an Indian and has his picture made with kids."*

His picture made with kids. Was it possible? I went to the closet and pulled down our most recent family album which has the pictures from the last five or so years. Fred and I are both terrible about taking pictures, even remembering our camera. And when we do, we forget to take the film to have it developed. We slink into Harco's with rolls of film so old that we feel the necessity to apologize to the clerk. The pictures that manage to survive we stick into albums in the envelopes, swearing that someday we'll arrange them. The only person in the family who is bothered by this is my daughter-in-law, Lisa. Her picture albums are perfect.

So she could have gone right to the pictures that I lucked into finding, pictures of her two sons, Charlie and Sam, taken about five years earlier at Crystal Caverns. Then about six and eight, they stood proudly, one on each side of an Indian chief. There were two other photographs, one of each child standing in front of the

48

chief. Charlie held a drum in his picture, Sam a tomahawk. I remembered those souvenirs had cost us a fortune.

I sat on the sofa and studied the pictures. Was it Chief Joseph? I hadn't gotten a good look at the face of the man on Meernaw's floor. In fact, I had looked at him as little as possible. But he was small and dark like this man who peered straight at the camera, his feathered headdress pushed back just a fraction too far, giving him a slightly cocky look I hadn't noticed when I first saw the pictures. *"Sure,"* he seemed to be saying. *"I'm chiefing. But you're the fools paying me ten bucks."*

I laid the photographs on the coffee table. I didn't want the body I had seen today to be this man who had posed with my grandchildren. Maybe that's why I'm terrible about pictures. When you look back at them, you already know too much about how the story will turn out.

I put the album back in the closet and tried to call Haley. She had sounded excited, and I had cut her off. Her line was busy, though. I couldn't call Debbie. She would know in a second that something was wrong by the tone of my voice. It's one of the things that makes her a good lawyer. So I tried TV. Rosie O'Donnell, one of my favorites, was interviewing Debbie Reynolds, also a favorite. I freshened my iced tea and willed myself to sit back and relax.

Might as well have willed myself to fly. I had to stay busy. Which is why I was in the middle of vacuuming the whole house when Haley arrived. I saw her car pull into the driveway, watched her go pat Woofer who was still curled in his cave. Such a pretty woman, her strawberry-blonde hair gleaming in the late August sun. She had once thought that she would have a long, happy life with her husband, Tom Buchanan. She would have his children, his love. A drunk driver put an end to that dream three years ago. For a long time, Fred and I thought we would never see our daughter happy again. And we know now that we'll never see the Haley we knew before Tom's death. But the lovely, confident woman crossing our backyard had accepted and moved beyond her grief. In fact, she looked radiant. I opened the door and hugged her.

"Any news?" she asked.

"No. Nothing except what I told you." I led the way into the den. "You want a Coke?"

"A beer." Haley got one from the refrigerator and followed me. She pointed to the vacuum cleaner in the middle of the floor. "Your recipe for nerves."

I wound the cord around it and put it in the closet. "Yep."

"Tell me what happened."

So I told the story of the day's events, ending by passing the photographs to Haley.

"Lord!" she said. "You think this was the man?"

"I don't know. Maybe."

"And Meemaw didn't know him?"

"Said she didn't. I believed her."

Haley placed the pictures back on the coffee table. "So she's gone for twenty minutes and when she gets home there's a murdered man she's never seen before in her trailer and her granddaughter's missing."

I shivered. "Or worse."

The phone rang. Haley answered it. "Wait a minute, Aunt Sister. I'll ask her." She turned to me. "What are you having for supper, Mama?"

"What?"

"She wants to know what you're having for supper, Mama."

"Turkey sandwiches and lemon meringue pie. Has she talked to Ray?"

"Turkey sandwiches and lemon meringue pie, Aunt Sister. And have you talked to Ray?" Haley listened for a moment. "Yes, ma'am. I'll tell her. Okay. Bye."

"She's coming over. She says she's starving, and Tiffany, the Magic Maid, brought her some homegrown tomatoes and she'll bring some for the sandwiches. She hasn't talked to Ray, but she's got call forwarding."

"Blood, death, and guts, and that woman wants to eat?"

"It's her reaction to stress, Mama." Haley placed the phone back on the end table. "By the way, Philip and I are getting married Saturday. It's what I came to tell you."

Penney's was having a white sale, too. We could use another light cotton blanket. I wondered how their prices compared to Sears'.

❀ ❀ ❀

"What I can't figure out is why the woman doesn't ask Gabriel where Sunshine is." Mary Alice picked up her second turkey sandwich and took a bite. She, Haley, and I were sitting at the kitchen table eating supper. Fred had called again saying he would be later than he had originally thought. Haley had talked to him and hadn't mentioned Sunshine's disappearance or her own wedding on Saturday. A little job for Mama; Fred would have a fit.

"Did you ask her?" Haley asked.

"I can't remember. Did I, Patricia Anne?"

I shrugged. I sure as hell didn't know.

"I mean, what good is a channeler if he can't do useful things like finding people?" Mary Alice looked at her sandwich. "Didn't I have a turkey sandwich for lunch?"

I looked at my own sandwich. So far I had managed to take one bite. "I don't remember. The waitress's name was Blenda, though."

"Blenda. That's a cute name." Mary Alice turned to Haley. "You're sure you're not pregnant, sweetie?"

Haley grinned. "Not yet, Aunt Sister."

"So the hurry-up wedding really is for convenience?"

If I had said that, Haley would have been on me like a chicken on a June bug. Coming from Sister, it didn't bother her.

"Well, we were going to do it eventually. So when Philip got the invitation to teach a semester at the medical school in Warsaw, we figured it would be a wonderful honeymoon."

I had already said, "But it's so sudden," at least a dozen times. This time I kept quiet; Mary Alice said it.

"I know, Aunt Sister. We'll have a big party when we get back, maybe even have another wedding. But this Saturday, Judge Bennett is going to meet us in his chambers at ten o'clock. Just Philip and me and you and Mama and Papa and Philip's kids if they can make it."

Dr. Philip Nachman's grown kids. I'd known this was coming for several months, but the over twenty-year age difference still bothered me. Not so Mary Alice whose three husbands had all been twenty-eight years her senior. And *so* rich.

"Well, I think it's grand. My niece and nephew getting married." Mary Alice chomped down on her sandwich. "I hope they've found Sunshine by then."

"I hope so, too," Haley agreed. "Maybe Ray will be home by then and they can come to the wedding."

I was eating supper with two absolute dingbats. How much sense did it take to add up a dead body, a missing girl, and a bloody nightgown to realize you were probably going to be minus a wedding guest on Saturday?

"My niece and nephew married. That's nice. I'll bet that doesn't happen often," Sister said.

"Depends on which part of the state you live in." I got up and poured each of us more tea. Actually, Dr. Philip Nachman, an ENT, ear, nose, and throat specialist, was the nephew of Mary Alice's second husband, Philip Nachman. He and Haley had met at their cousin Debbie's wedding where Dr. Philip (the nephew, the uncle having long been dead) had given the bride away. "It's just downright cozy," Mary Alice says. Most people find it confusing.

The phone rang and I answered it.

"Hey, Aunt Pat. Have you met my Sunshine yet?" Ray sounded as if he were in the next room.

"I have, and she's darling. Here's your mother, honey." I handed the phone to Mary Alice quick as a hot potato and walked toward the bedroom. I didn't want to hear this conversation. In a moment, Haley followed me.

"You've had a god-awful day, haven't you, Mama?"

"Pretty bad."

We sat on the bed and looked at each other.

"Maybe you and Papa can come over for Christmas. Wouldn't that be wonderful? I think it snows a lot in Warsaw."

I swallowed hard. "What are you wearing Saturday?"

"My peach linen suit, I think."

She wouldn't make it to the courthouse without it being so wrinkled it'd look like she'd slept in it. But I just nodded. I wondered if Mary Alice was telling Ray everything that had happened or was sparing him some of the details.

"Haley," I said, "I think Sunshine's dead."

"I know," she said.

We were sitting on the bed holding hands when Mary Alice came to the door. "It's a twenty-hour flight," she said. "He'll be here tomorrow." She sat down on the bed beside us. "He sounded upset."

"Did you by any chance mention the bloody nightgown?"

Sister nodded.

"That just might have done it then."

"I guess so." Mary Alice took Haley's other hand. "What are you wearing Saturday?"

"My peach linen suit."

"Well, put it on in the restroom at the courthouse and don't sit down or you'll look all wrinkled in your pictures."

"We hadn't planned on any pictures. Maybe Papa can bring his camera."

"You have to have wedding pictures." Mary Alice patted Haley's hand. "Don't worry. I'll take care of it."

Haley looked up and started to say something, but Mary Alice was on a roll.

"And I think you ought to change the time to noon. That way I could give you a wedding luncheon, maybe at the Tutwiler."

"Ten o'clock was the only time the judge could work us in on Saturday."

"Then we'll make it a champagne breakfast. That'll be nice, too. And you'll have to have a wedding cake. Two tiers so you can freeze the top one."

Haley turned and looked at me. I smiled innocently. I've lived with Sister a lot longer than she has.

"I declare," Sister said, mulling over wedding plans and suddenly remembering something that might interfere. "I hope Sunshine's all right."

So did I. I could hear Meemaw declaring, *"She's my heart. Always has been."* I could only imagine her pain. It made my worry over being separated from Haley for six months seem trivial.

54

Still talking wedding, Mary Alice and Haley left about nine o'clock. They were hardly out of the house when the phone rang. Probably Fred again. Dammit, he shouldn't be working these long hours. The whole point of merging his Metal Fab with a large Atlanta firm had been to make his job easier. I picked up the phone and said hello impatiently.

"Mrs. Crane?" a man asked.

"No, this is Mrs. Hollowell, her sister. She had her phone forwarded here, but she's left."

"Well, you can take the message, Mrs. Hollowell. This is Eddie Turkett, Sunshine's uncle."

I sat down on the sofa, my knees suddenly weak. "Yes, Mr. Turkett. What's happened?"

"Junior Reuse has had to call off the search tonight because it's dark. But he wants to start again in the morning, said to get volunteers. I'm out at the compound with Mama and Papa calling people. Do you think maybe you and Mrs. Crane could come help us?"

"Of course we can. Do you want us to bring some other people?"

"If you can. The sheriff's going to divide the area between here and the river into sections and then organize groups for each section."

"What time?"

"First light and before it gets too hot. Four-thirty?"

"We'll be there." I paused. "Mr. Turkett, how's your mother?"

"Holding up pretty good, everything considered. My sister and brother should be getting in from Atlanta in a little while, and she's baking them a pound cake. I told her to go on to bed, but she won't listen. Says they've got to have a pound cake."

"Let her stay busy if she wants to."

"Guess I don't have a choice."

I was sure he didn't. "We'll see you in the morning, then."

"Okay. And Mrs. Hollowell? If you've got any boots, you might want to wear them."

"Boots?"

"For snakes."

Oh! I said I would definitely wear boots, that we would all wear boots.

After he hung up, I tried to call Mary Alice. She wasn't home yet, and I couldn't remember her car phone number. Damn.

The kitchen door opened and Fred came in, looking mighty chipper for someone who had been at work since seven that morning. "Hi, sweetie," he said, looking into the den where I was sitting with the phone in my hand. "What's happening?"

"You want the good news first or the bad news?"

"The good news."

But I couldn't think of any.

Chapter 6

WE WERE LATE GETTING TO THE TURKETT COMPOUND the next morning. It was all of five o'clock and I had a rip-roaring headache when we turned onto the dirt road that ran through the briar patch.

"You sure this is it?" Fred asked.

"Of course it is." I answered crossly, but Fred didn't seem to notice. He was busy trying to keep the car in the deep ruts formed by years of drivers avoiding briar scratches. A small cloud of red dust hung in the air above the trail; a larger one billowed behind us.

"And Mary Alice drove her Jaguar down here?"

"Very carefully. She kept saying 'shit' a lot." The first rays of the sun popped up over the horizon and hit me in the eye; I cringed.

The whole night had been surreal. First I had had to explain everything to Fred, everything from the chief's body impaled on Meemaws linoleum to Sunshine's disappearance and the bloody nightgown. And then—I don't think you'd call it the icing on the cake—I had to tell him about Haley and Philip Nachman, their imminent wedding and departure for Warsaw.

He sat in his recliner, leaning toward me, listening intently, not interrupting. I related the day's events, beginning with running into Meemaw at the restaurant and ending, I believe, with the two-tier wedding cake, the top tier to be kept in the freezer and to be eaten on anniversaries. I took a deep breath, closed my eyes, and waited for his reaction. Nothing. After almost a minute of silence, I opened my eyes. He was still leaning forward; there was a slightly puzzled look on his face.

"Say what?" he said.

So I had to go through the whole thing again. This time I got the questions such as "What were y'all doing out there in the first place?" which you would have to be pretty dense not to figure out, to "Warsaw? The place where they sell insurance?"

After that, it was downhill all the way, ending with a call from Sister around two-thirty in the morning asking me if I had her big straw hat, the one she had gotten at Kmart for fifty cents last winter. She had been planning on wearing a safari hat, but that might not be enough. And did I have any Deep-Woods Off? God knows we didn't want to come down with Lyme disease and Henry said those woods were crawling with ticks. He was going with her, incidentally, as was Tiffany, the Magic Maid. And someone should bring some food, shouldn't they? Maybe the restaurant up there would deliver, considering it was an emergency.

Fred rolled over. "Mary Alice?"

I nodded. He took the phone from me, said into it, "Go to sleep," hung it up, and then took it from its cradle. "There."

"That was rude."

"I know."

In a few minutes, I could hear him snoring lightly. But I was wide awake. I got up, went to the den, and lay down on the sofa. I read for a while and had just dropped off to sleep when Fred came to tell me it was time to get up.

The dirt road widened and we were at the Turkett Compound.

"Hey, look at those trailers in a circle," Fred said. "That's neat."

"They're manufactured homes," I snapped.

"You need some more coffee, don't you, honey?"

A uniformed man pointed toward a field on the left which had been turned into a makeshift parking lot. At one time it must have been a cotton field. We bounced over the rows, past ten or twelve cars, including Mary Alice's. One of her best traits is her punctuality. If she says she'll be somewhere at a certain time, then by damn, she'll be there. Fred says it's because she's scared she'll miss something. Whatever. I think it's admirable.

"Looks like there are quite a few people here," Fred said. "Did Haley have any idea when she could make it?"

"She said they had a couple of bypasses this morning and it depended on how they went." Haley is a scrub nurse with a cardiac surgical unit. I wondered how she was going to work it out with them, leaving so suddenly.

58

"Philip had a full schedule today. Trying to get everybody's sinuses unstopped before he leaves, I guess."

"I looked up Poland in the atlas last night. It's not so far. You can probably get direct flights from Atlanta."

"Uh huh."

Fred turned off the ignition. "Listen, honey. Chances are this thing today isn't going to turn out very well. I want you to be prepared and not get too upset. Okay?"

"Well, at least it's not the wrong time of the month for me." I smiled sweetly and got out of the car. I knew which one of us would have to be resuscitated if things didn't turn out well, a nice way of saying if we found Sunshine's body.

Fred caught up with me and took my hand. "I know you're just tired and need something to eat."

How can my feelings for this man, after all these years, be so wildly vacillating? One minute I'm furious, and the next minute I'm mushy. Go figure.

About forty people were gathered in the circle that the trailers formed. Apparently no instructions had been given by the sheriff as everyone was milling around aimlessly. I spotted Mary Alice, Henry, and Tiffany sitting on the steps of Pawpaw's trailer and waved to them.

"You're late," Sister greeted us.

"Doesn't look like we missed much." I looked around. "Is there any coffee?"

"I'll get y'all some," Tiffany volunteered. She turned and banged on Pawpaw's door. When he stuck his head out, she held up her Styrofoam cup and two fingers.

"Cream and sugar?" Pawpaw asked.

"I want cream and sugar," I said.

Tiffany held up one finger; Pawpaw nodded and disappeared.

"Y'all sit down." Henry moved over to make room for

us on the steps. "We're waiting for the sheriff. He's over in that trailer"—Henry pointed toward Kerrigan's—"talking to Sunshine's mother."

"Doing something to Sunshine's mother," Sister said. "He's been in there a half hour."

"Where's Meemaw?"

"She went over to Howard's trailer while ago. Probably cooking him breakfast. I keep smelling bacon."

I sat on the narrow metal step and wished for some bacon. For some more aspirin. For coffee. Fortunately the last wish was granted as Pawpaw opened the door and handed Tiffany two Styrofoam cups which she handed down to us. We thanked him profusely.

"You want some more, pretty lady?" he asked Mary Alice.

"No, but I'd like to use your bathroom."

"What?"

Mary Alice stood up and pointed toward the open trailer door. "I have to pee," she said loudly and bluntly.

Pawpaw smiled broadly. "You just come right on in."

We all moved so Mary Alice could get up the steps. She was courting disaster if Meemaw happened to be looking out of Howard's window.

"How was Debbie this morning?" I asked Henry.

"She was still asleep when I left. In fact, she was asleep when I went to bed last night. I called several people to see if they could come out here today and I had to explain to all of them what had happened. Some of them are coming, though. Dwayne, the guy who was at Mary Alice's the other night, the one who walked out, is already here. I think that's some of his buddies he's with over there by the trailer with the Christmas tree lights."

"That's Eddie Turkett's trailer," I explained. "Meemaw says he works at the chicken plant in Trussville."

Henry looked up, surprised. "Eddie Turkett? Hell, he *owns* the chicken plant in Trussville. And one in Cullman. And a turkey plant in south Alabama."

"Are his turkeys by any chance the stress-free ones, raised in the shade of pecan trees?"

Henry grinned. "I don't know about that, but the man's made millions on them."

Hmmm. A millionaire and a movie star. Now if Howard Turkett were by any chance a professor . . .

Fred interrupted my casting of *Gilligan's Island* by standing up. "I'm going to walk around some. Has anybody heard anything new this morning?"

"Not that we know of." Tiffany ran inch-long acrylic nails through her blonde curls. "I wish they'd get the show on the road, though. I'm already sweating."

So was I. My jeans were tucked into my old rubber rain boots, the only boots I owned, to protect against snakes and ticks, and I had on a long-sleeved shirt and a sun hat so large I had had to pull it off so the raveling straw edges wouldn't blind one of my fellow step-sitters. Fred was similarly decked out in his fishing boots and hat. Fair-skinned Southerners, we are still paying for our youthful fun in the sun. Literally. The demands for the services of Alabama dermatologists run a close second to that of ENTs. Henry and Tiffany were also adequately covered. Tiffany's hat, which she held on her lap, was larger than mine. I was glad to see they had learned from their parents' mistakes.

Several cars had come up since Fred and I had arrived. Dust rose and settled as the drivers were ushered into the cotton field. A white pickup, however, was directed into the space between Meemaw's and Pawpaw's trailer. When a woman got out, I recognized Blenda from the Starlight Cafe. She waved. "I've got sausage biscuits and coffee."

61

She was talking to the three of us on Pawpaw's steps, but it was amazing how many people heard her and descended on the truck. I watched her handing out the food and wondered aloud if Mary Alice had called her at two-thirty this morning.

My question was answered by Sister who opened Pawpaw's door and said, "Oh, good. Blenda's here. I wonder what she brought."

Tiffany moved over so Sister could come down the steps. "She said sausage biscuits."

"Good. We're all going to need our energy. I'll go help her." Sister swished by me. Her go-hunt-for-a-dead-daughter-in-law's-body-in-the-woods-in-August-outfit was one I had seen her wear line-dancing, a blue silk jumpsuit and rhinestone-studded boots. The woman wouldn't make it as far as the cotton patch. And how on God's earth had she been able to locate Blenda in the middle of the night?

"That woman is scary," I said. Henry and Tiffany both laughed. For some reason they thought I was joking.

Lady Bountiful and Blenda were handing out biscuits and little packets of grape jelly when the door to Kerrigan's trailer opened, and the sheriff and a woman so beautiful that Henry said, "Wow!" came out.

"Okay, everybody," Sheriff Reuse said loudly. "Gather 'round."

"He reminds me of a P.E. teacher I had once," Tiffany said, getting up. "We better go or he'll start blowing a whistle."

I looked around for Fred. He was gathering 'round just like the sheriff had requested. Right up at the front of the crowd by Kerrigan Dabbs at whom he was smiling. My head hurt too much to bother; let the old fool enjoy himself.

"You want a sausage biscuit with grape jelly, Sheriff?"

Mary Alice called. That made me feel better. I followed Henry and Tiffany and stood at the back of the crowd awaiting instructions. I was already discovering I wouldn't be able to wear the rubber boots very long. Given the certainty of my feet feeling like they were on fire and the uncertainty of a snake bite, I'd have to opt for the snake.

"Y'all know what happened here yesterday," the sheriff said, "and we appreciate your coming." Kerrigan began to cry. My Fred handed her a tissue.

"How did Uncle Fred get up there?" Henry murmured. I gave him a hard look.

Sheriff Reuse continued, "We can't leave any rock unturned until we find Sunshine."

"Well, she crawled out from under one. Maybe she crawled back." A whisper in my ear. Grape-jelly breath. For a moment, the remark didn't register. By the time it did, and I whirled around, there was no one close enough to pinpoint as the whisperer. A redheaded girl moving away was a possibility.

I grabbed Henry's arm. "Who was behind me?"

He was startled. "What?"

"Did you just see anybody right behind me?"

"I wasn't paying any attention. Why?"

Tiffany turned. "What's the matter?" Several people were looking our way.

Sheriff Reuse, pulling an old schoolteacher trick that I knew well, hushed talking and simply looked our way.

"Nothing," I whispered. "I'll tell you after while."

"We're going to divide into groups of five and walk toward the river. I want you to stay an arm's length from each other and walk slowly. If you see anything that looks suspicious, don't touch it. I've got some whistles here, one for each group. Blow it, and we'll come."

"I told you," Tiffany said. "I could just look at him and

63

tell he was a whistle blower."

"Suspicious like what?" a man asked.

"A shoe, anything."

"Sunshine was barefooted," Meemaw called. I didn't realize she had come out of the trailer until I heard her voice. She stood to the right of the group between two very large bearded men who looked like the Smith cough-drop brothers and must be Eddie and Howard.

"Good morning, Meemaw," the sheriff acknowledged her, then turned back to the crowd. "Like I said, anything at all. Just use your common sense."

Tiffany grinned. "Big order."

"How come he doesn't have dogs out here?" Henry murmured. "Wouldn't that be simpler?"

I shrugged. "Ask him."

"Sheriff," Henry called. "How come you aren't using dogs?"

"We'd have to borrow them from Jefferson County and mainly what they've got is drug-sniffing dogs. Dogs can't do as good as people, anyway." He slapped his hands together. "Okay, divide up into groups of five. Remember how hot it is today. If you've got any health problems, don't try it."

There was instant confusion as the group tried to sort itself out.

"Wait for me," I told Henry and Tiffany. "I'm going to go get Fred."

He was still consoling Kerrigan who, at closer glance, was even more beautiful than she had appeared from a distance.

"Hey, honey," Fred said, and the beautiful Kerrigan, who by this time had her face burrowed against his arm, looked up. Elizabeth Taylor eyes brimmed with tears and were framed with eyelashes like those most women have to buy at cosmetic counters. But not Kerrigan. Her pale skin was slightly flushed, and her shiny brown hair was pulled back in a barrette and cascaded to her waist.

"This is Kerrigan," he continued, looking a little sheepish. "Patricia Anne is Ray's aunt, Kerrigan."

I've always laughed at novels where one tear slides down the heroine's face. But damned if that isn't what happened. One big tear plopped over the bottom of Kerrigan's left eye and glided down her cheek. I was amazed.

"Oh, Patricia Anne. What's happened to my Sunshine?"

"She's fine. We'll find her," I lied.

The tear reached a dimple. Kerrigan flicked it out with her thumb. Amazing.

"It's all so bizarre, an Indian none of us knew getting killed in Mama's trailer and Sunshine disappearing. And"—she leaned her head toward Sheriff Reuse—"I don't think Junior knows what the hell he's doing."

"Of course he does." Fred lied, too. "We're going to get organized here in a few minutes."

And we did, somehow, in spite of Sheriff Reuse. Small groups formed and were conducted by deputies across the cotton field and to the edge of the woods. Our group was the last one because I had to stop by the car and swap the rain boots for tennis shoes. Plus, we had to wait for Mary Alice who insisted on giving everyone a bottle of Evian to take with them to ward off dehydration.

"I had to open up the club before dawn this morning to get that stuff," Henry said when I mentioned the Evian was a good idea. Like I said, sometimes my sister is a scary person. But all of us stomping through the woods on a manhunt armed with bottles of Evian was just one more surreal facet of the morning.

"Meemaw said they had a perfectly good well, thank you, ma'am," Mary Alice said when she caught up with us. "That woman's got a burr up her butt." She pulled the blue silk of her jumpsuit away from her legs. "I may have made a mistake wearing this. But I didn't have anything else decent, did I, Tiffany?"

"No ma'am." The girl knew which side her bread was buttered on.

A young deputy came over to us and pointed to the woods. "Straight through there, arm's width apart. When you get to the river, turn, move to the right, and come back. Then move to the left and back to the river. Got it?" He handed Fred a whistle. "Y'all take your time; look under bushes and dead trees."

"I hope we don't find anything," Mary Alice said.

We all agreed fervently and stepped into the woods.

Chapter 7

THE WOODS WERE LOVELY, DARK, AND DEEP AND IT was at least ten degrees cooler in the heavy shade for which I was grateful. I rubbed the cold bottle of Evian against my aching head.

"Y'all go ahead," Mary Alice said. "I'll wait right here for you on this stump." She took a handkerchief from her pocket, spread it on a stump and sat, blue silk jumpsuit packed with Mary Alice butt hanging over the sides. We all looked at her.

"What do you mean *us* go ahead?" I asked.

"Well, you heard the weatherman. It's really not healthy for people to be out in this heat."

I nodded. "You're right, he particularly said the elderly. So I guess you'd better stay here."

"Why don't we all sit down a minute and drink some of our water," Henry, the peacemaker, suggested.

"Good idea," Fred agreed. "Those sausage biscuits are heating up my belly."

I reached into my ultralight fanny pack I'd ordered from L.L. Bean and passed around a package of Tums. Everybody took one.

"I told Blenda"—Mary Alice chewed on her Tum—"I said, Blenda, sausage biscuits are a mite heavy on an August morning with an inversion going on. And she said she thought so, too, but it was what Eddie Turkett said to bring, that it was turkey sausage."

"You didn't order them?" I asked.

"Sausage biscuits? Lord, no. I didn't even know the woman's phone number. How could I have ordered them?"

I shrugged.

"Drink your water, everybody," Tiffany reminded us. "We really need to get going."

Mary Alice got up, grumbling. "We're not going to find a damn thing in here."

She was wrong. We found huge thornbushes and vines so heavy that Tarzan, Cheetah, and Jane could have swung together. When we reached the river, we found plastic milk cartons and a few dead fish.

"Look," Henry said. He pointed across the stream where two red foxes were looking at us in surprise.

We sat down for a moment and drank some more water. Sister reached in her pocket and pulled out a tiny phone. "Gotta check my voice mail."

The rest of us laughed. There was something so incongruous about struggling through the woods and then checking your voice mail.

"Let's sit on that rock and put our feet in the water,"

Fred said. It sounded good to me. To Henry and Tiffany, too. But we hadn't made it to the rock when Sister screeched, "Shit! Blow the whistle, Fred!"

"What?" all four of us asked.

Sister was doing a dance, thrusting the phone out first to one of us and then the other. "Come here. Listen. You're not going to believe this. Blow the whistle, Fred."

Henry got there first. "Punch four," Sister said, handing him the phone. He listened and began to grin. "I'll be damned."

"Let me hear." I took the phone from him and punched four.

"*Mother Crane.*" Sunshine's voice came over the phone clearly. "*I'm all right. Tell Ray I'm all right.*"

"What is it?" Fred and Tiffany were standing by me.

"It's Sunshine." I handed the phone to Fred. "She's okay."

"Where is she?" Tiffany asked.

"She didn't say. She just said to tell Ray she was all right." Tears of relief sprang to my eyes. I brushed them away and grinned.

Fred handed the phone to Tiffany and blew the whistle several times. "I hope everybody stops hunting when they hear that," he said.

"They'll probably think we've found the body," Mary Alice said happily.

She was right. Sheriff Reuse, followed by a deputy, was running across the cotton patch as we exited from the pines.

"Sunshine's okay," Mary Alice called.

The sheriff slowed to a walk. "You found her?"

Mary Alice held up the phone. "Got a message."

By this time, the sheriff had reached us. He leaned over, breathing raspily with his hands on his legs. And this was

68

the man we didn't think sweated.

I held out my bottle of Evian. "You want some water?" I asked. "Pour some on your wrists and then splash some behind your neck."

"I'm fine," he said. He obviously wasn't, but if he wanted to pass out in a cotton patch being macho it was his business. "What did she say?"

"Said she's fine. Here." Mary Alice handed him the phone. "Punch four."

He straightened up and took the phone. In a minute, he nodded his head and said, "Blow your whistle, Leroy."

Leroy, redheaded with the beginnings of a sunburn across his nose, asked how many times he should blow it. What signals had they decided on?

"We didn't decide on any, though we should have." Mary Alice took the phone from the sheriff. "Look, y'all. Here come the Turketts. Jump up and down and look happy so they'll know it's good news."

"Lord," Fred grumbled.

"You can just wave and smile, Fred." To my amazement, he did what Sister said.

Kerrigan was the first to arrive. Our message had gotten through because, hand on her heart, she said, "It's good news, isn't it?"

"The best," Sister assured her.

Kerrigan turned to Eddie, Howard, and Meemaw who was making surprisingly good time across the cotton rows. "It's good news!"

"Oh, thank the Lord." Meemaw caught up to the group. "Howard, honey, run tell your papa we've found Sunshine. He's worried sick."

"Where is she?" Howard Turkett asked.

The sheriff mopped his face with a handkerchief. "We don't know. Mrs. Crane got a message on her voice mail

69

from Sunshine saying she's okay. It was made about an hour ago. That's all we know."

"Here." Mary Alice handed the phone to Kerrigan. "Punch four."

Kerrigan beamed when she heard the message and handed the phone to Meemaw.

"You still want me to blow the whistle, Sheriff?" Leroy asked. "You never did say how many times."

"Just blow it a bunch of times. They'll get the idea. And let's go get in some shade."

By the time we got back to the Compound, other groups were emerging from the woods, most of them expecting the worst. Pawpaw, however, alerted by Howard, emerged from his trailer smiling. He looked, I realized, exactly like a prospector in the movies, one who's been down by the creek too long. He made a beeline for Mary Alice and hugged her. "Our baby's all right," he said.

Fred had realized the same thing I had about Pawpaw. "He reminds me of Gabby Hayes," he whispered.

Mary Alice seemed to think so, too. She was looking around rather wildly, perhaps as fearful that Meemaw would see what was going on as anything else. But Meemaw had disappeared into her trailer.

"Old fool." Kerrigan went over and tapped her father on the shoulder. A very sound tap. "Behave yourself, Paw."

He turned and Mary Alice seized the opportunity to move away faster than I thought she could move. So fast it made me right proud.

Leroy was still blowing the whistle though the sound was getting weaker, more like a chirp. Sheriff Reuse told him he could quit which he did and went to sit by Kerrigan's trailer fanning himself with his hat. Henry took

70

him another bottle of Evian.

"Are we going home now?" Tiffany asked. Some of the cars were already leaving the cotton field.

"I don't see why not." Fred looked around. "Where did Mary Alice go?"

"Probably hiding from Pawpaw." I looked at my watch. It was a few minutes after seven. Lord! I had thought it was at least noon.

Meemaw came out of her trailer holding a large pitcher and a stack of Styrofoam cups. "Hawaiian Punch!" The crowd surged forward.

There was such a feeling of relief in the air, it was almost palpable. Given the circumstances of Sunshine's disappearance, there wasn't a person there who hadn't feared what he would find with his next step into the woods.

"I'm going to go get some punch," Tiffany said. "Y'all want some?"

"Sure. I'll go with you." Fred turned to me. "Honey?"

"Bring me some." I sat down on an old wheelbarrow that was turned upside down and looked around. The gathering was turning into a party, with laughing and joking, celebrating the fact that Sunshine was all right. But—a tiredness settled over me—something terrible had happened here yesterday, and Sunshine's disappearance was part of it. Her body might not be in the woods, but she was definitely not all right.

Kerrigan sat down on the ground beside me. "You want some punch?" She held up a Styrofoam cup.

I shook my head no. "Fred's bringing me some."

We sat silently for a moment. Then Kerrigan said what I'd been thinking. "My baby's in terrible trouble, isn't she?"

"I don't know. I don't have any idea what's going on."

71

"Will you tell me about yesterday? I've heard Mama's version a dozen times, but none of it makes sense. None of us even knew the guy who got killed. He just showed up murdered in Mama's trailer and Sunshine was gone. Plus, everything in my trailer was messed up."

"I'll tell you all I know." I went through the sequence of events starting with us running into Meemaw at the restaurant (I didn't tell her how we happened to be at the restaurant) and ending with us nearly getting killed at the highway.

Kerrigan listened quietly, sipping her Hawaiian Punch, not interrupting a single time.

"And thats it," I finished.

She nodded. "That's pretty much Mama's story. It's just crazy, though."

What could I say? The circumstances had made no sense; the violence had been obscene.

"Mrs. Hollowell, I know he's your nephew, but I have to ask you if there's any chance Ray could be involved in any way. I mean, I know he's not here, but could something be going on that he's part of? Something that Sunshine's gotten caught in?"

I put my hand on her shoulder. "Ray's not involved in this. He's the sweetest, nicest one of all our children." He was also the only one who had ever been arrested, but I didn't think that his and some of his fraternity buddies' plot of marijuana in the Bankhead National Forest was part of the problem here. He had gotten off with a fine and 100 hours of community service. His main punishment had come from his mother who had urged the whole family to hold up our heads in spite of what Ray had done. "No," I said again. "This has nothing to do with Ray. Sunshine can count her blessings with him."

"That's good to hear." Kerrigan smiled up at me.

Perfect teeth, skin that glowed, those violet eyes. I thought of Meemaw and Pawpaw. Lord, there's no accounting for genes.

Sheriff Reuse came up, red in the face. "Kerrigan, I need to talk to you." He motioned toward her trailer and walked toward it.

"Shit." Kerrigan got up in one graceful movement. "That man drives me nuts. Thinks he's Sunshine's daddy."

"Is he?" It just popped out.

"I hope not."

Fred and Tiffany came up with the Hawaiian Punch. Kerrigan gave them a little wave and left.

"Why is your mouth open, honey?" Fred asked.

The crowd, having received their cups of Hawaiian Punch, began to disperse quickly. There was still no sign of Mary Alice, and Henry, also, had disappeared.

"I'll just go on with you," Tiffany said. "They'll show up."

"She always does," Fred agreed.

I was ready to go, too, but first I wanted to go tell Meemaw that if there was anything else we could do to help her, we were available. After all, it was only polite.

Meemaw had gone back inside her trailer to mix some more punch, and though I could see her through the door, I knocked.

"Come in," she said when she looked up. "Just don't step on the man. I swear, he's right in the middle of everything."

I already had the door open when she said that about the man, or I wouldn't have set foot in there. What she was talking about, I saw immediately, was a chalk outline of Chief Joseph, the kind you see in the movies. He had been stepped on several times. Stepped on and tracked

73

into the kitchen.

"What the hell is this?" I asked. "Why didn't they put up some of those yellow ribbons and not let anybody in here?"

"Junior Reuse wanted to, but I told him I couldn't sleep anywhere but in my own bed and Kerrigan told him that was true. So he just drew that picture. Did a whole bunch of scraping on the floor after they got the body out. Sprayed stuff around. It was okay after I got everything aired out, though." Meemaw pointed to the floor. "You can come in long as you don't step on the chalk lines."

"That's okay. I just wanted to tell you we were leaving, but you have our phone number. If you need us for anything, call."

"Is your sister leaving, too?"

"Probably in a little while. I don't know where she is."

"She's over in Howard's trailer. I saw her and that son-in-law of hers sneaking in while ago."

"Sneaking in?"

"Well, I guess not. Howard was holding the door open."

"I'll get her," I said. "Where's Pawpaw?"

"Taking a nap back yonder." She pointed toward the bedroom end of the trailer. "Hold the door open for me, will you?"

I don't know much about anatomy, but I figure Meemaw stepped right on Chief Joseph's bladder as she came through the door with the pitcher. I motioned to Fred that I was going over to Howard's trailer. He seemed to be happy with Tiffany and the Hawaiian Punch.

There is no one on earth with a laugh like Mary Alice's. It's a bellow, I swear. And that's what I heard when I got near Howard's trailer. Henry saw me coming up the steps and opened the door. "Come in, Aunt Pat. Howard's telling us a story you're going to love."

I smiled at Howard. He was the Turkett I had seen the least of. Probably under all that facial hair, I decided, was a handsome man.

"He's telling us how Pawpaw lost his hearing," Mary Alice said. She had made herself at home, I noticed. Boots off, she was leaning back in a recliner with the air-conditioning unit blowing right on her. "Start over, Howard. I don't want Patricia Anne to miss any of this."

Howard offered me the stool he was sitting on and leaned against the kitchen counter, grinning.

"Well, you know Papa worked for NASA. He was a rocket scientist, a damn good one, too, so I understand. One of Wernher von Braun's right-hand men. When we were little, I remember he was gone all the time.

"Anyway, they all went to Cape Canaveral to see *Apollo 11* launched. I mean, this is what they had been working for years for, right? A man on the moon?"

We nodded.

"Well, they took the guys from Huntsville out to see their handiwork, got them front-row seats for the launch. I mean those guys were in rocket scientist heaven.

"The only problem was that Paw made one little mistake. He decided to use one of the Port-o-Johns out by the launchpad and he got locked in. Can you imagine? The man designs spaceships to go to the moon and he can't get himself out of a Port-o-John. In all the excitement, nobody missed him, and he says he finally got so tired, he just propped his head over on the toilet paper and went to sleep. And then the rocket launched."

"One giant leap," Mary Alice bellowed. Henry was laughing so hard, he was gasping. And, I'll have to admit, I was laughing as hard as they were. I had this cartoon image of Pawpaw, hair on end, arms and legs stretched to the corners of the Port-o-John while man blasted to the moon.

"He came out of there a changed man," Howard continued when we were quiet enough. "Said he wasn't ever going to do anything again but fish. And that's when we moved down here close to the river. Started out with two trailers."

Howard was a good storyteller. He paused. "We ate a lot of catfish."

Mary Alice and Henry continued to laugh, but there was a slight change of tone in Howard's voice that, old schoolteacher that I am, I caught.

"What's Pawpaw's name, Howard?" I asked.

"Melvin. His name is Melvin."

In a few minutes, I was back with Fred and Tiffany.

"Are you laughing, honey, or crying?" Fred asked.

"I'm not sure." And that was the truth.

Chapter 8

AS WE WERE LEAVING THE COMPOUND, EDDIE Turkett came over to thank us for coming. One thing about these Turkett men—they could grow hair. Eddie was as fully bearded as Howard, and, like Howard, was probably a handsome man under that mop. Eddie's beard, I noticed, was sprinkled with gray.

"You're very welcome." Fred shook Eddie's hand. "Sunshine's our family, too, now."

What a nice man.

"Anything we can do to help, just call." Tiffany reached over and put one of her Magic Maid business cards in Eddie's shirt pocket. I frowned at her as he walked away.

"What?" she asked. "He's the rich one, isn't he?" The

child had been around Mary Alice too long. I could just hear Sister saying, *"Smart move, Tiffany."*

Which reminded me. "You'd better go tell Sister you're going home with us."

"Hey." Tiffany reached out and grabbed Deputy Leroy's arm as he walked by. "You know Mrs. Crane in the blue jumpsuit?"

He nodded.

"Tell her Tiffany's gone home with her sister. Okay?"

"Sure."

"Let's go," Tiffany said to Fred and me.

There is nothing as hot as a car that's been parked in an Alabama cotton patch in August. We opened the doors and turned on the air-conditioning, but the leather seats were still a danger to any exposed skin. Finally, we were able to get in and back over the rows.

Tiffany pointed toward the Turkett Compound. "That's a strange place back there."

"How so?" Fred asked. He was trying to drive without holding the hot steering wheel. Quite a feat.

"Tiffany, there's a towel back there on the floor. Hand it to Fred."

"Here." She passed it over the seat. "I don't know. Just sort of spooky. Out in the woods like that and nobody living in the same trailer."

"They moved out here because Pawpaw lost his hearing. All he wanted to do after that was fish, so Howard said."

"How did he lose his hearing?" Fred asked.

"Well . . ." I related the story just as Howard had told it. Fred and Tiffany were an appreciative audience.

"A Port-o-John? Oh, God." Fred was laughing so hard I thought I was going to have to make him pull over so I could drive.

Tiffany slapped the back of the seat. "I can just see him.

77

I'll bet he thought he'd died and gone to hell."

I was giggling. "It's not funny, y'all, and we ought to be ashamed. He can't hear it thunder now."

That set them off even more. "Oh, God, I'm going to pee my pants," Tiffany squealed. "Stop at the next gas station, Mr. Hollowell."

Fortunately, it wasn't far to the interstate and a huge Exxon station. Fred and Tiffany, still laughing, both rushed to the rest rooms. I fished change out of the bottom of my purse and headed for the Coke machine. A large round thermometer hanging where a flower had probably once hung and died from heatstroke stated that the temperature was 105 degrees. Subtract five for the heat of the pavement, hell, subtract ten, you still had an egg-frying day. We would have been dropping like flies tromping through those woods.

Clunk. The Coke dropped down, wonderfully cold. I turned it up and chugalugged about half the can.

An old green car pulled up and Dwayne Parker got out. "I need one of those," he said, pointing toward my Coke. "That sausage biscuit is still giving me trouble." He fished around in his pocket for change. "You're the aunt, aren't you?"

"I'm the aunt. I'm Patricia Anne Hollowell."

He put the money in the machine. "I'm Dwayne Parker. I'm the one who left the party the other night."

"I know." He was also the one who had nearly run us down the day before. I recognized the car.

"I guess I shouldn't have left Mr. Lamont like that." He took the Coke from the machine, opened it, and gulped it like I had mine.

"You were upset when you found out Sunshine was there. That's understandable."

"I guess so." He studied the Coke can as if it held some

78

great secret. "Well, I'll see you, Mrs. Hollowell."

"Okay. I'm glad we heard from Sunshine this morning."

"Yes, ma'am. I am, too." He turned toward his car. He had on an Atlanta Braves baseball cap which hid his crew cut, but his ears stuck out below it. Dwayne wasn't going to have any trouble finding some girl who, like me, thought those ears were wonderful. Some girl who would be more than willing to pass them along in the gene pool. I hoped he realized that but knew he probably didn't.

By the time we dropped Tiffany off and got home, it was almost eleven and had been a long time since the sausage biscuits. Fred took a shower while I fixed tuna-fish sandwiches. He took his with him, though, saying he needed to get to work. I took my sandwich into the den and turned on *Jeopardy!*. The answer to the final question was Madagascar which I knew. I always feel smart when I get the Final Jeopardy question. It's even better when someone's around who knows when I get it. Fred's always pleased; Sister says it's a rerun and I've already seen it.

I put my plate in the dishwasher and admired the cabinets I'd painted. A new floor would be nice, a white one. Maybe I should go look at samples. I tapped on the window for Woofer, but he stayed in his igloo. Just as well. On the corner of the TV screen the temperature was posted: 100 degrees.

Sunshine was okay, hopefully, and my Haley was marrying a man she loved. I should be happy. I should be ashamed not to be happy. But Haley wouldn't be home for her birthday, or for Christmas, or maybe not even when Debbie's baby was born. She wouldn't be popping in to see what we were having for supper. I undressed and got in the shower and bawled. My life was changing big-time here, and I don't cope with change well.

79

By the time the water began to cool, though, I was beginning to pull myself together. Six months. It was only for six months. And we would go visit her. Warsaw must be a wonderful place to visit. We could do all kinds of sightseeing. The only other time I had been to Europe had been with Mary Alice, a trip to Scandinavia which happened to coincide with the explosion of Chernobyl. We saw one fjord before we were forced to stay inside the hotel while the radioactive cloud passed overhead. Everyone was furious because we had all had a good dose of radiation before the Russians admitted what was happening. Mary Alice kept telling the Swedes she thought it was downright tacky that they hadn't been informed immediately. I think they translated "downright tacky" without any problems.

I got out of the shower, wrapped a towel around me, stepped into the bedroom, and screamed.

Mary Alice, sitting on my bed in a semi-yoga position, dropped the tuna-fish sandwich she was eating. "Shit! What's wrong with you?"

"You just scared the hell out of me." I sat on the end of the bed and burst into tears again.

"Well, my Lord!" Mary Alice handed me a paper napkin. "I thought you'd cried yourself out in there in the shower."

I snatched the napkin from her and wiped my eyes. "How long have you been here?"

"About fifteen minutes." She picked up the pieces of her sandwich and started putting them back together. "Is this bedspread washable?"

"Why didn't you tell me you were here?"

"I didn't want to disturb you."

"You just scared me to death instead."

"Listen. A normal person would not be scared to death

and yelling if they walked into their bedroom and saw their sister sitting there eating a tuna-fish sandwich."

"What do you mean 'a normal person'? I'm normal." I thought for a moment. "Besides, it's one person; you should have used 'she.' If 'she' walked into 'her' bedroom."

"Hmmm." Sister examined her sandwich and took a bite.

"What are you doing here, anyway? I thought you were going to stay out at the Turketts' for a while, talk to the sheriff."

"They all got in a fight." She drank some tea and put the glass back on the nightstand.

"Put something under that. It'll circle. Get a coaster out of the drawer."

"Anything else interesting in there?"

"I'm sure you know. You've been here fifteen minutes."

"Testy, testy." But she got the coaster.

"Who got in a fight?" I asked.

"Howard and Eddie mainly. Howard told Eddie he had peanut *cojones* and Eddie took it personally. Men are so fixated on their balls. You know?"

"How come he told him that?"

"Best I could tell—I wasn't paying much attention until Eddie hit him—Howard thinks Eddie ought to expand his business and Eddie doesn't want to chance it."

"He hit him?"

"Knock-down, drag-out, much as you can have in a trailer. Meemaw came in yelling like a banshee and broke them up. I swear, Patricia Anne, I half expected that woman to turn them over her knee and spank them."

"Where were the sheriff and Kerrigan? Still in her trailer?"

"I don't know where she was. He was talking on the

81

phone in his car and I told him Henry and I were leaving." Sister took another bite of her sandwich. "That is one more dysfunctional family out there, Mouse."

"Did you see Pawpaw any more?"

"We saw him hightailing it across the cotton patch as we were leaving. Probably heading toward the river fishing."

I got up and got underwear, khaki shorts, and a white tee shirt from the chest of drawers. The mirror above it showed a face that had been crying for a long time.

"You need to put some ice on your eyes," Sister said. "Did I tell you I checked on flights to Warsaw?"

I shook my head no.

"We could fly the Concorde to Paris and be in Warsaw in five hours. Just about as long as it takes to get to Pensacola. Think about that. You wouldn't bat an eye if she was going to Pensacola for six months, now would you?"

"I can't afford the Concorde," I said.

"I can. Besides, it's the idea of the thing. Just knowing the possibility. True?"

"True." And I did feel better. I turned and gave Sister a grateful smile.

"The seats are kind of little on the Concorde but Fred's not big, and you're not big as a flea. The three of us will do fine."

Fred, Sister, and me, halfway across the Atlantic, the point of no return, squashed together in three little seats. My smile faded.

"Anyway, I came by to tell you that Gabriel says Sunshine's in a dark place but okay."

"You talked to Meemaw's channeler?" I began to dress.

"Of course not. Meemaw talked to him." Sister leaned back against the headboard. "How much do you weigh?"

"Enough. What did Gabriel say?"

"He told Meemaw that Sunshine's in a dark place. I just said that, Mouse."

I zipped up my shorts. "Did he give any details?"

"I have no idea. I told Meemaw that Henry and I were leaving and to call if she needed us, and she said she had just been communing with Gabriel and Sunshine was okay in a dark place." Sister took the last bite of her sandwich. "I hope it's not a cave. Remember those snakes in *Raiders of the Lost Ark?*"

"Lord, yes." I sat on the bed and looked at Mary Alice. We've been sisters for sixty-one years. She had no more stopped by to tell me Gabriel said Sunshine was in a dark place than she could fly. "Want to tell me why you're really here?"

"I knew you were upset at Haley leaving so suddenly."

"And?"

"And I found something in my pocket I don't know what to do with." She handed me a lined index card, the kind you write recipes on, that had been folded in half. On the top was a cartoon turkey saying *From the kitchen of Mary Louise Turkett.* Below that, someone had printed in pencil, *Chief Joseph sends his regards to your son.*

I studied the card, turned it over to make sure I hadn't missed anything.

"It's a threat, isn't it?" Sister reached over and took the card back. "They're saying Ray's in danger, aren't they? That the same thing could happen to him." She shivered. "It's cold in here."

"No, it's not. And I don't know what it means." Of course it was a threat, but I didn't want to upset Sister more. "It just showed up in your pocket?"

"When Henry and I got in the car, I felt the corner of it sticking me, but I just thought it was the tag on my new

83

underpants."

Made sense to me.

"But when I let Henry out at his house, I went in to see about Debbie and reached in my pocket and found it." Sister studied the card. "Reckon I ought to call the sheriff?"

"Probably. But let's think about it a minute. The first thing he's going to ask you is if you have any idea how it got in your pocket."

Sister looked at me as if I didn't have walking-around sense. "Somebody put it there, Mouse."

"But who?" I took the card back. The printing, though done in pencil, was very neat and precise.

"Well, it's Meemaw's recipe card."

"Did she have a chance to put it in your pocket?"

"I don't think so. We sort of kept our distance from each other."

"Pawpaw?"

"He had the opportunity. But so did Eddie and Howard. They each hugged me when I went in Howard's trailer." Mary Alice thought for a moment. "But you know, Mouse, it could have happened any time we were crowded around listening to the sheriff. It could have been anybody there."

I suddenly remembered the smell of grape-jelly breath, of someone's whispering that Sunshine had crawled out from under a rock. "What time is Ray's plane?" I asked.

"Around seven. Why?"

"Because he's walking into a mess." I reached into the nightstand, got a notepad and a pencil. "Okay. Let's start with Sunshine. What do we know about her?"

"She looks like a Barbie doll."

I wrote down *Barbie.* No one looks like a Barbie doll naturally. Or cheaply.

84

"She's a nursing student at Jefferson State, lives with her grandmother because her mother's a porn actress."

"Aha!" I wrote down *Frances Zata*. My best friend and recently retired counselor from Robert Alexander High had just taken a part-time counseling job at Jeff State. Said she wasn't cut out for retirement. Frances doesn't mind sharing a little information occasionally.

"Lives in a trailer with her grandmother," I muttered. "What about clothes?"

"What are you talking about?" Mary Alice asked.

"Where does Sunshine keep her clothes? I didn't see much closet space in that trailer."

"Maybe she doesn't have many."

"At twenty and looking like she does? Get real, Sister. Besides, I've got an idea that Kerrigan makes a lot of money. A whole lot." I wrote *clothes* and *money*. Then I added *car*. "Her car doesn't fit either."

Mary Alice yawned. "The main thing is she's missing and left a bloody nightgown by a body."

I looked up from my notes. "The nightgown was by the body? I don't remember seeing a nightgown, do you?"

"No. But I wasn't paying much attention, to tell you the truth, to anything but the Indian guy. Anyway, that's what Eddie Turkett said, and he could have been wrong."

Nevertheless, I wrote down *nightgown*.

Mary Alice yawned again. "Look, I don't think I got a wink of sleep last night. All I want you to do is tell me if you think I ought to call the sheriff about this note."

"I said probably."

"Then maybe I will."

"Okay."

"It could be a joke."

"Could be. Not likely."

"I'll see." Mary Alice stood up. "You know what,

85

Mouse?"

"What?"

"We know Meemaw's name now." She ambled out of the door. I hoped she made it home before she went to sleep.

❁ ❁ ❁

Frances Zata is the most elegant-looking woman I have ever known. Hair a beautiful color of blonde pulled back into a chignon, face unlined, eyes round and blue, she's a sixty-year-old paean to chemistry, cosmetics, and surgery. She's also a dingbat at times. She's currently madly in love with a pink Victorian house on Choctawhatchee Bay in Destin, Florida, and its owner. In that order, I suspect. He's grieving over the death of his fiancée and Frances is keeping close tabs on which step he's on in his grief. I'm predicting a spring wedding as he seems to be bearing up very well. In the meantime, Frances has taken the job at Jeff State. I picked up the phone and called her.

"Hey, Patricia Anne," she said. "Good thing you called today. I'm off Fridays and Mondays so I can go to the coast."

"How's Jason?"

"He's way past denial and anger. Getting into acceptance."

"That's good."

"Coming right along. What's up with you?"

"You got an hour or so?"

"I think I'm the only one on the whole campus today. Tell me."

So I told her about Haley and Philip. Frances commiserated with me; her only son lives in London. Then I got into the Ray-Sunshine story, described the dinner party, the snooping trip Mary Alice and I took, and Chief Joseph.

"You were there?" Frances interrupted. "My Lord. I read about that in the paper. A hog-butchering knife?"

"Stuck to the linoleum." I heard Frances gasp as I segued to Sunshine's disappearance, the bloody nightgown, the search through the woods.

Frances is a good listener which makes her a good counselor, but I didn't want to push my luck. I left out a few details like Gabriel and the Port-o-John and the porn movies. Interesting details that she would enjoy someday soon when we had an afternoon to visit.

"Anyway," I finished, "I wonder if you could look Sunshine's record up for me. See what kind of student she is, if she's in any kind of extracurricular activities, if she cuts class much."

"I've already pulled her record up, Patricia Anne. These used to be confidential, you know. Now anybody with a computer can get to them. We'll probably have to go back to the old-fashioned manila folders in file cabinets someday. Give me a minute. Let me see what we've got."

I could hear clicks from her computer.

"Pretty good grades," Frances announced. "Came for tutoring in chemistry."

"Did she cut class much?"

"My Lord, Patricia Anne. They don't have that old three-cuts-and-you're-out rule like they did when you and I were in school back in the Ice Age."

"They don't keep attendance?"

"Nope. Not like we had to, girlfriend."

"Extracurricular activities?" I waited for the search.

"Don't see any. That's not unusual, though. These are day students who go back to jobs or their neighborhood pursuits."

"The only thing to pursue in her neighborhood is rabbits."

"In Redmont?"

"She lives in Locust Fork, Frances. In a trailer. Are you sure you have the right girl?"

"How many Sunshine Marie Dabbs would be enrolled here? It gives her address as 30535 Redmont Crest. Now isn't that up on Red Mountain close to Mary Alice? One of those fancy houses?"

"Maybe they moved," I said lamely.

"Well, she's a pretty girl, even in this school picture. Reminds me of Audrey Hepburn. Remember how we all went out and got Audrey Hepburn *Roman Holiday* haircuts, Patricia Anne?"

"She's got short dark hair?"

"She did last fall."

I'd read somewhere that hair grows a half inch a month. It was possible, I supposed, that Audrey Hepburn could have turned into a blonde Barbie in eleven months. Though if you were an Audrey Hepburn, why would you want to?

"Do you see anything else interesting? Who's listed as her father?"

"They don't have to give that anymore, Patricia Anne. I guess they think people might be snooping in these records."

God forbid.

"She does say in case of emergency to contact Edward Turkett."

"That's her uncle."

"Well, he's listed at that same address she gave on Redmont."

"That's strange."

"Not so strange. A lot of these kids live with relatives."

I wasn't about to explain Meemaw and the trailer to Frances. I thanked her for the information and promised that I would give Haley her love and wish her every happiness. Lunch soon.

Lord! None of the pieces of this jigsaw puzzle fit. Who in the world were the Turketts? What I needed was a Gabriel to tell me. I closed my eyes and thought of all I would ask him.

Chapter 9

IT WAS A MISTAKE CLOSING MY EYES. WHEN I WOKE UP, it was three o'clock and my morning headache had come back full blast. I groaned and went into the kitchen for aspirin. The television in the den was still on, and in the corner of the screen the temperature was posted, 103 degrees.

I heard a car door slam, and a moment later Haley came up the back steps. I opened the door and told her to bring Woofer in, 'tweren't fit for man nor beast out there. Haley grinned. When she was in the sixth grade, she had a starring part in the class play, a melodrama. Her brothers loved it, mimicking her " 'Tain't fit fer man nor beast" until Fred put his foot down.

She was back in a minute, pushing a reluctant Woofer. "He was all the way back in his igloo, Mama. He didn't want to come in."

I set down a bowl of water with ice in it. Woofer took a few laps and then stretched out on the floor. "I feel better with him in."

Haley looked at me suspiciously. "Have you been crying?"

"Nope. I've just had a nap that lasted way too long and I have a headache. You want some tea? I'm having some."

"I'll get it. Why don't you go sit in the den, Mama?"

89

I got my aspirin and did what she said because I felt like I was going to cry again and that wouldn't do. I had to be happy for Haley. I *was* happy for Haley.

"I talked to Debbie," she called from the kitchen. "I know what happened this morning." She came into the den and handed me a glass of tea and a napkin. "What do you think's going on?"

"I don't have any idea. That's a strange bunch of folks, honey. They've even got Sheriff Reuse sweating."

"Lord, I can't believe that."

"It's the truth. Kerrigan Dabbs says the sheriff thinks he's Sunshine's father."

"Really?" Haley thought about this a moment. "Did she say whether he was or not?"

"She said she didn't know."

Haley was truly shocked. "Was she serious?"

"Seemed to be."

"Well, Lord have mercy."

I laughed at the expression on Haley's face. "She's a gorgeous woman, Haley. Elizabeth Taylor eyes. Very little makeup."

"And a porn star."

I nodded yes.

Haley put her tea down and sat back on the sofa. "I want to hear some more in a few minutes, but let me bring you up to date on the wedding. For starters, it's not going to be in the judge's chambers; it's going to be in the little chapel at Trinity Methodist."

"Uh huh." Somebody, namely Mary Alice Crane, had been busy with more than looking for a missing daughter-in-law. Why was I not surprised?

"And I'm not going to wear my linen suit. Aunt Sister had the personal shopper from Parisian bring over some dresses for me to try on. There was one—you'll just love it, Mama—that's a pale pink silk that I just fell in love with. The lady called it blush, but I don't think they should call it that. It's not dark enough." Haley stopped for a moment, envisioning the dress. "It's pretty simple. Short. But it's got about a half an inch of pearl beading around the neck and the sleeves. But the unbelievable thing"—she held up her foot, a foot encased in dirty white canvas Keds—"is that there are shoes to match. Pale pink shoes with beading around the toe and heel.

"And then we're all having lunch at the Merritt House. Aunt Sister said she would have asked Henry to do it at her house, but Saturday is his busiest day at the club. We're going to have chicken Kiev."

"Chicken Kiev," I repeated, almost out of breath. Here sat my intelligent daughter totally oblivious to the fact that her every wedding plan had been changed by her aunt. Awesome.

"Little new potatoes, those green beans they do so good." Haley droned on while I thought about what the world would be like if Sister had been born a man. Boggled the mind.

"What do you think, Mama?"

"It sounds lovely." It really did. And my daughter was happy. So I hadn't been included in any of the planning. So what? I had a sudden memory of Mama saying, *"Remember, Patricia Anne, your sister always means well."* I didn't know about that "always" bit, but in this case, she had. I let go of my resentment and asked what kind of wedding cake Sister had planned. I couldn't resist.

Haley, bless her heart, laughed. "She *has* sort of taken over, hasn't she?"

"And done a good job, it sounds like. Just remember it's yours and Philip's wedding, though."

"I will." Haley leaned over and patted Woofer. "Mine

91

and Philip's wedding." She was tasting the words.

There was a long moment of silence. Then Haley jumped up. "The dress is being altered, but the shoes are in the car. I want you to see them, Mama."

I grabbed a paper napkin and mopped up a few fresh tears while she ran to the car. The phone rang and I answered it.

"You've been crying some more," Sister said.

"No, I haven't. I just woke up. Haley's here."

"She tell you about the wedding?"

"Every little change."

"It's a lot nicer, isn't it? Who wants to get married at the city hall?"

"A lot of people. Didn't you and Roger get married at the city hall?"

"And we shouldn't have. It was by far the least memorable of my weddings. The main thing I remember is the judge had about three hairs pulled all the way over from one ear to the other. I swear, I can't figure out why men's wives let them get away with that. I told Roger right after the ceremony that I didn't care how much balder he got, he wasn't going to pull his hair all the way over his head."

"I'm sure he appreciated that."

"He seemed to. I hope Ray doesn't get prematurely bald like his daddy did."

"Prematurely bald? Roger was sixty, Mary Alice."

"He'd been bald a long time. Has Haley got her outfit with her?"

"She's gone to the car to get the shoes; the dress is being altered."

"Well, listen. I'll pick you up around six-fifteen."

"For what?"

"To go to the airport to pick up Ray."

92

"You want me to go with you?"

"Ray wants you there. When I called to tell him we'd heard from Sunshine, he said for me to be sure to bring you to the airport."

"When did you talk to Ray?"

Haley came in with a shoebox, sat down, and began to pull off her Keds.

"This morning."

"How could you talk to him this morning? He was forty thousand feet over the Pacific Ocean."

"I picked up the phone and dialed him, Mouse. Simple. Anyway, I'll pick you up around six-fifteen. Tell Haley I want to see her outfit." The phone went dead.

Haley held up a beaded shoe for my admiration.

"Beautiful," I said, nodding. "You know what? Your Aunt Sister says she called Ray on an airplane halfway across the Pacific. Doesn't that boggle your mind? Forty thousand feet up there in the air and the phone ringing?"

"They just bounce it off a satellite."

Yeah. Just bounce if off a satellite. She was dealing here with a woman who still hasn't figured out how they squeeze all the voices onto the wires.

"Aren't these pretty?" Haley got up and walked around. Even Woofer looked up to admire the shoes.

"They're awesome." They really were.

"I'll bring the whole outfit by in the morning for you to see. Or tonight. I'm picking up the dress around five."

"Call. It seems I'm going to the airport with Sister to pick up Ray at seven. She said he wants me there. I can't imagine why. I'll be glad to see him, though."

"Ray knows his mama. He wants you there so he can find out immediately what's going on with Sunshine."

The answer pleased me, but I felt I had to take up for Mary Alice just like our own mother had. "She means

93

well, Haley."

"I know she does, Mama. But you hone right in. In Aunt Sister's version, Sunshine would just get lost in the story somewhere between Gabriel, Pawpaw, and Chief Joseph."

I swear the correction just popped out. "Among, Haley. Sunshine would get lost *among*. You've got three people."

Haley grinned. "I rest my case."

❀ ❀ ❀

"I could not leave him another Lean Cuisine. The man needed vegetables, Sister. Green leafy vegetables like collards."

"You got Fred collards? They'll never make it past his hiatal hernia."

"They will if he walks around during the Braves game. I left him a note to do that."

"Walk from the television in the den to the one in the bedroom?"

"He just has to keep moving."

"Lord."

It was a couple of hours later and we had plenty of time to get to the airport, but Sister was acting a fool. Absolutely. Just because I had run to the Heights Cafe to get Fred some supper and she had to wait five minutes for me.

"That's probably Ray's plane coming in now," she said.

We were hauling down the interstate with a clear view of the runways. A Cessna was landing. Not another plane was in sight.

"I don't think so," I said.

One of the things that surprises first-time visitors to Birmingham is the fact that the airport is practically in downtown. Granted, it's on the left of Interstate 59-20 if you're heading to Atlanta, and the downtown high-rise buildings are on the right, but runways and interstate run parallel. Somehow, thanks to chain-link fences and flashing arrows, it works. And it's convenient.

This late August afternoon, Jones Valley, where downtown and the airport are located, was simmering. You could see the heat rising from the pavement and fogging around the buildings. The sun setting to our left was a smoky red.

"What did it get up to today?" Mary Alice asked.

"A hundred four, they said on the five o'clock news."

"Did they say anything about Chief Joseph's murder?"

"Didn't mention it. Mainly talking about a couple of banks got robbed. And the heat."

"The dog days. Have you ever noticed how many banks get robbed during the dog days?" Mary Alice took the airport exit and turned left.

I'd never noticed a connection so I changed the subject. "We've got plenty of time," I said as she swung into the parking deck. I looked at my watch.

"We probably have time for a sandwich. I'm hungry."

"You are not. You're never hungry." Mary Alice slowed down. "Watch for a place. I swear I wish they hadn't done away with Saint Christopher. He always found me a parking place."

"I don't think they did away with him. Just demoted him."

"How can you demote a saint, Mouse? Besides, what did the man ever do to deserve demotion anyway?"

I shrugged. I sure didn't know.

"Just confuses people," Mary Alice grumbled.

I thought about advising her to write to the Pope and complain but decided it would be wiser not to since she was already peeved about having to wait while I got Fred the collards.

Fortunately a car was backing out on the second level. We parked and walked across to the terminal. It was a short walk, but it was still over a hundred degrees and we were sweating when the doors slid open and cool air rushed out to greet us.

Ray's flight, Delta 180 from Atlanta, was listed as being on time. It may seem strange that someone flying in from the west has to fly to Atlanta, change planes, and come back west to Birmingham. It seems strange to us. A favorite expression in Birmingham is that you can't go anywhere, not even to hell, without going through Atlanta. Having flown over my house numerous times on the way to Atlanta, I believe it.

The Birmingham International Airport is a pleasant place, not hustle and bustle like Atlanta's. More shuffle and pause. But that's fine. We rode up the escalator and made our way to the waiting area for Concourse C where a few people sat watching *Wheel of Fortune.*

"How come they call this an international airport?" Mary Alice asked, sitting in one of the connected chairs and dropping her purse on the floor with a thump. "You ever hear of an international flight coming in here?"

"Maybe one stopped one time on their way to Atlanta. Hijacked or something."

"Yeah, sure. Can't you just see a hijacker bursting into the cockpit and demanding that the pilot take him to Birmingham, Alabama?"

"It's a nice place."

"It is," Sister agreed. "Maybe Ray will decide to stay."

"After he meets his new in-laws? Dream on, Sister."

"They're just a little eccentric."

No way I was going to touch that one.

Across from us and down a couple of seats, a young woman sat knitting a green afghan.

Mary Alice leaned forward. "Our mother was a hooker," she informed her.

The woman looked up in surprise.

"She means she hooked rugs," I explained. "Beautiful ones." I turned and frowned at Mary Alice.

"Well, she knew what I was talking about. Good Lord, Mouse." Sister turned back to the young woman. "You knew what I was talking about, didn't you?"

"I guess so." The woman concentrated on a stitch she had dropped, retrieved it, and looked up with a lovely smile. "You just startled me."

"She does that a lot." I quickly tucked my legs as far under the blue fiberglass chair as I could to avoid the kick I knew was coming.

But Mary Alice just pointed toward the green afghan. "It's so nice to see a young woman doing handwork."

"Vanna White crochets afghans," I said, looking at the TV.

"And that's nice, you know? Good practice for turning letters. Things going in the right slot."

The woman smiled as if Sister had made sense. "I enjoy it." She stretched her fingers and then bent to her work again. The conversation had obviously worn down for her.

But the subject matter hadn't. "Patricia Anne," Sister said, "you know how the prettiest one of Mama's rugs is the one with the Easter lilies on it? I'm thinking about giving it to Ray and Sunshine. I think they'll appreciate it, don't you?"

"On a boat? No way. Give it to one of the girls."

"I guess you're right." Mary Alice glanced at her watch. "You must need batteries. We sure didn't have time for a sandwich." She got up and walked to the window. Just at that moment, a voice on the intercom announced the arrival of Delta flight 180 from Atlanta. I joined her to watch the plane taxiing in.

Ray was the first person up the ramp and we let him walk right by. We had seen the wedding tape and knew he had a beard, but we weren't expecting a Viking. We were waiting for the Ray who was still our youngest child.

"Mama. Aunt Pat." He stood behind us, at least fifty pounds heavier and grinning through a bush of golden blond hair. "You didn't recognize me."

Mary Alice clutched her chest. "My Lord." Ray hugged her, almost picking her up. Me he nearly threw over his shoulder. Then he gave each of us a big kiss which surprisingly, considering all the hair, was a familiar Ray smack.

"Y'all okay?" He looked around. "Sunshine's not here?"

"We haven't heard any more from her," Sister said, coming in for another hug. "Hey, my darling. How was your trip?"

"Long." He waved at someone over our shoulders. We turned and saw a huge bearded man walking toward us. Had I missed something? Were beards coming back in style? The last couple of days we had certainly seen a lot of them.

"Mama. Aunt Pat. This is my good buddy Buck Owens. Buck's my right-hand man on the boat."

"Ladies. I've heard a lot about both of you." Buck appeared to be about twenty years older than Ray, in his early fifties. His hairline was receding from his bronzed creased forehead, and there was as much gray in his beard as there was brown. Like Ray, he was wearing jeans and a tee shirt. His smile was that of a much younger man, though—a flash of white, even teeth.

"Here, Ray," he said, handing him a large paper sack. "Hold my Georgia suitcase for me and let me get hugs."

He was a very competent hugger. I even got a little pat on the behind, and I think Sister did, too. She looked at me, grinning. Sometimes I think the whole feminist movement missed us.

"Heard any more from Sunshine?" Buck asked as we were walking toward the baggage claim.

"Nothing," Sister said. "There's sure been a lot happening, though."

"Buck knows all about it, Mama."

"Yeah. Sounds like a mess. I grew up in Nectar, and I know the Turketts, every one of them. Nice people. Course Meemaw's a little strange since she saw the flying saucer, but that happens sometimes. You know?"

"Of course," Sister agreed. Just an everyday occurrence.

We reached the baggage carousel and waited.

"The funny thing," Ray said, "is that Sunshine had been on the boat for two days before Buck realized he knew her family."

"Didn't recognize the name Dabbs. Like to have had a fit when I found out she was Kerrigan's daughter." There was a buzz and the bags clunked down the ramp and began to circle. "I said, 'Lord, Lord, what a small world.' "

"Here, Buck." Ray reached over, grabbed a bag, and handed it to Buck.

"Thanks. I'm so jet-lagged, I'm cross-eyed."

"Are you going out to Nectar tonight?" Mary Alice asked. "Do you want us to take you?"

He nodded. "My mama's expecting me. She's the main reason I came home. I came to help Ray, too, but the main reason is my mama. I've been away too long. And I appreciate the offer, but I'll grab me some coffee and rent a car. It's no distance."

"We'll be happy to take you."

"Thank you, ma'am. But I'll be fine, and I'll need a car up there." Buck Owens picked up his bag. "I'll call you tomorrow, Ray."

99

"Okay, Buck. Thanks."

"Bye, ladies."

I watched him walk away carrying the suitcase, paper sack under the other arm. I didn't know how long Buck had been working on boats, but he had the slight roll of a sailor. Nice man, I thought.

"If that man lost a hundred pounds, he'd be a knockout," Mary Alice said to Ray. "Did you meet him in Bora Bora or did you already know him?"

"I met him in Bora Bora. In fact, I bought his boat. I saw it advertised and went to see him. When I opened my mouth, he said, 'Man, you've got to be from Alabama.' We got a kick out of that."

"How come he was selling the boat?" I asked.

"He'd never had the money to fix it up for dive groups coming from the United States and Australia. They want nice accommodations and good food and they're willing to pay good money for it. Old Buck's a great diver, but he's not much for the amenities." Ray reached over and grabbed a bag. "Anyway, he stayed with me and it's worked out fine for both of us." He straightened. "Okay, let's go."

Mary Alice pointed to the bag. "That's all you brought?"

"I've got a closet full of clothes at home, Mama, unless you've given them to the Goodwill."

"They're there." And they would all fit a man several sizes smaller. Ray had forgotten about that.

"Jeez!" he exclaimed as we stepped through the door. "What's the temperature?"

"I think it made it to a hundred five." Mary Alice looked at Ray with concern. Sweat was streaming down his forehead, the only part of his face we could see. "Are you okay?"

"Jet-lagged to hell and back. And you're sure it's only a hundred five?"

"That's not counting the humidity," I said. "The heat index is something like a hundred fifteen."

"Well, good. I thought I'd suddenly been hit by a truck."

"You look like it, too," Mary Alice said. "Let's get you where it's cool and get some fluids down you."

"And tell me all about Sunshine. You're sure she's okay?"

"Positive," we both lied.

Chapter 10

AN HOUR LATER, WE WERE SITTING IN SISTER'S AIR-conditioned sunroom. The plants and white wicker furniture make it an oasis on a day like this. Below us, Jones Valley simmered in deep twilight.

Ray, showered and dressed in shorts and tee shirt, an outfit he must have brought with him because it fit, sat on the sofa eating pasta salad and drinking iced tea.

"I didn't think I was hungry," he said. "But I guess I am."

"Here, have some more tea, sweetheart." Mary Alice filled his glass. "That's what you need when you're jet-lagged. And eat those apple wedges. They're good for you, too."

I had eaten while Ray was showering and now I had my chair turned sideways so I could see the whole valley and the statue of Vulcan guarding it. Behind Vulcan, down a tree-lined street, was a man walking from his den to his bedroom trying to digest collards and keep up with the Braves game. I had called him as soon as we got to Sister's

101

and he said the vegetables were delicious and he had eaten every bite. "Walk," I reminded him. "And take some Maalox."

Ray put his plate on the coffee table. "Thanks, Mama. That was great. Now y'all tell me everything that's happened."

"We don't know," I said.

"I mean everything in general, Aunt Pat. I think I'm missing a lot of what's been going on."

"That's for sure." Sister looked over at me. "I'll tell him about the dinner party, Mouse, and you tell him about the dead Indian. Okay?"

"Sure."

Mary Alice sat down across from Ray. "Well, Henry did the cooking and we had Rock Cornish hens, but Debbie didn't feel like coming so I invited Haley who, incidentally, is marrying Dr. Philip Nachman Saturday and going to live in Warsaw for six months. Bless her heart. They were going to the city hall and having a judge do it but I stepped in and said, 'Listen, Haley, a person doesn't get married very often so you ought to make it special.'"

Ray reached over and patted his mother on her knee. "What about Sunshine, Mama?"

"Well, she had on a pink sundress with spaghetti straps and looked just like a Barbie doll. Her Meemaw is something else, though. I hope your children don't look like her, Ray. Little squenchy eyes." Sister made little binoculars with her fingers and held them to her eyes. "Real squenchy and her face all puffy. You know how steroids do you?" She turned to me. "I hadn't thought of that, Mouse. Did Meemaw say anything about taking steroids? I swear so much has happened I can't remember it all."

I shrugged that I didn't know.

"Anyway, it doesn't matter except we don't want something wrong with her that your children could inherit." Mary Alice paused. "Where was I?"

"The dinner party," Ray said.

"Of course. Well, we were sitting in here having drinks and Sunshine said she had a tape of the wedding for us to see, but she'd left it in the car which she should have known better than to do because they warp in this heat. But anyway, she went and got it, but it wasn't a tape of your wedding. It was a movie her mother starred in." Sister looked at me for help but she got it from Ray.

"She told me her mother makes porn movies."

"But she's real nice, son."

"And beautiful," I added.

"Okay, tell me about the dead Indian."

It was my turn. I told him about running into Meemaw and going to the Compound, about the dogs—

"Pick up a stick if you go out there," Sister interrupted.

I told him about the Indian who really wasn't an Indian but who chiefed at Crystal Caverns, about the hog-butchering knife, and Sunshine's disappearance. And Pawpaw.

Together Sister and I told him about the morning's search, and he listened to Sunshine's message.

"I'm more jet-lagged than I thought," he said. "None of this is adding up. I guess I thought Sunshine would have shown up by now with some explanations. Unless she's really been kidnapped. But"—he pointed toward the phone—"if she were, she wouldn't have left that message."

"Well, we're not going to solve it tonight and you need some rest." I got up and stretched. "Are you going to take me home, Sister, or do you want me to call Fred?"

"I'll take you. Let me find my keys."

I kissed Ray and told him to sleep well. He followed me down the hall toward the front door.

"Thank you, Aunt Pat, for everything."

"I've done nothing, darling. I wish there were something I could do."

"I found them," Mary Alice called.

Ray opened the front door and I stepped out and fell flat. I don't mean a sort of glide-down or stumble-around. I mean flat, right on the terrazzo tile and the welcome mat.

"My God, Aunt Pat. Are you all right?" He stepped out to help me and ended up on the tile, too, though I could tell from the noise and the fact that he didn't land on top of me that his fall was the stumble-around-before-you-settle variety.

"What are y'all doing down there?" Sister asked.

"Don't come out, Mama." Ray touched my shoulder. "Are you all right, Aunt Pat?"

"I just don't know." I moved my arms and legs. They were working. There was no sharp pain in my hips. I saw only one Sister and Ray, and I knew who the President was. I turned on my side and felt a squishy mess under my stomach. I reached down and touched it. "Maybe you'd better call 911. I think my intestines are falling out." I don't even remember being afraid, just surprised that my insides had suddenly gushed out.

"Yuck," Ray said. "It's a dead turkey."

"Roll over, Mouse. You've killed a turkey. Are you okay?" Sister knelt down with much groaning. "Lord, I'm getting out of shape."

I rolled over and sat up gingerly. All my bones still seemed to be connected. There was a burning sensation on my forehead, though. I reached up and felt a knot already popping up. Ray and Mary Alice were examining a

104

turkey which, as far as I could tell, was split down the middle, viscera spilling out. I closed my eyes against sudden nausea and held on to a pot of geraniums.

"I didn't kill that turkey," I managed to say.

"What the hell kind of deal is this?" Ray stood up, brushing himself off.

Sister poked at the turkey. "And he was just lying here when y'all stepped out?"

"Of course, Mama. How come you think Aunt Pat and I ended up on the porch?" This reminded Ray. He came over and gently lifted me to my feet. The world whirled around dizzily.

I held on for dear life. "Don't let me go."

"God, look at that goose egg," Ray said.

Sister looked around. "There's an egg, too?"

"On Aunt Pat's head, Mama." He picked me up and carried me in to the den sofa. "We've got to get some ice on that."

Sister followed us, looking worried.

"I'm okay," I told her.

"No, you're not. You're going to look awful at Haley's wedding."

The wedding. I felt my forehead. She was right. I was going to have the shiner of all times.

Ray was back in a minute with ice wrapped in a paper towel. "Maybe we ought to take you to the emergency room," he said. "That's really a big bump."

"Get the flashlight out of the junk drawer and let's see if her pupils are dilated," Sister said. Ray trotted off and was back in a moment shining a big yellow flashlight in my eyes.

"What do you think?" He turned the light off and on while he and Sister watched to see what happened in my eyes.

"I think you're crazy." I snatched the flashlight away and sat up. The room was reasonably still. "I'm going home. I'm going to take a very long hot shower and throw these dead turkey clothes away. Yuck. And then I'm going to take a whole bottle of aspirin and put an ice pack on my head and go to bed. Is that clear?"

"I'll take you," Mary Alice said.

❀ ❀ ❀

Fred was asleep in his recliner when I went in which was a relief. I wanted to get cleaned up before he saw me. The knot on my head would be bad enough; I didn't want him to see dead turkey all down the front of my good beige linen pants which, regardless of what Mary Alice said, I bet the cleaners couldn't do a thing with.

I crept into the bedroom, closed the door quietly so I wouldn't wake him up, and shucked off the bloody turkey clothes which I figured were probably strep and staph incubators by now. I took the plastic liner from the bathroom wastebasket and wrapped them in it. Then I got in the shower and, for the second time that day, began to bawl. My head ached, I was going to have a black eye, and every joint in my body was stiffening. Every bit of it was Sister's fault.

The hot water felt good on my neck and shoulders. I put my head back far enough so some of it ran down my forehead and blended with the tears. It actually felt soothing going over the bump. I wet a washrag and draped it over my head and forehead. Haley was to blame, too. Springing a wedding on us and moving to Europe like that.

Mary Alice and Haley. If I ended up on Prozac, they'd be to blame. If I ended up in Brookwood Hospital's psych ward, it would be their fault. "*No*," I would say to Fred. "*Tell Haley she mustn't come all the way across the Atlantic to see about me even though I know she's eaten up with guilt."*

I began to feel a lot more cheerful. *"And tell Sister that the doctor says she is to remember my fragile emotional state. No more bossing me around or calling me Mouse."*

"Yes, my darling. You're the cornerstone of this family. We all know that now." Fred would lean over and brush my lips with a kiss. *"You just get your head back on straight."*

Hmmm. He could have phrased that better.

The shower door opened just a little. "Can I get in with you?" Fred asked.

"You can get in but not with me. I'm getting out."

"That's okay. I've already had a shower."

I turned off the water and reached for a towel.

"I'll dry your back," Fred said helpfully.

"Not until you see my head." I stepped out and pushed my wet hair back so he could get a good look.

"My Lord, honey, how'd you get that bruise?"

"I fell over a turkey."

He held me by my shoulders. "Come over here in the light where I can get a good look at that thing. What do you mean you fell over a turkey?"

"I mean there was a turkey on Sister's porch. A dead one. I fell over it." I closed my eyes as Fred tilted my head toward the fluorescent light over the medicine cabinet. "It's all Sister's fault."

"I'm sure it is, honey." He circled the bump gently with his fingers. "Do you feel okay? Dizzy or anything?"

"I was at first. I'm okay now. Except everything hurts."

"Well, damn." He handed me my nightgown which was hanging behind the door. "Here, honey, put this on. I think I'd better call the doctor."

But I had an inspiration. "Why don't you call Haley?"

"Good idea. She needs to come over and check you

out." Fred held out my summer robe. "And I want you to come sit in the den until she gets here or until I get the doctor. I don't think you ought to go to sleep."

I was feeling much better. "Haley is probably at Philip's, you know."

Fred led me gently down the hall. "I'll find her. I can't believe Mary Alice didn't do something about this."

Much, much better.

"A turkey?"

Maybe I imagined I heard a tiny snicker.

❊ ❊ ❊

"Advil's about the best you can do for something like this, Mama. You got any?" Haley sat on the edge of the couch in the den.

"I've got a little package that came in the mail with some coupons."

"Well, take a couple of them. I really don't see any signs of a concussion. You might want to check with the doctor, but I'm sure he'd just say call him if you have any symptoms like nausea."

"That's some knot, isn't it?" her father said admiringly.

"If that turkey had been an ostrich, she'd be dead." Haley and Fred both giggled. I knew I'd be hearing *"Remember the time Mama fell over the turkey?"* until the day I died.

I shifted the ice pack to my other hand. "I'm going to look like hell at your wedding."

"So am I at the rate I'm going. I'm only halfway packed and I keep thinking of things to do, like stop the paper."

"What are you doing about your job?"

"Della St. Clair is coming back. She quit when her little girl was born, but she's three now and Della jumped at the chance. By the way, Mama, y'all will keep Muffin for me, won't you? She's not a bit of trouble. I don't think she and

108

Woofer will bother each other at all."

"Sure we will," Fred agreed. "But no heating pads on the kitchen counter."

They both laughed at that. Mary Alice's fat cat, Bubba, sleeps on a heating pad on her counter. Not only is it a terrible fire hazard, but it's a wonder all of us don't have hair balls.

"Back to the turkey, though. It was split down the middle?" Haley asked.

"With its insides falling out. It was awful."

"No way it could have flown up there and banged into the door? There are wild turkeys all up there in those woods."

I looked at my daughter with my good right eye. "If that's what happened, that particular turkey had the San Andreas fault right down his middle waiting to erupt. No, Haley, he was cut and put there as a warning for Ray that that's what will happen to Sunshine if he gets too nosy or doesn't follow instructions. Not that there have been any. Or to one of the other Turketts." I paused. "I reckon." I shifted the ice pack to my other hand. Damn, it was cold. "That's pretty much what happened to that dead Indian guy. Split down the middle."

"He wasn't an Indian," Fred said.

"I know. He was Mexican or something."

"His name was Dudley Cross and he lived in Bradford." Fred seemed pleased with himself.

"How did you find that out?" Haley asked.

"It's in tonight's *Post-Herald*. Here." Fred reached over and got the paper. "It's on the second page. It says a body found stabbed in a mobile home in the Locust Fork community has been identified as Dudley Cross, fifty-three, of Bradford. Mr. Cross frequently worked at Crystal Caverns as an Indian chief, posing for photographs."

"Dudley Cross," Haley said. "You know, I'll bet all his life people called him Double Cross." She took the paper from Fred. "Does it say anything else? Anything about his family or about the Turketts?"

"Doesn't even say he was killed in Meemaw's trailer or that Sunshine's missing." Fred pointed out the article to her. "Is Ray calling the police about the turkey?" he asked me.

"I don't know. Maybe. What he ought to do is call Sheriff Reuse. I'm sure he'll do that. Or Sister will."

"That ought to get some action." Fred stood up. "I'll go get the Advil. Where are they, honey?"

"In the corner by the coupon box. A little sample package."

Haley handed me the paper, but I didn't have my reading glasses. There was nothing new there, anyway, except the Indian's name, and learning his name saddened me. Dudley Cross who lived in Bradford was a real person who had lived a life for fifty-three years. Damn.

"Is Ray okay?" Haley asked.

"You mean about Sunshine? He seems to be accepting her message that she's all right." I took the pills Fred handed me and washed them down with Coke. "He looks good. A big beard and about two hundred fifty pounds."

Haley was surprised. "I can't believe that. Ray's always been skinny."

"Not anymore. Not by a long shot. He looks good, though. And the guy who works with him, Buck Owens, weighs at least three fifty. He came home with Ray. He lives out in Nectar and said he needed to come see his mother and that maybe he could help Ray. Seems he knows the Turketts."

"And he let Ray marry Sunshine?"

"She seems like a nice girl, Haley."

"That's true. I ought to be ashamed of myself. She just didn't strike me as being authentic, somehow." Haley shook her head. "I don't know. Maybe she was just nervous."

"Having Mary Alice for a mother-in-law would do that," Fred agreed.

"This morning up at the Compound someone said Sunshine had crawled out from under a rock." I took another sip of Coke. "I didn't see who it was."

"Well, that's interesting." Haley stood up. "I hope they're wrong, and I hope I'm wrong. I want Ray to be happy." She leaned over and kissed the bump on my head. "You'll feel better tomorrow, and don't worry about how you look, Mama. Somebody, maybe Merle Norman, has some makeup with a greenish tint to it that's supposed to cover up bruises. People use it after face-lifts and things."

I'd rather not think about the "things."

"I'll check with you in the morning. Y'all get some sleep now."

Fred locked the kitchen door after she left and came back into the den. "Think you can sleep?"

"Probably. It's been a long day."

But long after we were in bed and Fred's breathing had become a light snore, events of the last several days played themselves over and over in my mind like one of those avant-garde films that skips from one scene to the next and they assume you figure out the relationship.

"*His name is Gabriel,*" Meemaw said.

"*Sunshine's not here?*" Ray asked.

"*Hey, pretty lady.*"

"*Tell Ray I'm fine.*"

"*A Port-o-John.*"

"*Stress-free turkeys.*"

The last thing I remember before sleep finally claimed

me was an image of Sunshine climbing out from under a big, big rock.

Chapter 11

FRED WOKE ME UP THE NEXT MORNING TO MAKE SURE I was all right before he went to work.

"More aspirin," I groaned. While he went to get them, I got up and went to the bathroom. The mirror over the medicine cabinet gave me bad news. "Damn," I murmured.

Fred came back with the aspirin. "Maybe you can sleep some more. If you want me, I'll be close to the office."

"Okay." I took the aspirin and promptly went back to sleep.

"Psst."

I opened my green bloodshot eyes and stared into Mary Alice's brown ones which were about two inches away.

"Are you okay? You don't look so good."

I rolled over and pushed my face into the pillow. "Go away."

"What?"

"I said go away. What time is it anyway?"

"It's about nine-fifteen. The sheriff's here to talk to you. I told him you weren't very pleasant in the morning, but he said it would save him another trip to town."

"Sheriff Reuse is here in my house?"

"In the kitchen drinking coffee. It was the last cup, but I've made some more. Are there any sweet rolls in the freezer?"

I slapped the air where I thought Sister was. Pain arced through my stiff shoulder.

"I'll look and see," she said. "You can come out when

you're ready."

I lay there for a few minutes hoping that, by some miracle, Sister's appearance had been a bad dream. The smell of coffee and sweet rolls put an end to that illusion, though. Plus, the coffee smelled wonderful. I finally got up, combed my hair, brushed my teeth, and went into the den.

"Here's Miss Slugabed," Mary Alice said cheerfully. She and the sheriff were sitting at my kitchen table in my bay window drinking my coffee and eating my sweet rolls.

"Morning, Mrs. Hollowell. That's some bruise you've got there. Mrs. Crane didn't do it justice."

"I'm getting some green makeup today," I said. I headed for the coffeepot with as much dignity as a knot on my head and a bathrobe that needed hemming would allow.

"What kind of green makeup?" Sister asked.

"Some Haley told me about. It has a greenish base that hides bruises. She thinks Merle Norman has it."

"If they don't, I'll bet you could get some at an undertaker's." The sheriff reached for another sweet roll.

I looked at him. He was serious, unfortunately. "Thanks. I'll remember that." I put sugar and cream in my coffee and sat down at the table between them. "Okay. What can I do for you?"

The sheriff stuffed a whole sweet roll in his mouth, wiped his sticky fingers on a paper napkin, and whipped out a notepad. "Just need to clear up a few things. Mrs. Crane said you wouldn't mind if we came over."

This was the reason children are taught not to talk with food in their mouths. "There's icing on your chin," I said.

He swiped at it with the back of his hand. "Thanks. Okay, tell me about finding Dudley Cross's body, Mrs. Hollowell. Just free-associate here. You may remember

113

something that surprises you. I may ask a few questions, but mainly I want you to just talk."

"Has Mary Alice done this?"

"Yes."

"I didn't remember a whole lot," Sister said.

"Well"—I took a sip of coffee—"Meemaw fell over him and we fell over her and didn't even know there was a body there for a minute. It was just a bunch of confusion. Then Meemaw started screeching about her hog-butchering knife and we saw the body." I looked over at Sister. "Mary Alice got sick. She didn't throw up or anything. She just rooted up against the sofa."

"And Mr. Cross?"

"Had on a gray wool suit, jacket and all, and it was burning-up hot. He had on a red tie, maybe striped, and a white dress shirt that looked like it had been done at a laundry. There wasn't much blood on it." I stopped. "But you already know this."

"What was Meemaw doing?"

"Sitting there. Sort of moaning. Then she started looking for Sunshine." I waited for another question but the sheriff was quiet. "The dogs were there," I added. "If a stranger had come up or someone who didn't know about the sticks, they'd have eaten them alive." I paused, trying to remember the details of the scene.

"Anything else?"

"It didn't look like there had been a struggle in there. The Chinese checker game Meemaw and Sunshine had been playing was still on the table, not even bumped. And everything looked tidy, except for the Indian, of course. Mr. Cross."

"What do you know about him?" Mary Alice asked the sheriff.

"Nothing much. He'd been in a few minor scrapes.

Caught for speeding once and they found a little marijuana, not enough to be peddling it. Couple of shoplifting charges. None stuck. A man at the caverns swore he took his wallet, but they never could prove anything." The sheriff shrugged. "Just piddling stuff. In the army a while, in Vietnam. Rented a garage apartment from a man out in Bradford said Cross didn't have any family he knew of." The sheriff picked up his notepad. "Sorry. Go on, Mrs. Hollowell."

"Well, Pawpaw showed up and started flirting with my sister here."

"He's pretty good at it, too," Mary Alice said.

I gave her a hard look. "Anyway, it made Meemaw mad and she said Mary Alice had been coming on to him."

Sister grinned. "Old coot."

"And then you said leave and we left. Nearly got ourselves killed when we got to the road. This car came over the rise going about a hundred. It was that Dwayne Parker kid. I saw his car at the Exxon station yesterday and recognized it."

The sheriff wrote the name down. "Who's Dwayne Parker?"

"One of Sunshine's old swains, best we can make out. I think he lives out there somewhere. Drives like greased lightning, too. He was out there with the search party yesterday."

"I'll check it out." The sheriff made a note and studied it as if he had just written something important.

"I know. I know what happened." Sister put her sweet roll down and clasped her hands together. "Sunshine was in the trailer and the man came in and attacked her. She grabbed Meemaw's hog-butchering knife to protect herself and hit him a little too hard." Sister paused. "Well, a lot too hard. She panicked and called Dwayne to come rescue her. Which he did. But being madly in love with her, he's holding her captive. Sunshine"—she opened her arms expansively—"is a prisoner of love."

The sheriff looked amazed.

"She's been taking creative writing classes at UAB," I explained. "She's doing pretty good with them, too."

"I can tell." The sheriff pointed his pencil at Sister. "A few loose ends here, though. For instance, what happened to Mr. Cross's car?"

"Sunshine drove it somewhere and Dwayne met her. She was in his car when they nearly hit us."

"Did you see her?"

"She was hiding on the floor."

"Her bloody nightgown was found in the woods. How do you account for that?"

"I thought it was by the body."

Lord, it was too early to be sitting here listening to this. I got up stiffly and poured another cup of coffee. The thermometer on the back porch already read ninety-four degrees and there was no sign of Woofer. I knew he was in his igloo, perfectly fine, but I needed to check on him anyway. An old animal becomes more precious each day.

"I'm going to go see about my dog," I said and stuck a couple of dog biscuits in my pocket. The two at the table paid no attention. They were having a good time.

"It's like a great puzzle each time," the sheriff was saying as I opened the door and stepped out into what felt like a blast furnace.

Woofer condescended to come out for the treats. He was as stiff as I was.

"Let's walk around a minute," I said. So we strolled around the yard examining the shrubs and flowers. Only the hardier flowers make it through the summer heat in Birmingham. By August the petunias and impatiens have had it. But begonias, geraniums, periwinkles, and the tall purple coneflowers have staked their claim to be around until frost. In this morning's heat, though, even the coneflowers were drooping. I turned on the hose and laid it on the ground so it would water the roots but not the foliage. Tonight, I promised myself, I would turn on the sprinkler if we didn't get an afternoon shower.

"Haley's getting married tomorrow," I informed Woofer who had just marked his territory on the apple tree. He turned and went back into his igloo.

"I know how you feel," I said. "I may go back to bed, too."

"But it had to be Eddie Turkett," Mary Alice was saying as I went back into the kitchen. "Who else could find a whole turkey, feathers and all? Everybody else would have a frozen Butterball one with the gizzards in a plastic bag."

"Not necessarily," the sheriff countered. "There are places all over Blount County where you can buy chickens and turkeys straight out of the yard. Some folks think they're better, but they're crazy. Most of them are stringy as all get-out when you cook them. Just like wild turkeys. No ma'am. Give me a storebought freezer one anytime."

I had obviously not been missed. "Excuse me," I said. "I'm going to go get dressed." Neither of them looked my way.

"Maybe it was Meemaw left the turkey. Trying to scare me away from Pawpaw."

It seemed to me that this murder investigation was being conducted very casually, to say the least. What had happened to DNA and fingerprints? And that stuff you sprayed around for hidden blood? When I left the kitchen, the sheriff and Mary Alice were laughing cozily over Meemaw's jealousy.

I slipped on a loose knit dress I had ordered from Lands' End and a pair of sandals. I brushed my hair, penciled on some eyebrows, and applied an apricot-colored lipstick. By the time I got back to the two chums in the kitchen, I didn't look much better, but I felt better.

Their conversation seemed to have wandered to Ray's dive ship.

"I don't know how big it is," Sister was saying. "But they take as many as ten people out for a week. So it must be pretty big."

"What kind of a crew would you have to have for a trip like that?"

"Three or four. A cook, of course, and a dive master. Ray says you have to have a top-notch dive master, because the safety of the divers depends on him knowing the waters."

"I'd love to make a trip like that," the sheriff said. "I've just started taking diving lessons in the Homewood pool. It would cost a bundle, though."

"Ray'll give you a discount."

I started loading the dishwasher. I hoped the sheriff didn't show up a year from now demanding his discount from Ray.

Sister licked her finger and stuck it into the crumbs on the sweet roll plate. "You may know his dive master. His name is Buck Owens and he lives out at Nectar. He owned the boat Ray bought and he stayed on as a crew member."

"Don't know him."

"Well, he came in last night with Ray. I thought that was real nice. He said he'd check on his family and be available if Ray needed him."

"He's huge," I said. "Looks like he'd sink to the bottom."

Both of them looked up in surprise. I was right; they'd forgotten I was there.

Sheriff Reuse glanced at his watch. "Good Lord. I've got to go. I've got an appointment with Eddie Turkett in fifteen minutes."

"You ask him about that turkey," Sister said. "I'm still trying to figure out what it meant."

The sheriff pushed his chair back and stood up. "It meant you need to stay away from Locust Fork until we get this thing cleared up."

"We won't have a problem doing that," I assured him.

Mary Alice walked with him to the front door and came back to inform me that she was going to the Big, Bold, and Beautiful Shoppe to get something to wear to the wedding.

"What are you wearing?" she asked me.

I hadn't thought about it. Other than green makeup. "I've got lots of stuff," I said. I put the last cup and saucer in the dishwasher and closed the door. "I'll go with you if you'll stop by Merle Norman's, though. I haven't seen Bonnie Blue in ages." Bonnie Blue Butler's becoming a friend of ours is the only good thing that came from Mary Alice's losing her mind and buying the Skoot 'n' Boot, a country-western bar out on Highway 78.

"Okay. Maybe she'll have lunch with us."

Lord. The woman was stuffed with sweet rolls and already thinking about lunch.

✼ ✼ ✼

"How was Ray this morning?" I asked as I got in Sister's Jaguar and the seat belt grabbed me. When the car was brand-new, I made the mistake of getting in with a Styrofoam cup of coffee in my hand. Sister swears the car still smells like Folgers.

"He was still asleep when I left." Sister backed out of

119

the driveway. "He called the police last night about the turkey. A man came by and looked and said it was probably kids."

"Sheriff Reuse seemed to be taking it a little more seriously."

"He is. I gave him that note somebody put in my pocket, the one that said Chief Joseph sent his regards to my son, and he thinks somebody's trying to scare us off. Now if we could just figure out what they're trying to scare us off of."

"And still no word from Sunshine?"

"Nope."

"Maybe she's hiding out at her Uncle Eddie's house. I think she lives there at least part of the time, anyway. It's the home address she gave at Jefferson State."

"How'd you find that out?"

"Frances Zata. She's working out there part-time. Incidentally, Sunshine's grades are pretty good, too."

Sister looked interested. "Is it legal for Frances to be telling you this?"

"If I had a computer, I could probably get it myself without going through her." I looked in my purse and found the bank deposit slip on which I had written Eddie Turkett's address. "He lives up close to you. You want to go check it out?"

"That's probably where the sheriff was going."

"I'll bet he wasn't. I'll bet he was going out to Eddie's office in Trussville."

"What's the address? We'll just ride by."

A ten-minute drive through hot, deserted streets brought us to the top of Red Mountain. The valley was hazy, still under the influence of the inversion. Sister turned onto Redmont Crest and checked the mailboxes.

The houses up here sit far back on well-kept lawns.

Sister's house is in this neighborhood and is similar to the others. They have no backyard since they are on the crest of the mountain. A couple of the more adventurous homeowners have had their houses built on poles so the houses seem to float out over the valley. That would make me nervous as hell. When I step out of my back door, I want to step on the ground, not into thin air.

Eddie Turkett's house was not one of the modern ones. It was a large dark red brick, two stories, probably built in the 1920s and perfectly maintained. The huge lawn of St. Augustine grass didn't seem to be wilting in the heat, and the two old oak trees that sat on either side of the driveway had been there when Jones Valley was settled. Across the front of the property was a black wrought-iron fence, the kind with little spears on it at intervals.

The street was deserted so Sister stopped. "Look, Mouse. Lightning rods in the trees. That's what I should have gotten for that big oak of mine I'm still trying to save."

I looked at one of the trees and saw what looked like a TV antenna sticking up.

"It's costing me a fortune trying to save that tree." Sister pointed. "And look at that fountain."

In front of the house, the driveway circled around a fountain that was spitting water into the air.

"Not much water pressure," I said.

"But Eddie Turkett's not on his way to the poor-house, is he?"

"I'd say not. It's a beautiful house."

"An expensive one, anyway. What did Meemaw say about Eddie's wife?"

"She said something like he and Howard occasionally had wives and children and that's why they needed the trailers as a getaway."

"How can you have an occasional wife?"

I shrugged. Mary Alice occasionally has husbands,but I thought it best not to mention this. Instead I said, "There doesn't seem to be anybody at home now." This was true. The house seemed deserted. In fact, the whole neighborhood seemed deserted. No one was out in the yards, not even the Chem-lawn people. Not a single car had passed us; no dog barked, I thought of my own neighborhood. Certainly not as fancy, but people were walking down the sidewalks and cars were passing.

"It's nice up here," Mary Alice said as if she were reading my thoughts.

"It's too isolated."

"Not really. Everybody up here's got binoculars and a telescope."

"Dear Lord," I said. "You need to get married again."

Sister giggled. "Maybe you're right."

That got my attention. "Is there something I need to know?"

"Not really." She giggled again. "Well, maybe." A long pause. "Bill's back again."

Bill Adams is Mary Alice's off-again, on-again line-dancing boyfriend, a handsome man in his early seventies. Several times I've thought they were getting serious and each time they drifted apart. Bill spends the winters in Florida, for one thing, and Sister doesn't tolerate separation well.

"Good," I said, knowing full well that if Sister did get married again, it wouldn't be to Bill.

"He's been calling me all summer but I kept telling him I had other plans. I figured he'd catch on after a while. And then you know what he did?"

"What?" I really wanted to know. This sounded romantic.

"He developed a kidney stone. Had them call me from

122

the emergency room at Brookwood Hospital. In all that pain and he wanted me. Isn't that the sweetest thing?"

"Precious."

"Well, it was."

"Is he okay now?"

"Oh, sure. Good as new. They smushed it with sound waves."

"And they say, 'Say it with flowers.'"

Another giggle. Maybe I was wrong about how serious Sister was about Bill.

She pointed toward Eddie Turkett's house. "You really think Sunshine might be hiding up there?"

"I don't have any idea. I just know she lives there part of the time."

"At least she has room to hang up her clothes."

"Obviously."

"Hmmm," Sister said. "You want to go knock on the door?"

"No. Besides, she wouldn't come if she's hiding."

"She's not hiding from us. She's hiding from the person who killed the Indian."

"What if somebody else comes to the door, like Eddie's wife?"

"We'll tell them we're Jehovah's Witnesses."

"Absolutely not."

Mary Alice reached in her purse and pulled out a small pair of binoculars which she aimed at the house.

"Put those up!" I grabbed at them.

She ducked. "I'm just looking, for heaven's sake."

"You're spying."

"Well, of course I am. Why else did we come up here?"

I thought about that for a moment while Mary Alice focused the binoculars and looked. "See anything?" I asked.

"No. But I'll tell you, Mouse, it's damn confusing. I

just can't figure out exactly if these people are trash or not. I hate not being able to figure that out, don't you?"

"Hmmm." Having binoculars trained on a house was pretty trashy. Best not say anything.

"I think somebody's up on the second floor looking through the curtains. See what you think."

Trashy or not, I took the binoculars. "I don't see anything."

A white car pulled up beside us and a familiar figure got out.

Officer Bo Mitchell of the Birmingham Police Department motioned for Mary Alice to let down her window.

"I was listening to the dispatcher and I told myself, I said, 'Bo, girl, that can't be who it sounds like, two women in a Jaguar skirting around looking for a house to hit on Redmont Crest.' But I was wrong, wasn't I? It's y'all. Is this the house you've decided on?"

"Hey, Bo," we both said.

"Everybody on the street's called."

"Doesn't look like anybody's at home."

"Don't kid yourself." Bo wiped her forehead with a handkerchief she took from her pocket. "Let me in your backseat. I'm dying out here."

Mary Alice unlocked the door and Bo got in.

"Lord, what a day." She leaned forward and grinned. "Well, hello, my two favorite felons. What's going on?"

"You've lost more weight," I said.

Bo nodded. "One hundred thirty-two. If Oprah can do it, I can do it."

"You look great." She did. Bo's skin is the color of light chocolate, and her wide-set eyes have a slightly Oriental slant to them.

"You don't. What'd you do to your head?"

124

"Fell over a turkey."

"Sounds reasonable to me." Bo laughed. "Y'all want to tell me what you're up to?"

"It's a long story," Sister said.

"I love to hear y'all's stories. Let's go down to Hardee's and you can take your time. I could use a Coke and a potty."

"My house is closer," Mary Alice said. "And this really is a complicated story."

"Do, Jesus. A complicated story. I'll follow you."

Chapter 12

RAY WAS SITTING IN THE SUNROOM EATING CEREAL and watching *The Price Is Right* when we came in. He had on khaki shorts and a faded blue shirt that looked as if it had seen many a diving trip. He looked considerably more rested than he had the night before.

We introduced him to Bo Mitchell who informed him she had apprehended us lurking around on Redmont Crest.

"It's where Eddie Turkett lives," Mary Alice explained to Ray. "Sunshine gave that as her address at Jeff State, so we were just looking around."

"Clue me in." Bo leaned back in a wicker chair and took the Coke I offered her. "Take your time."

"It's a long story," Mary Alice repeated.

"Suits me."

So we told her the whole story of Sunshine (with help from Ray), of the Turketts, all of them, and of the dead Indian who wasn't an Indian but a man from Bradford named Dudley Cross which probably meant everybody called him Double Cross. Sister showed her the note that said regards to her son, and I told her about the turkey and how I nearly knocked my brains out falling over it.

Bo looked pleased as we finished our story. "Y'all are the only people I know that keep falling over dead bodies. It's just a real talent."

"It's not me. It's Mary Alice," I insisted. "She gets involved with weird people."

Ray hopped to his wife's defense. "Sunshine's not weird."

"No, she's not," I agreed. "I didn't mean Sunshine."

"That whole trailer camp's weird, though. Wait till you see it, Ray." Mary Alice poured him some more orange juice. "You have to have a stick in your hand so the pit bulls won't attack you."

Ray put the juice glass on the table. "You have to hit the dogs?"

"No. Of course not. You just show them the stick. And you have to yell at Pawpaw because he was in a Port-o-John when a rocket went off."

"Which was sad," I added.

Bo turned to Ray. "You listen to these women. You realize how lucky you are? How blessed among men?"

Ray grinned. "Sometimes."

Bo held out her Coke glass for a refill. "Lord, it's hot today." She held it up, said "Cheers," took a big swig, and burped slightly. "Rockets and pit bulls aside for the moment, you think this sweet child's wife is really over there at her uncle's house?"

"It's a possibility," I said.

Bo drained the rest of her Coke. "Let me go potty and I'll check it out."

"How will you check it out?" Sister asked.

"Do what any normal person would do. I'll knock on the door and ask if Sunshine Dabbs Crane is there. And if they say no, I'll say it's too bad because she's been elected Miss Jefferson State and I'm there to deliver her tiara."

"I don't think they'll buy that," Sister said.

Bo sighed. "I know it. I'll try to think of something else on the way over there." She got up and headed for the bathroom. "Maybe you could be dying, Mary Alice, and asking for her."

"Try something else," Sister called down the hall.

Ray was wiping his beard with a paper napkin.

"Are you sure all that hair is sanitary?" his mother asked.

Ray thumped his chest. "Me Tarzan."

"Tarzan didn't have a beard." Mary Alice turned and looked at me. "How come Tarzan didn't have a beard, Mouse?"

"Jane wouldn't put up with it."

"No. I mean how could he shave? Seems like I remember seeing Jane cut his hair once. And that's another thing. Where did she get scissors?"

"I have no idea," I said. "I was too busy worrying about somebody finding the elephants' graveyard."

"The alligators always scared me," Ray said. "Just lying around the edge of the water waiting on Tarzan."

"And how come lightning didn't hit them up there in that tree? Or the tree house get blown down? Don't you know everything stayed soaking wet?" Sister was getting into this. "And think how Cheetah must have stunk. And he slept right there with them. Loaded with fleas, I'll bet you. Do they have fleas in Bora Bora, Ray?"

"Sure. Ticks, too."

Mary Alice rubbed her forehead. "Ticks. I hadn't thought about that. It's a wonder Tarzan and Jane didn't die of Lyme disease."

"And Boy, too," I added.

127

"I never liked Boy," Mary Alice said.

Bo came back in. "You're right," Ray told her. "I'm blessed among men."

Bo hoisted her purse to her shoulder. "I'll call you if I run up on anything. The neighbors up there'll know what's going on. I'll ask around."

"We'd appreciate it." Ray stood up. "I'll walk out to your car with you."

"Hmmm," Sister said as the front door closed. "I wonder what that's about."

"He's just being polite."

"Ray? Don't be ridiculous."

"He's a very polite man."

"Did I say he wasn't?"

This was getting us nowhere. "Get your purse," I said. "I need that makeup."

"You sure do," Sister agreed.

We were headed out the door as Ray came in. "What are you going to do this morning, son?" Mary Alice asked.

"I'm going out to the Turkett Compound. Buck's going with me."

"Well, carry a big stick."

"And walk softly," I added.

"How come he needs to walk softly?" Sister asked.

"It's just what Teddy Roosevelt said. 'Walk softly and carry a big stick.'"

"What does Teddy Roosevelt have to do with the Turketts?"

"Not a damn thing. Get in the car."

❁ ❁ ❁

The Big, Bold, and Beautiful Shoppe always smells wonderful, flowery but with a delicate citrus undertone. The perfume is never overwhelming; you catch a whiff of it as you enter and then it becomes simply part of the

128

pleasure of the shop. Mary Alice wanted to buy some and was taken by our friend, Bonnie Blue Butler, back to a storeroom where a small machine stuck on the wall went *psst* every hour and spit out the perfumed air cleanser. When Sister found out it was from a janitorial supply house, she changed her mind, though it seems to me a smell is a smell. And this one is good. It was especially good and cool on this hot day.

Bonnie Blue was glad to see us. She had worked at the Skoot 'n' Boot and nearly gotten herself killed along with us. Now she's manager of the Big, Bold, and Beautiful Shoppe and loving it. Her very words are, *"I could eat these clothes up."*

She came to us with her arms outstretched for hugs. "Lord have mercy. Mary Alice, you been beating up on this child again?"

"Not enough. She's still sassy."

Bonnie Blue examined my forehead. "How'd you do that?"

"Fell over a turkey."

"Figured it was something reasonable. Let's sit down and have some coffee. I want to hear about this." Bonnie Blue pointed to a corner where there was a nice seating arrangement. "We're not overrun with customers this morning. Anybody comes in, Katrinka can wait on them." She grinned. "Katrinka. And they say us black folks give their kids funny names. You rather have a Coke?"

"I would," I said.

"I'll be back in a minute. You here, Mary Alice, to buy a whole fall wardrobe, I hope?"

"Haley's getting married tomorrow. I'm looking for a dress."

"Haley's marrying that doctor?"

We nodded yes.

"Great. And we got a big summer sale going. You just wait."

We watched Bonnie Blue disappear into the back, and if Sister was thinking what I was, it was how fond we were of this large black woman who had come into our lives under such traumatic conditions and become a friend.

"Okay." Bonnie Blue put the Coke and a plate of cookies on the coffee table. "It's not diet, either. You need all the calories you can get, Patricia Anne. You're not big as a flea." She poured Sister and herself coffee. "Now tell me what's been going on."

We took turns telling about the Turketts, and Ray's marriage to Sunshine, and finding the body.

Bonnie Blue put her coffee down. "Old Double Cross? The one who chiefs down at Crystal Caverns? I know him. He used to come in the Skoot 'n' Boot all the time. Always ordered boilermakers."

"You know anything about him?" Sister asked.

"Not really. Seemed like a right good old fellow. I think everybody liked him pretty good. He'd always have on a suit. Or at least a tie and dress shirt."

"He had on a suit when he was killed," I said. "A gray one." Goose bumps popped up on my arms. "It's cold in here."

"No, it's not." Sister leaned forward and helped herself to a couple of cookies. "Did he have any special friends?"

Bonnie Blue shrugged. "I don't know. I couldn't keep up with everybody. I just remember the boilermakers."

The door opened and a definite potential customer came in. Katrinka, blonde and a size four, maybe, came from the back smiling.

"Are you sure Katrinka's good for business?" Mary Alice whispered to Bonnie Blue.

"You just watch. That woman will buy the store out."

"I hope not. I've got to get a dress for the wedding."

"And I know just which one. Now y'all tell me what else has been happening. How's Debbie's morning sickness?"

"Lasting all day," Sister said.

"Bless her heart."

"She's going back to the doctor today. I hope he can help her."

"And Haley's moving to Warsaw." Tears welled up in my eyes.

"You mean like in Poland?" Bonnie Blue asked.

"Just for a few months," Sister said as if it were nothing.

"Well, do."

Do, indeed, I thought. I brushed my eyes with the back of my hand.

"Let's look at those dresses," Bonnie Blue said. "When you said wedding I thought about this off-white one, a two-piece with real fancy pearl and gold buttons." She got up. "Patricia Anne, I can't do much about fitting you, but the new *People* magazine just came in."

"That's fine." I took the magazine she handed me and settled down to wait. Mary Alice usually doesn't take a long time trying on clothes and chances were that if she liked the dress Bonnie Blue was talking about and it fit, she would buy it.

Not even the article on the clinic for sexually addicted movie stars interested me, though. For one thing, my eyes were blurry. I took off my glasses and rubbed my eyes, wincing as I hit my bruise. I blinked and looked outside and then blinked again. Sunshine Dabbs was walking down the sidewalk across the street. There was no mistaking her. She was even wearing the pink sundress that she had worn to the dinner party.

"Mary Alice!" I yelled, jumping up and dropping the

magazine. "It's Sunshine!" And even as I was yelling, the pink-clad figure disappeared into a hardware store directly across the street.

I didn't wait for Sister. I ran out of the dress shop and crossed the street, holding up my arm for cars to stop. Fortunately, it was not the busy time of the day and I made it to the other side with only a couple of obscene gestures aimed at me.

I barreled into the hardware store expecting to see Sunshine. Instead, all I saw was a middle-aged woman sitting on a stool at a cash register reading the same *People* I had just thrown down.

"A girl in a pink sundress just came in here." I was out of breath from my run. "Did you see which way she went?"

The woman shrugged. "Didn't notice." She continued her reading.

No help there. I scouted across the front of the store, looking down each aisle. No Sunshine. In fact, I didn't see another woman. Several men were browsing through tools and strange-looking pipes and fittings. One man was counting nails into a small paper sack. "Excuse me," I said. "Have you seen a girl in a pink dress go by here?"

He frowned at me. "Sixty-seven, sixty-eight."

Well, okay. I hurried down the aisle toward the back of the store and realized to my dismay that there was a rear exit that led to a parking lot. There was also another checkout counter at the back entrance where a clerk and a customer were talking.

"Y'all seen a girl in a pink dress?" I asked.

The clerk pointed toward the back door with the fishing rod they were discussing.

Damn. I ran outside just in time to see a pickup backing out of a parking space. The driver had blonde hair.

"Wait," I screeched. But the truck took off, easing into the traffic of Twentieth Street.

"Where is she?" Mary Alice came rushing out of the hardware store.

"She left in a pickup before I could catch her."

"You sure it was Sunshine?"

I nodded. "She even had on that pink sundress."

"And you're positive it was Sunshine?"

"Damn it, Sister. It was Sunshine." The asphalt of the parking lot was sticky it was so hot. My run hadn't helped matters either. "Let's get somewhere where it's cool."

"I never did get to try my dress on," Sister said.

"Tough," I grumbled. We walked black through the hardware store.

"Assuming," Sister said as we reached the sidewalk, "that it was Sunshine—"

"Assume it, damn it."

"Which way was she coming from?"

I pointed toward my left.

"Then she was at"—Sister shaded her eyes—"a florist, an antique shop, a clothes consignment shop, or a drugstore."

"And she wasn't gone long because somebody was waiting for her, and it's too hot to wait long."

"Then while I'm trying on my dresses, why don't you check in those stores and see if you can find out what she was doing?"

I was about to say, "Do it yourself" when Sister added, "If you're sure it was Sunshine."

"I've got to get a drink of water first," I said.

"Lord have mercy, Mrs. Hollowell. You're red as a beet around that green knot on your head."

"Thank you, Katrinka." I took the glass of icewater she

was offering and gulped it down.

"You shouldn't drink it that fast when you're hot. My granddaddy did that and dropped dead."

I took a piece of ice from the glass and held it against my forehead. "I'll remember that."

"He came in from plowing and drank three glasses of icewater and fell over." Katrinka listed to the side. "Just like that." She listed some more; her voice lowered. "Dead. About your age, too."

"Katrinka. Come here, girl," Bonnie Blue called, fortunately. "Bring me that green silk jacket. Twenty-four."

"Yes ma'am." Katrinka gave me an appraising look, decided I wasn't going to pull her grandfather's stunt, at least not this moment, and went to get the jacket. Holding the ice against my forehead, I walked outside and looked at the shops across the street. Might as well start with the drugstore on the corner.

This time I crossed at the light and, remembering Katrinka's description of my face and her grandfather's demise, walked slowly.

"Nope," said the cashier in the drugstore. "I'd have remembered somebody who looked like Barbie in a pink dress. Ask the pharmacist. Maybe she picked up a prescription."

"No ma'am. I've got some ice packs you put in the freezer, though. Fit right over your ears kind of like glasses. They'd do wonders for that bruise. How'd you do it, anyway?"

I walked into the consignment shop carrying the ice pack.

"Barbie?" The woman's hair was so black you could hardly see it. It made her face look startlingly white. "You must be kidding. We tend to run low on Barbie sizes."

I thanked her and left. It had been cool in the consignment shop, but there had been a faint odor of cigarette smoke that made you realize that the sign ALL OUR CLOTHES HAVE BEEN CLEANED wasn't true. Unless the woman was a nicotine fiend.

The antique shop smelled of lemon furniture polish. I could have spent the day in here happily. A very handsome young man came forward to help me, asked if I would like to sit down, or if I would like something to drink. Some coffee? A Coke?

A Coke would be lovely. We sat in two chairs that were marked $2,500 and which I thought was $25 until I finished my Coke without spilling it, thank God.

"Priceless." The nice young man rubbed his hands over the carved back of the chair as we got up. But they weren't, of course. They were $2,500. Lord!

And no, he hadn't seen Sunshine.

That left the florist. I thanked the man and told him I would recommend him to my sister. Actually, I wasn't sure even Mary Alice would pay those prices.

I was glad I had saved the florist for last. Cool, white, fragrant, it was a wonderful place to enter from a hot August sidewalk.

No one was in the showroom. The sound of voices led me to a work area, though, at the back of the store where three women were working on flowers for a wedding. Independent Presbyterian, they explained, a big wedding. One of the women held up a small bouquet. "Fussy Mussies for the bridesmaids."

I caught my breath. For a few minutes I had repressed the thought that I was going to a wedding in the morning. Now it came back painfully. I should be doing something about flowers and all sorts of details. After all, I was the bride's mother.

"Would you like a Coke?" one of the women asked.

"Some aspirin?"

"Would you like to sit down a minute?"

Lord, I must look awful.

And no, they hadn't seen a girl in a pink sundress.

A bell over the door rang and Mary Alice walked in carrying a plastic hanger bag from the Big, Bold, and Beautiful Shoppe.

"Have mercy," she said, looking around. "We forgot about flowers for the wedding, didn't we?"

"What wedding?" the ladies wanted to know.

"My daughter's," I said firmly. "Tomorrow morning at Trinity Methodist Chapel."

Three astonished faces confronted me. "And you don't have any flowers?"

"It was rather sudden," I explained.

The women looked at each other. Two of them shook their heads. The third one, probably the owner of the shop, said, "We could probably rustle you up some white glads and a couple of ferns."

"We'll need a wedding bouquet, too," Mary Alice said.

"Don't you think you ought to talk to the bride?" one of the ladies suggested.

I shrugged. "She's forgotten, too."

"We could probably rustle her up a Fussy Mussy in white," the shop owner said. "I think we've got enough white roses. We might have to stick something else in."

So we rustled Haley up some flowers. It didn't make me feel a bit better. A wedding should be planned and looked forward to, not rustled up.

"What have you got in your sack?" Mary Alice asked as we left the florist.

I showed her the ice pack. "And nobody had seen Sunshine in any of the shops."

Sister shrugged.

"But I saw her."

"I believe you. You still want to go to Merle Norman's?"

"I need all the help I can get."

We were quiet all the way to the nearest mall.

Chapter 13

I COULD HEAR THE PHONE RINGING AS I UNLOCKED the kitchen door. I picked it up as the answering machine started its "We are unable to come to the phone" bit. I'm never quite sure how to handle this, usually ending up shouting "Hello" over the message so the caller won't hang up.

"Mama? I was just about to hang up."

Haley sounded tired. "Are you okay?" I asked.

"That's what I called to ask you. How's your head?"

"Feels better and looks better. I'm just coming in from getting my makeup."

"Good."

"Are you at work?"

"Just left. It made me sad."

"I'll bet. Your Aunt Sister and I bought flowers for tomorrow, one arrangement for the chapel and a bouquet for you. Just a small one. White. You haven't already gotten some, have you? Because we can cancel ours if you have."

"Thanks. I forgot about flowers." Haley really sounded down.

"We were in a flower shop and remembered. Sure you're okay?"

"Tired. Can I bring Muffin over after while? The

137

packing and confusion are making her nervous."

"Sure." We talked for a few more minutes, mostly about the cat's likes and dislikes. Muffin had never struck me as being a strange cat, but after listening to Haley I wasn't sure. I had hung up before I realized I hadn't told Haley about Sunshine.

Mary Alice had wanted to stop somewhere and have lunch, but I had declined. What I wanted, needed, was something light. Something to fortify me.

I peeled what was probably the last Alabama peach of the season and sliced it into the blender. A cup of peach yogurt and a few ice cubes (Henry adds whipping cream), a few seconds on blend, and I had a wonderful fruit shake. I poured it into a large glass, went into the den, and turned on *Jeopardy!*. It was over and I was greeted with Men Who Sleep with Their Stepdaughters Or Some Other Family Member They Shouldn't Be Messing With. I changed quickly to an episode of *M*A*S*H* that I knew by heart, the one where Colonel Potter arrives. The Korean War was more soothing than the Men Who Sleep with Their Stepdaughters, Etc. Fred says the people on those shows are paid and make it all up. I haven't figured out if this makes me feel better or worse.

The doorbell's ring made me jump so hard, I realized I must have been on the verge of dozing. I glanced at my watch and went to the door expecting the postlady. She's a cute brunette who wears shorts that I'm sure aren't regulation length. But when I opened the door, there stood Meemaw Turkett. The Chevy Bel Air's fins flared defiantly in my driveway.

"Well?" she asked. Not even a hello.

"Well what?"

"Don't you have something to tell me?"

I had no idea what the woman was talking about, but I

tried to be helpful. "I saw Sunshine this morning. She was across the street from me, but she looked fine."

"That's all? You saw her across the street?"

I opened the door farther. "Why don't you come in where it's cool?"

"Don't mind if I do." Meemaw stepped inside. "I could use a glass of water."

"Sure. Come on back to the den." I started down the hall with Meemaw behind me.

"You look like you got hit by a Mack truck," she said. "What happened to your head?"

"I had a fall last night." No use going into the details. "Have a seat. Would you rather have some tea?"

Meemaw sank onto the sofa. "Water's fine."

"Say Sunshine looked okay?" she called while I was getting the ice from the refrigerator.

"Sure. She had on her pink sundress."

"She looks pretty in that."

I came back into the den. "She looks pretty in everything."

Meemaw took the water and drank about half of it. "She does," she agreed. I had noticed when I opened the door that Meemaw wasn't wearing her usual housedress. Instead she had on cream-colored polyester knit pants, too long to be shorts, just below her knees, and not full enough to be culottes. Now she said, "Lord, it's hot today," and unstuck the polyester knit from her ample thigh. Then she ran her fingers under the elastic waistband. "I'd like to just dump this ice right down me. I'm sweating like a whore in church."

To hide my grin, I glanced at the outside thermometer. "It's sitting right on a hundred."

"Maybe it'll rain after while." Meemaw drank the rest of the water.

"Did you see Ray this morning?" I asked.

Meemaw looked puzzled.

"Ray Crane. Sunshine's husband. He was going out to Locust Fork."

Meemaw shook her head no. "Kerrigan's there, though. And Pawpaw and Howard. I told them I had to come in to see you."

The light dawned. "Let me guess. Gabriel sent you?"

"Said you had something to tell me. Very specific about it. More specific than usual. In fact, lot of the time he's downright vague."

"I can imagine."

Meemaw looked up sharply.

I felt a twinge of guilt. "I mean he's got to be vague, considering the territory he's covering."

The Cabbage Patch eyes nailed me. "What do you know about Gabriel's territory, missy?"

"Not much," I said sheepishly. "Would you like some more water?"

Meemaw held out her glass. I escaped to the kitchen.

"I just want to know what it is you've got to tell me," she said as I handed her the refilled glass.

I could at least be truthful this time. "I don't know anything except I saw Sunshine this morning. Don't you expect that's the message?"

"No. There's more."

"She got in a pickup and drove off."

"What kind of pickup?"

"An old red one." I hate to admit I can't tell one vehicle from another. "She'd been to a drugstore, a consignment shop, an antique dealer's, or a florist. I asked in all of them, though, and none of them had seen her."

Meemaw looked interested. "A clothes consignment shop?"

"Yes. The lady who runs it looks like she dyes her hair with tar. Does that ring a bell?"

"Nope. I just like consignment shops. I got these pants at one in Oneonta."

"This one's called Play It Again."

"I'll look into it."

Okay. A deep silence settled between us. I thought I heard the last of the peach shake hit my stomach.

"I could go to sleep here," Meemaw said finally. "I haven't been sleeping worth a damn since all the commotion."

"I didn't get much sleep last night myself." I touched the knot on my head which felt huge. I'd forgotten about the ice pack I'd bought at the drugstore. I'd put it on as soon as Meemaw left.

Silence stretched out again. This time I broke it. "I guess you heard they found out the dead Indian's name. Dudley Cross from Bradford."

"The sheriff told us. I don't know the man from Adam's house cat." Meemaw put her empty glass on the coffee table. "I think if I'd known him, it wouldn't have been so bad."

"I think I'd rather find the body of somebody I don't know."

"Not stuck to your own linoleum with your own hog-butchering knife."

"Especially stuck to my linoleum."

"Well—" Meemaw fanned herself with the damp paper napkin that had been around the water.

I got up and turned on the ceiling fan. "Are you okay?"

"Oh, sure. I'm just heated up. I'm easy to heat up."

But she didn't look okay. She looked like an old lady packing too much weight and stress on the hottest day of the year. If the enlarged varicose veins coursing up to the

141

polyester shorts were any indication, I'd best keep my finger on the 911 button.

"Let me get you a cold washrag," I offered. "You could hold it against your forehead."

"Thanks, but I'll just suck on some ice." She fingered a cube from her water glass.

"Don't chew it," I said out of habit.

Meemaw and I smiled at each other at this mothers' refrain which, so to speak, broke the ice between us at this point.

"Do you have any inkling why Gabriel sent you to me?"

Meemaw sucked the ice thoughtfully. "Said you had something to tell me."

"Well, how about I just say things. Like my daughter Haley's getting married tomorrow."

"That's not it."

"I know." I gave her my schoolteacher look. "Just listen and you might catch the message."

Meemaw was quiet so I continued. "She's marrying an ear, nose, and throat doctor named Philip Nachman who's the nephew of my sister Mary Alice's second husband. His name was Philip Nachman, too, which confuses people sometimes, but Mary Alice calls him Nephew so we can usually keep it straight. The nephew, not the uncle-husband who was the father of Debbie, Henry's wife who's pregnant. You met Henry the other night. He cooked the supper.

"They're going to go live in Warsaw, Poland, for several months, Haley and Nephew are, and it's the most jumped-up wedding I've ever been involved in. They didn't even have any flowers. We bought an arrangement of glads and one of those little bouquets that you hold in your hand. They call them Fussy Mussies. Did you know that?"

Meemaw shook her head no.

"We were at the Big, Bold, and Beautiful Shoppe this morning buying Mary Alice a dress for the wedding when I saw Sunshine, and I went running out and nearly got myself killed on Twentieth Street, but she went out the back door of a hardware store. Then we went to Merle Norman's and bought me some makeup for this horn on my head. It helped, but I'm still going to look horrible at the wedding. My grandchildren are going to look at the pictures and say, 'What's wrong with Grandmama?' and everybody's going to laugh and say, 'She fell over a turkey.' Even my unborn grandchildren will know." I paused. "Dear Lord, I'll bet they don't have anybody to take pictures either. I'd better check into it."

Meemaw had moved forward and was sitting on the edge of the sofa. "You hurt your head falling over a turkey?"

"Right on my sister's stoop. I could have killed myself. A whole turkey, not a frozen one, but feathers and all, just lying there with its insides hanging out." I shuddered. "Yuck."

Meemaw shook another piece of ice into her mouth and stood up. "Thanks, Patricia Anne."

"For what? Was the turkey the message?"

"Probably."

I got up, too. "What does the message say? We figured it was some kind of warning."

"I don't know, but I saw a light."

"I used to see lights when I was getting a migraine. Zigzag like a zipper lights. Hormonal, so I don't get them anymore."

"This is a flash."

"Are your retinas okay?"

Meemaw actually giggled as we walked toward the

143

door. "They're fine."

Heat poured through the door as I opened it. "You going to be all right out here?" I asked.

"Sure. Thanks." She unstuck the polyester shorts from her rear end.

"Will you let us know when you find out what the message means?"

"Soon as I find out."

I watched her walk toward her car. Sunlight was bouncing off the car's fins. As she drove off, I wished that I had called her back, fixed lemonade, had her tell me about her life. For I realized as she gave me a wave and backed the car out of my driveway, that I liked Meemaw Turkett. A bubble out of plumb, maybe, but I liked her a lot.

The slight doze and the peach shake had revitalized me. I checked the answering machine and didn't have any messages which made me feel bad. Mary Alice's phone is always full of messages. Of course she belongs to every organization in town and is on the board of half of them. Probably doesn't know what meeting she's attending half the time.

I checked the utility room. The washer and dryer are in there, but Muffin's litter box could go in the corner under a shelf. There'd be room for her to get in. We'd have to leave the door cracked, but it was either there or the guest bathroom.

A plastic bag lying on top of the washing machine reminded me that I had done nothing with my turkey-spattered clothes. I opened the bag, holding my breath, and took out the shirt, underwear, and linen pants. By the time I got the Spray 'n Wash down, though, I was forced to breathe. There was a definite odor, but it wasn't as bad as I had thought it would be. I sprayed the washable

144

things, added a few more clothes from the hamper, and turned the machine on. The linen pants needed to go to the cleaners right now; I shouldn't have waited this long.

Holding them away from me, I went through the pockets. A stick of Freedent, a receipt from the Piggly Wiggly, a Kleenex, a pebble, a Tum, two pennies. I dumped the stuff on the kitchen table, grabbed my purse, and went to the cleaners.

"Turkey?" the lady asked, looking from my forehead to the pants. "You're sure?"

I nodded that I was sure.

"Because I've got a number right here"—she opened a drawer—"a domestic violence hot line."

"My husband's the most nonviolent man in the world."

She looked at me speculatively. "You got children?"

"Hey, it's turkey blood. Clean it."

"Well, it could be evidence, you know."

This woman was going to have Fred or the kids in jail before nightfall at this rate. But she truly looked worried.

"It's all right. But thank you."

She seemed to believe me. But I left the cleaners knowing more about domestic violence in our neighborhood than I had wanted to know.

I checked my watch. I had time to stop by the grocery and get some shrimp. Shrimp salad would be good for supper. Split a croissant and put the salad on it with a couple of slices of tomato on the side, and Fred would think I'd been cooking all afternoon. I ran into Mitzi Phizer at the store, though, and had to explain my forehead. I didn't mention the turkey, just that I had fallen on Mary Alice's porch. "Witch hazel," she recommended. "You need to keep dabbing witch hazel on it."

Haley was sitting at the kitchen table drinking a beer

when I got home.

"Sorry," I said, putting the shrimp into the refrigerator. "You been here long?"

"Just a few minutes. Muffin's hiding in the closet in your bedroom."

"I thought I'd put her litter box in the utility room."

Haley pushed her hair back with both hands. "Okay. Everything's out in the car." Her voice was teary.

"She'll be fine."

"I know. It's just everything's happening so fast."

I pulled out a chair and sat down. "You can get married when Philip gets back. That way you'll have plenty of time to plan everything."

Haley looked up in horror. "Mama!"

I grinned. "Then go get Muffin's stuff and let's get her settled. Do you need any help?"

"I can get it."

In a few minutes she was back and came into the utility room where I was putting the clothes in the dryer.

"This food. Where shall I put it?"

I pointed to a shelf. "Guess what. I've seen Sunshine and Meemaw both today."

"Really? Sunshine's showed up?"

"Not exactly." I related the story of Sunshine and the pickup truck and Meemaw's visit.

"Does Ray know about it?"

"Probably your Aunt Sister's told him by now. She doesn't know about Meemaw's visit, though."

"That's really strange that she thought the turkey was some kind of sign." By this time we were back at the table and Haley reached for the stick of Freedent. "Can I have this?"

"Sure. I guess it's okay. It was in the pocket of the pants I had on last night. All this stuff was." I pointed toward the little pile of things I had removed before I took the pants to the cleaners.

"I don't know. Maybe I'd better throw it away. I sure don't want food poisoning on my wedding day." Haley picked up the rock. "What's this?"

"I think it came from Meemaw's trailer. She and Sunshine were playing Chinese checkers and were using pebbles for some of the checkers I guess were lost."

"That's sad, Mama."

"It's their choice, Haley." I filled her in on Eddie's wealth. "And Pawpaw's got to be drawing a good amount of disability, and Kerrigan and Howard are both doing well."

"But maybe, some way, Meemaw is left out, scapegoated. Maybe that's why she needs a Gabriel."

I couldn't see Meemaw in the role of scapegoat, but I supposed it was possible. The lady at the cleaners had reminded me that all families are not what they appear on the surface. And Meemaw had said that if she had known the dead man on her floor, it would have been better.

"Mama." Haley's eyes widened suddenly. "There are two big men with beards coming up the back steps."

I turned to see Ray waving through the glass top of the kitchen door.

"It's Ray, Haley."

"Well, I see it is now." She was out of her chair, opening the door, and throwing herself into his arms before I could get up.

"Little Ray, you've got a beard."

"And you're getting married." Ray picked Haley up and held her by her elbows as if she weighed nothing. "Somebody's marrying himself a feisty redhead tomorrow."

"And somebody's already married himself a beautiful

blonde."

"But sweet, not feisty. I swear I think I better go call that doctor and tell him what he's getting into."

Buck Owens had come into the kitchen behind Ray and was smiling at the reunion.

"Hi, Buck," I said. "Come over and have a seat."

He ambled over and pulled out a chair. "I'd say those two are glad to see each other."

"They're the two youngest. They've always taken up for each other."

"Hey, Aunt Pat." Ray deposited Haley in a chair and leaned over to kiss me. "Haley, this is Buck Owens. Buck, Haley Buchanan who this time tomorrow will be Haley Nachman. I didn't know I was coming home to a wedding."

Haley chuckled. "Neither did I, but I'm certainly glad. Y'all want a beer?"

"Sure," Ray said. "I'll get it. Buck?"

"Got any Diet Coke?"

"In the pantry, Ray." I turned to Buck and asked him if they had been out to Locust Fork.

"Yep. Ray met his in-laws, all of them except Meemaw and Eddie."

"Interesting folks," Ray said, disappearing into the pantry. He reappeared in a moment with a can of Diet Coke. "Buck's in love with Kerrigan."

Buck gave an aw-shucks grin. "Best-looking woman I've ever seen."

"She's beautiful," I agreed. I turned to Ray. "Did your mama tell you I saw Sunshine this morning?"

"She said on Twentieth Street in a hardware store." Ray brought the Coke to Buck and sat down. "That's why we came by, to find out the details."

I repeated the story again and was asked by Buck what

kind of pickup it was.

"Mama doesn't know one car from the other, let alone a truck," Haley explained.

"I know Meemaw's car. It's an old Chevrolet, a Bel Air with fins."

"Those things are worth a fortune," Buck said. "Is it in good shape?"

"It runs," I said. Then I explained that Meemaw had been by because Gabriel had sent her, which called for more explaining.

Haley pushed her chair back. "I've got to go, Mama. Gabriel's going to take a while and I've still got a million things to do." She kissed me on the forehead. "I'll call you after while. Muffin will come out when she's ready."

It was just as well the two men were there. It kept me from crying when she went out the back door.

"Meemaw's channeler?" Ray nudged me back onto the subject. "Is she serious?"

"Absolutely." I repeated Meemaw's story of the flying saucer she had seen on the way home from bingo. "He told her to come here today," I said. "Told her I had a message for her."

"Did you?" Ray asked.

"Not that I know of. I finally just started talking, and when I told her about falling over the turkey, she said that was the message."

"A message about what?"

"I don't know. She just said that was the message and left."

Buck and Ray both smiled. Smart alecks.

"Hey, she believes it." The phone rang and I got up to answer it.

"Mouse," Mary Alice said. It was her tight voice, the one that always means something's very wrong.

"What?" I held my breath.

"Bo Mitchell just called me. They answered an emergency call at Eddie Turkett's house, and apparently Meemaw's had a stroke."

"Oh, Lord," I said, leaning against the counter. "It's my fault."

"How come? What did you do?"

"Let her go out in the heat."

"Don't be ridiculous, Mouse. You couldn't very well sit on her."

"She looked awful, though."

"Well, of course she did. She was sick as a dog."

This wasn't making me feel any better. "How bad is she?"

"I don't think they know yet. Bo called me because she said Meemaw was asking for me. So she's not unconscious; that's a good sign."

"Was Eddie there? Did he call the rescue squad?"

"I have no idea. Bo says they're taking her to University, though. I'm going on down there. Is Ray still at your house?"

"He's right here."

"Let me speak to him a minute."

I handed Ray the phone. "It's your mama. Meemaw's had a stroke." I sat back down at the table. "It's my fault," I told Buck. "I thought I was going to have to call 911 while she was here."

"A heatstroke or a stroke stroke?" Buck asked.

"I don't know. She's conscious but she's not thinking right. She's asking for Sister."

Ray hung up the phone. "I'm going down to University Hospital to meet Mama. Buck, if you'll drop me off, you can use my car to go home."

"Sure thing." Buck drank the last of his Coke and stood

up. "These folks are having their share of troubles, aren't they?"

"Yes, they are," I agreed. And part of them were my fault.

Chapter 14

THE SMELL OF SHRIMP BEING PEELED BROUGHT Muffin into the kitchen. She's a large calico that Tom and Haley found as a kitten abandoned in a Winn-Dixie parking lot. It was instant love. The apartment complex where they were living didn't allow pets so they moved. Muffin was anemic and had flea allergies; she was given vitamins and allergy shots, was combed every day. She became sleek, and then plump. She was put on a special diet. Now middle-aged and shiny with good health, she leaped gracefully to my kitchen table and looked at me.

"You're not allowed on the kitchen table," I said.

Muffin looked surprised and hurt.

"I'll give you just one shrimp if you'll get down."

The deal was struck. I took the shrimp into the utility room and put it in her bowl.

"This is your apartment," I explained. "Bathroom, kitchen, and bedroom."

Muffin dragged the shrimp from the bowl and onto the floor where she proceeded to tear it into small bits before she ate it. We were going to have to discuss this some more. I hoped Haley had checked out how Philip felt about cats.

The back door opened and Mitzi Phizer called, "Patricia Anne?"

"I'm in here with Haley's cat."

Mitzi stuck her head around the door. "What are you

151

doing?"

"Making sure she understands the rules."

Mitzi snorted. "Rules for a cat?"

Muffin walked by both of us and leaped onto the kitchen table again where she began an elaborate grooming session.

Mitzi laughed. "That's what I want to come back as. A big fat cat." She held out a bowl. "Here's some fruit salad. I figure the next couple of days are going to be hectic for you and it'll come in handy. You want me to put it in the refrigerator?"

"Thanks. I've got shrimp on my hands."

"Go ahead and finish peeling them." Mitzi put the salad into the refrigerator and sat down at the kitchen table. She and Muffin both looked at me.

"Actually," I admitted, "I don't have much to do at all. The wedding is just sort of happening." I offered Mitzi a shrimp. She shook her head no. "Alan and Lisa are coming over from Atlanta but are going straight back home. One of their boys is in a baseball tournament. Freddie's out of town, and Debbie may not feel like coming." I shrugged. "It's certainly different from Haley's first wedding."

"But they'll be just as married." Mitzi rolled the pebble that was still on the table toward Muffin. Muffin ignored it.

"Of course they will." But I didn't want to talk about the wedding. I told Mitzi that Meemaw had been here earlier and might have had a stroke, that they had taken her to University Hospital, and that she had been asking for Mary Alice.

"Maybe she wants to confess to her that she killed the Indian guy." Mitzi shuddered. "Lord, I'm glad I didn't walk in on that."

"I wish I hadn't." I peeled the last shrimp and put the shells in the plastic bag they had come in. "Nope, I don't think Meemaw did it. I think she knows a lot more than she's telling, though." I soaped my hands. "I think maybe she's scared it's Howard or Eddie. Or even Kerrigan."

"What makes you think that? And why would Sunshine have run from one of them?"

I rinsed my hands and dried them on a paper towel. "I really don't know," I admitted. "Just a feeling."

"It could have been Sunshine."

"She was there by herself," I agreed. "I suppose the fellow could have been breaking in. But it doesn't make sense that she'd run." I got the celery from the refrigerator, pulled it apart, and offered Mitzi one of the tiny stalks from the center.

"Sure."

I rinsed it and handed it to her. I took one, too.

"Maybe"—Mitzi crunched into her celery—"maybe it was all of them like that Agatha Christie movie where Mia Farrow and Ingrid Bergman were going down the Nile." She chewed thoughtfully. "I don't even remember who they killed. I just remember it was all of them and Mia Farrow looked pitiful in it. You know how washed-out she looks when she doesn't have on eye makeup."

"I don't think that's the right movie," I said. "Wasn't it the one on the Orient Express? And was Candice Bergen in it?"

"I don't remember. I just remember Candice Bergen hanging around Gandhi all the time. He'd be trying to say something wise and here she'd be taking his picture in those droopy diaper pants." Mitzi took another bite of celery. "I know he was one of the greatest men who ever lived, but I declare, Patricia Anne, the man should have worn some sure-enough pants."

We were both quiet for a moment, as quiet as we could be while eating celery. The mention of nice pants suddenly reminded me of the clothes that Dudley Cross had been wearing, the neat gray suit. Mitzi's thoughts were obviously roaming in another direction.

"What kind of pants did Jesus wear, Patricia Anne? Do you remember?"

"How come I should remember what kind of pants Jesus wore?"

"From the pictures on the front of the Sunday school weekly readers."

"There were always children gathered around him."

"That's true. I don't guess it matters anyway, does it?"

"I don't think so." I began to chop the celery. "You can look it up in the *World Book.*"

"I want to get on the Internet."

The phone's ring was welcome.

"Mrs. Hollowell? Jed Reuse here. I'm looking for your nephew Ray and thought you might know where he is. I've tried your sister's."

"Have you found Sunshine?"

Mitzi looked up from scratching Muffin's chin.

"No, I'm afraid not. I'd like to get in touch with him this afternoon, though."

I shook my head no to Mitzi who nodded and continued the scratching.

"He's at University Hospital. Meemaw Turkett had what they think is a stroke and he's down there."

"Meemaw had a stroke? A bad one?"

"I don't know any of the details except she's at University."

"Well, Lord, I hate to hear that." He sounded like he truly was upset. Sometimes I like Jed Reuse.

"I hate it, too. She was here this afternoon and looked

154

terrible. I never should have let her go out in the heat."

"You let her go out? It's a hundred and two right now."

Sometimes I dislike Jed Reuse.

"Well, you can find them down at University."

He thanked me and I hung up. "Jackass."

"The sheriff?"

I nodded. "Thank the Lord he and Haley didn't hit it off. Gives me the shivers to think she might be marrying him tomorrow instead of Philip."

"Speaking of which, what are you wearing to the wedding?"

"I haven't decided other than a whole lot of green makeup."

"It'll be fine." Mitzi got up, gave Muffin a final pat, and hugged me. "Call me if you want some company."

"I'm fine," I said. The truth was I was so teary I could hardly see the celery I was trying to cut.

After the salad was in the refrigerator, though, I knew I had to make some decisions about the wedding. At least about what I was going to wear. I went into the middle bedroom and opened the closet door. This is where Fred and I keep what I still think of as our "dress-up" clothes.

I've never been able to figure out why people who built houses fifty years ago didn't think closets were important. One little, and I do mean little, closet in each bedroom. I've read articles on organizing them, bought shelves and rods from Kmart so I can hang skirts above blouses. But it boils down to three little closets. And in the one where I was looking, nothing looked like what I needed for a daughter's wedding during a heat wave. Not that anybody would notice anything about me except the knot on my head—I looked in the mirror—and oh, God, the black eye. Definitely the left eye was much darker than the right. I rushed into the bathroom and turned on the fluorescent light. No question about it. My daughter was getting married and moving halfway around the world, I had nothing to wear to the wedding, and I had a black eye. Well, hell. Time for some regrouping here.

I went to the freezer and got the last box of Girl Scout chocolate mint cookies and turned on the Movie Channel. *Fort Apache* was playing, with Henry Fonda, John Wayne, and Shirley Temple. Imaginative casting. I sat back, watched the movie, ate cookies, and simply waited for whatever was going to happen next in my life.

Which, of course, was a call from Sister. She was stuck at the hospital since Ray had gone to see Sheriff Reuse. She would be waiting outside for me in fifteen minutes. Fifteen. It was too hot to be kept waiting on the sidewalk in the sun.

"How's Meemaw?" I asked.

"Not too good. I think they're about to settle on a heatstroke. Fifteen minutes."

Okay. I turned off *Fort Apache.* It hadn't been hard to figure out what was going to happen to the Indians. Then I got my keys and headed for University Hospital.

No Mary Alice. I cruised slowly down Nineteenth Street past the front of the hospital, checked my watch. Maybe she had meant the emergency room exit. I turned on Sixth Avenue. A couple of ambulances were parked under the emergency room portico with people scurrying around, but no one was standing on the sidewalk. I went around the block. I went around the block five times, slowly. This is one of the most heavily traveled blocks in Birmingham. Consequently, I received several obscene gestures, a couple of them very imaginative, from other drivers. The sixth time around, I turned, came back the other way, and pulled in beside a valet parking sign. A man sat in a little booth furnished with a chair, a TV, and an air conditioner that was chugging rusty rivulets down the outside wall. Behind him were rows and rows of keys.

He raised a window and said, "Lady, I'm full up."

"So am I," I said. As I got out of the car and left it, I saw he was watching *Fort Apache.*

I jaywalked across Nineteenth, causing a few more gestures. My sandals stuck to the hot pavement with each step, *pop, pop,* against my heels. The cool lobby of the hospital was a blessing.

The woman at the information desk looked up in alarm. "The emergency room's down yonder, honey." She pointed toward a corridor clearly marked EMERGENCY. "You need some help getting there? It's a pretty long way."

"I'm fine," I assured her. "I just had a fall last night."

"You sure did. What happened?" She wasn't being nosy; she really wanted to know. And if I had told her, not only would she have understood, but would probably have had an aunt who had the same thing happen to her: *"Right over a turkey, smack in the middle of a family reunion."*

I swear I love this place.

But I didn't have time for conversation. "Fell on my sister's steps," I said. "And I'm okay."

"Stove up, I'll bet."

"You got that right." I moved my shoulders stiffly to assure her that I was, indeed, stove up. "I'm looking for my sister. She was supposed to be out on the sidewalk for me to pick up and I've been around the block so many times I'm getting dizzy."

"Could be a concussion."

"No. I'm okay. I just need to find my sister. She's here with a woman named Mary Louise Turkett. They brought her in this afternoon. Heatstroke, they think."

"I'll check." The woman, whose name tag identified her as Grace Oliver, picked up her phone. "Myrtice? It's

Grace." A pause. "Lord, don't I know it. A hundred and four last I heard." She settled back for a good talk.

I unstuck my sandals from the tile floor. The noise reminded her of the reason for her call.

"Listen, I've got a lady here looking for her sister. Names something like Turkey. Heatstroke. She in the emergency room?"

"Turkett," I said. "Mary Louise Turkett. She's the patient. My sister's with her."

"Mary Louise Turkett," Grace relayed. She smiled at me and mouthed, "Just a minute." Then, "Out of the emergency room? Okay. Thanks, Myrtice." Grace hung up the phone. "She's in intensive care on the seventh floor."

"Thanks." I headed for the elevator, slightly worried about Mary Alice. She had been so emphatic about the fifteen minutes and usually she's punctual. But as I walked into the intensive care waiting room, there she sat at a card table, playing gin rummy with Kerrigan and Howard.

Kerrigan saw me first. "Good Lord, Mrs. Hollowell. What happened to you?"

"I fell last night."

Sister looked up. "Is it fifteen minutes already?"

"Many fifteen minutes."

"Gin." She put her cards down; Kerrigan and Howard groaned.

"She's been whipping our tails off," Howard said.

I sank down on a sofa. "Hows your mother?"

"Pretty sick," Howard said. "They're pumping her full of stuff."

Sister shuffled the cards. "Doing something with electric lights."

"Electrolytes?"

"Whatever. I'm no doctor." Sister handed Kerrigan the

cards. "Nora, Eddie's wife, is in there with her now."

Kerrigan began to deal the cards. "Nora was at the house when Mama showed up sick. She and Eddie are temporarily separated, but she was there picking some clothes up. She was the one who called 911." Kerrigan stopped. "You want me to deal you in, Mrs. Hollowell?"

I shook my head no.

"Personally," Kerrigan continued, "I think Nora was there looking for Sunshine. They're real close. Nora's the one who helped her in the Miss Alabama contest."

This caught my interest. "Sunshine was in the Miss Alabama contest?"

Kerrigan nodded. "Last year and this year. Last year she was a brunette and didn't make the finals. So this year she went blonde. Still didn't make the finals."

Everybody picked up their cards and started sorting them.

"What's her talent?" I asked.

"Fly-fishing," Howard said. "She's great at it."

I thought about the stage at Samford University where the Miss Alabama contests are held. Fly-fishing?

"They play the music from *A River Runs Through It* and Sunshine does a little dance while she flips the rod and hits targets. This year she and Nora decided to do away with the waders and have her wear a bathing suit, but she still didn't make it to the finals." Kerrigan reached over and drew a card. "She wasn't too disappointed. She had the trip to Bora Bora coming up."

I got up and walked to the window. Everything seemed normal down there on Nineteenth. Across the street my car was gone from the valet parking booth. And I had no parking ticket, no way to identify it.

"Has anybody heard from Sunshine?" I asked.

"Nope. Gin." Howard slapped his cards down.

"Where are Pawpaw and Eddie?"

"Eddie had to go back to work, and we decided not to tell Pawpaw until we know what's what because of his spells," Kerrigan explained.

"How did you do that so soon?" Sister asked Howard. "You really got me that time."

A young couple pushed an elderly woman in a wheelchair into the waiting room.

"We've got to go, Sister," I said. "By the time we locate my car, we're going to be in rush hour traffic."

"Okay." Mary Alice pushed back her chair. "Y'all call us if we can do anything or if there's any change."

"We will," Kerrigan promised. "And you let us know if Junior Reuse wanted anything important with Ray."

"I will. I doubt he did, though. That man just likes to have people roll over when he says to."

"God's truth," Kerrigan agreed.

I apologized to them both for letting their mother go out in the heat.

Howard smiled. "Don't blame yourself. I'd like to have seen you try to stop her."

This assuaged my guilt slightly. Enough so that in the elevator when Mary Alice turned to me and said, "Fly-fishing?" I burst out laughing. We were laughing so hard when the elevator opened in the lobby, we were hanging onto each other. Everyone, I'm sure, thought we were crying. Which was more appropriate, given the location.

We jaywalked back across Nineteenth and rapped on the window of the valet parking booth.

"I need my car," I said. "A blue eighty-eight Chevy."

"Where's your ticket?"

"You know I don't have one."

"Gotta have a ticket." He shut the window and turned back to his TV. Mary Alice opened the window, lifted

160

several sets of keys from the wallboard, and dropped them into her purse.

"A blue eighty-eight Chevy?" the man asked. "I think I remember."

When he brought the car up, Mary Alice rewarded him with the keys she had snitched and a five-dollar bill. Then we got in and hauled.

"What did Meemaw want to tell you?" I asked her as we headed up the mountain.

"I don't know. All she kept saying was 'Sunshine turkey.' Just over and over, 'Sunshine turkey.' Didn't make sense."

"Well, maybe it did. Maybe she was saying that Sunshine left the turkey on your front porch. When I mentioned the turkey, she said that was what Gabriel had sent her to find out."

"Find out what?"

"Gabriel wanted her to know that someone left a turkey on your front steps. I think."

"Why?"

"Hell, I don't know. I'm not a channeler." I thought for a moment. "And this whole thing is tacky. I hate to say it, Sister, because they're your in-laws, but I think our dear mother would have said that whole Turkett bunch is common as pig tracks."

I didn't get the reaction I had expected. "You're right," Sister agreed. "But you've got to admit our holidays are going to be interesting from now on. Think about it."

I didn't want to.

Every sprinkler was on in the Redmont area where Mary Alice lives. Hers are timed to come on, rain or shine, as I assume most of the others are, too. It's disconcerting during a thunderstorm to see water shooting up from the ground.

"Want to come have supper with us?" I asked. "Shrimp salad."

"Thanks, but Bill and Ray and I are going somewhere. Maybe that new Chinese place at Brookwood."

I pulled into her driveway and stopped. "This time tomorrow, Haley will be married," I said.

"And maybe by this time tomorrow Sheriff Reuse will know which one of the Turketts killed the Indian, and Sunshine can come home."

"You really think it was one of the Turketts?"

"Oh, sure."

"Which one is your money on?"

"Howard."

"Why?"

"He's the quietest one. That's always the way it works, Mouse."

"And why did Howard kill him?"

"Now *that* I don't know." Sister opened the door and got out. "But I was watching him while we played gin. He's the one, all right. Even his eyes are a little shifty."

"Call the sheriff and tell him. Make his day."

"That martinet? He can do his own work."

I drove back down the mountain, past the statue of Vulcan with its huge bare butt reflecting the late afternoon sunlight, down streets lined with trees somnolent in the heat. Fred's car was in our driveway; I was home.

Chapter 15

FRED GREETED ME WHEN I OPENED THE DOOR WITH "That cat was on the table when I came in." He was reading the paper in his recliner, an open beer on the table

162

beside him. Across from him, on the sofa, Muffin, erect as an Egyptian cat, sat watching his every move. "He didn't get down when I told him to."

"It's a she, and don't scare her. She's bound to be nervous in a strange place. I'll teach her not to get on the table." I sat down beside Muffin who immediately jumped down and disappeared into the hall.

"Ha." Fred put down the paper and looked at me. And then looked more carefully. "Your eye's getting black."

"I know. Down at University Hospital, they thought I belonged in the emergency room."

Fred looked alarmed. "You've been to the hospital?"

"To get Mary Alice." I told him about Meemaw's visit and her heatstroke, about driving at least twenty times around the hospital waiting for Mary Alice to show up, and—at this I teared up—about having nothing to wear to the wedding tomorrow and looking awful.

Fred straightened his chair with a clunk, dropped the newspaper onto the floor, and came over to hold me. "Don't cry, honey. That won't do a thing but make your eye swell up more."

Which was true. Sad but true. I burrowed my head against his chest. He smelled like sweat and Gain detergent and the metals in his warehouse. I could hear the loud thump and the softer thump of his heart, steady, rhythmical. I could go to sleep, I thought. Right here. Right now.

"Let's go look in the good closet and see what we can find. How about the dress you wore to Debbie's wedding? That was pretty."

"Too dressy."

"Your red suit?"

"Too hot." Yes, indeed, I could go to sleep right here.

"Well, let's go look. Or we can go down to the mall

tonight and get you something."

"Okay." But I held on to him for a few more minutes before I let him move.

"What about this?" He pulled a green linen jacket from the closet while Muffin and I sat on the bed and watched. "Don't you have a white skirt?"

"An off-white."

"That'll look good."

I was beginning to feel more interested. "And I've got an off-white blouse. Almost the same off-white as the skirt."

"Let's see it."

In a moment, my wedding outfit lay on the bed.

"Now you can help me," Fred said.

"How about a navy jacket and khaki pants?" I was safe; that's what he always wears.

❊ ❊ ❊

I don't know why I thought the night would be busy. As it was, it was very quiet. I went out and walked Woofer around the yard a little and then brought him into the house for a visit and to meet Muffin. The cat bristled a little when she saw Woofer, but he couldn't have cared less that a cat was in his house. He drank some water and went into the den to lie across the air-conditioning vent, ignoring her.

We ate our shrimp salad and watched the ball game. Around nine o'clock Haley called to say she was still doing last-minute things. I didn't tell her about Meemaw.

"You need me to come over in the morning?" I asked. "Help you get ready?"

"Maybe get to the church a little early to check me out. We're not making this a big deal."

But it was a big deal. A very big deal that would change all of our lives.

164

"Haley," I told Fred as I hung up. He nodded but didn't say anything. Wise man.

The Braves trounced San Francisco but Fred didn't see it. Sometime during the seventh inning he began to snore. After the ten o'clock news (the weather was the number-one story), I woke him up to go to bed. I thought I would have trouble going to sleep, but the steady hum of the air conditioner was soothing. Muffin joined us, but Fred didn't know. As for me, I liked her purring.

The sound of the doorbell was part of my dream. I was at a wedding and a bell was ringing.

"What's that?" Fred grumbled. "The doorbell?"

It rang again. This time both of us came straight up. I turned on the light. Three o'clock. "Don't open it," I said to Fred who was looking for his robe. "It could be one of those home invaders. Some of them ring the doorbell."

"Home invader, hell. It better be an emergency."

Oh, God. An emergency. I grabbed my robe and followed.

Fred turned on the porch light and looked through the peephole.

"It's Sunshine," he announced.

"At three o'clock in the morning?"

"Right here."

"Well, let her in."

"How do we know it's safe?"

"Sunshine? You think Sunshine might be dangerous?" I looked through the peephole. Bedraggled, still dressed in the same pink dress, Sunshine still managed to look beautiful. And innocent. "Don't be ridiculous. She was almost in the Miss Alabama finals." I opened the door.

"Oh, Mrs. Hollowell, Mr. Hollowell." She began to cry. "I'm so sorry to bother you in the middle of the night, but I've got to find out about Meemaw. I just heard she

165

had a stroke and is in intensive care."

"You heard it at three o'clock in the morning?" Fred asked.

"I know it sounds crazy, and I shouldn't be here. I apologize. But I couldn't go to Mother Crane's. Ray's there. And I didn't even know which hospital to call."

I gave Fred a hard look. "Come on in, Sunshine. Your grandmother is in intensive care at University, but it's a heatstroke, not a stroke stroke. They think she's going to be okay."

Sunshine leaned her head against the doorjamb and cried harder.

"Come on in, honey," I repeated. "I'll get us some coffee."

"It's just all so terrible." Sunshine stepped inside, mopping at her face with her palms.

"I'll get you a Kleenex," Fred offered. As we got to the den, he came in with a whole box. "Here."

Sunshine took a couple, sank down on the sofa, and held them to her face. "I really should go. You're sure Meemaw's going to be all right?"

"She's pretty sick or she wouldn't be in intensive care, but she's not paralyzed or anything like that. It's a matter of getting her stabilized."

"Making sure she doesn't have brain damage," Fred added. I gave him another dirty look for that happy information.

"It's true," he insisted. "The body's cooling system shuts down, you quit sweating, and your temperature goes sky-high."

"Well, when she was here, she said she was sweating like a whore in church, so she couldn't have been shut down long."

Sunshine looked up with a slight smile. "That sounds

166

like Meemaw."

"She's going to be fine," I said. "Now how about I fix you some coffee?"

Sunshine sank into the sofa. "That would be wonderful."

"I'm going back to bed," Fred said and left.

I got the coffee going and came back into the den. I thought Sunshine was asleep, but she opened her eyes as I sat down.

"Mrs. Hollowell, is Ray all right?"

"Fine. Missing you."

"I'm sorry to do him this way."

"Then why don't you call him?"

"I can't. I really can't."

We were silent for a few minutes. Muffin came in to see what was going on and hopped up on the sofa beside Sunshine. Sunshine rubbed the cat with one hand and mopped tears with the other.

"You're staying with Dwayne, aren't you?" It was a guess, but a good one.

"I'm staying with a friend of his. He came and got me, though. At the trailer." Her voice lowered. "I called him."

"And he nearly ran us down as we were coming into the highway in Sister's Jaguar."

"Yes, ma'am. It scared him real bad."

"Us, too." Again there was a pause. The smell of coffee began to waft into the room. "Want to tell me why you ran?"

"I was so scared. I've never been so scared in my life." Sunshine shivered; obviously she was telling the truth.

"But what happened?"

She shivered harder. "Can I use your bathroom?"

"Down the hall. First door on the left. I'll get our coffee."

By the time she got back, I had fixed a tray with coffee and the rest of the Girl Scout cookies. Sunshine looked like she needed some sugar; I knew I did.

"Thanks, Mrs. Hollowell." She put sugar in her coffee, stirred it, and turned to me. It must have been the first time she had really looked at me because she said, "My Lord, what happened to you?"

"I fell over a turkey somebody left on my sister's front porch." I emphasized "somebody."

But it apparently struck no guilt chord. "How could you fall over a turkey?" Sunshine asked, her eyes wide.

"Easy. It was a dead feathered one, split down the middle and right in the front door." I picked up my coffee, keeping an eye on Sunshine. Old schoolteachers can spot in a minute when somebody's lying. "We figured it was a warning of some kind."

"Of what?" She looked sufficiently bewildered. Maybe she hadn't known about the turkey.

"We don't know," I admitted. "You got any ideas?"

She shook her head slightly. "Doesn't make sense. Are you okay?"

"Just bunged up." I sipped my coffee; Sunshine sipped hers. I ate a cookie; Sunshine ate one. The deep silence of 3 A.M. begged not to be disturbed, but there were questions that needed answering. I put my cup down. "You were going to tell me why you ran."

Sunshine put her cup down, too. "I was so scared. The man who killed the other man saw me. I was asleep and I heard all this commotion and opened the bedroom door and there he was. The man was on the floor with the knife in him"—Sunshine shuddered—"and this guy was looking right at me. I figured I was dead. I could hear him at the door when I crawled out of the window and ran toward the woods."

"You saw him?"

"Close as I am to you."

"Did you know him?"

"No idea who he is. I don't think he followed me, though. I hid and called Dwayne."

"You grabbed your cell phone on the way out of the window?"

"Yes, ma'am. And this one dress." Sunshine plucked at the material as if she were sick of it.

"Why didn't you call the police?"

"I was too scared. I just knew I had to get out of there and quick. I'm going to Sheriff Reuse tomorrow—today, I mean. I'd already decided that when Dwayne came in and said Meemaw was sick. He works at a bar on Southside part-time and doesn't get off work until two."

"What was the man like, or do you mind answering these questions?"

"Oh, no, ma'am. I don't mind." Sunshine picked up her mug and held it with both hands as if trying to warm them. "He was in his fiffies, partly bald. Had a big stomach, but he wasn't really fat. You know how men do sometimes. Get a beer belly." She bit her lower lip, thinking. "Probably almost six feet tall, and he had great big hands with the veins sticking out on them like he'd been working real hard."

"He had," I said. "He'd been sticking a hog-butchering knife through a man."

Coffee sloshed from Sunshine's cup onto her pink dress. She grabbed a Kleenex from the box Fred had left. "I'm still scared to death," she said.

That part I believed. The mystery-man story was so full of holes you could use it for a colander.

"Anyway," she said, mopping at her skirt, "I probably shouldn't have, but I ran."

169

"Sometimes it's the wisest thing to do." I got up and took her cup. "Here, let me get you some fresh coffee."

"I really need to go."

"Well, I was going to tell you some more about Meemaw."

"What about her?" She held out the cup. I went into the kitchen to refill it. "I was at the hospital this afternoon," I called. I came back into the den. Sunshine was stroking Muffin and crying again. "Your Aunt Nora was with her. Your mother and Uncle Howard were in the waiting room. And my sister. But your Aunt Nora was with Meemaw."

Sunshine nodded. "That's good. Aunt Nora's the best one of the whole bunch. I'm glad she was with her."

"But she and your Uncle Eddie are separated?" I was trying to be subtle and find out more about the family relationships. Sunshine was obliging.

"He works all the time. All the time. They've got that gorgeous house and if I hadn't been there with her most of the time since the boys left for college, Aunt Nora would have been rattling around up there by herself. The man's crazy. All he thinks about is money."

I took another cookie and sat down. "What about your Uncle Howard?"

"You mean does he have a wife? He's had six. Pawpaw says you've got to give Howard credit, he believes in the institution of marriage." Sunshine reached for a cookie. "Now Mama, on the other hand—" She didn't finish the thought, just sat back and nibbled on the cookie.

"But Meemaw raised you, didn't she?"

"Meemaw and Pawpaw." Her expression softened. "I guess my first memory is Pawpaw taking me fishing on the Tennessee River when we lived in Muscle Shoals."

"That's a nice memory," I said. "I remember my

170

grandfather taking me fishing, too. He only took Mary Alice once, though. He told my grandmother that Mary Alice needed the gulf to fish in."

Sunshine smiled. "She's an interesting lady, isn't she?"

"As long as she has the whole gulf to fish in." I stretched. My body was beginning to say 4 A.M.

"I need to go," Sunshine said. "I shouldn't have come here in the middle of the night, but I panicked when Dwayne came in telling me about Meemaw."

"It's going to be awfully hard for you to leave her to go to Bora Bora, isn't it?"

"It's going to break my heart." The words were simple and heartfelt.

"Listen," I said. "Why don't you just lie down here on the sofa and sleep for a few hours. Call Dwayne if you think he might be worried. Incidentally, does Dwayne have a redheaded girlfriend?"

Sunshine looked startled. "An ex-girlfriend named Leeann Skinner. Real redheaded. Why? How did you know?"

"I think she was in the crowd looking for you. Made a couple of remarks."

Sunshine managed a smile. "That would have been Leeann, all right. I'm glad she didn't find me. She thinks I beat her out for Miss Locust Fork, too."

"I think it's just as well, too." I smiled, too, thinking of the menace I had attributed to the "crawled from under a rock" whisper. "Why don't you curl up and let me spread the afghan over you. You look worn out."

"I am. You sure it's all right?"

"I'll get you a pillow. Or you can use the guest bedroom."

"Here's fine. Can the cat stay with me?"

"If she wants to. She decides."

By the time I got back, Sunshine was almost asleep.

"One more thing," I said. "This morning I saw you on Twentieth Street. I tried to catch you, but you went out the back door of the hardware store."

"Wasn't me," Sunshine said. She took the pillow. "Thank you."

"Have a good nap." I covered her and she sighed.

Chapter 16

SUNSHINE WAS GONE WHEN WE GOT UP THE NEXT morning which didn't surprise me. I wondered if she would go to the sheriff with the tale of the man who had killed Dudley Cross. I hoped if she did, that she would tell him about the man trying to come in the door of the bedroom as she went out the window. Not only did the "door" of the bedroom consist of blue-and-white-striped fabric, the windows were small and high. Sunshine, while not large, would have had a hell of a time getting out of one of those windows with a murderer chasing her.

But why had she lied about it?

I put on a fresh pot of coffee, poured myself a glass of cranberry juice, and went out to see about Woofer. He was so far back in his igloo that I had to kneel down to reach in and wake him up.

"Listen," I said when he ambled out, "Haley's getting married today. I think you ought to get a bath and put on your diamond collar."

He wagged his tail in agreement.

Woofer's diamond collar is a family joke. A distant cousin of mine died without a will and with no direct heirs. So one day, out of the blue, a check arrived for me, my part of his estate, for $257. This is mine, I thought, a

172

gift to buy anything I want. A new dress, shoes, books.

I spent a whole day trying to spend that money. Every time I'd see something I wanted, I'd think that if I spent the money then, I'd see something I wanted more later. What I finally bought was the rhinestone collar for Woofer. That was all. $20. Mary Alice bought a beautiful birdbath with her $257, St. Francis of Assisi blessing the birds with an outstretched hand that Sister swears stays full of bird crap. But it still looks good in the flower bed under her dining room window. I wish that was what I had bought. I don't know what happened to my money except for Woofer's diamond necklace.

"I'll be back in a minute," I said. "Let me go get some hot water." We bathe Woofer in a child's wading pool, and I like to have the water slightly warm. Well, he *is* an old dog.

"What are you doing?" Fred asked. He was pouring himself a cup of coffee.

"Fixing to put on my Woofer-washing shorts. He's dressing up because it's Haley's wedding day."

Fred squinted at the outside thermometer. "Another hot one, too."

"You got that right." I finished my cranberry juice which was still on the counter.

"What time did Sunshine leave?"

"Don't know. She slept for a while on the sofa but was gone when I got up. Told me a cock-and-bull story about the murderer trying to break down the bedroom door of the trailer and her having to climb out of the window."

"Sounds smart to me. I'd run like hell, too."

I put my glass into the dishwasher. "No door."

Fred looked up from pouring milk into his coffee. "No door?"

"Meemaw's trailer is one of those old ones that just has

173

curtains between the bedroom and the other areas. And those windows are so little, Sunshine couldn't even get her boobs through them." I poured myself a cup of coffee. "You ask me, that girl's got more than a passing acquaintance with a plastic surgeon."

"Probably the same one her mother's acquainted with."

"Touché." I grinned at Fred. Sometimes the old fellow still surprises me.

"You want me to help you with the dog?" he asked, looking pleased with himself.

"No. Just read the paper. If Mary Alice calls, tell her Sunshine was here last night and I'll call her when I finish bathing Woofer."

"You don't think Sunshine went over to Mary Alice's house?"

"No. She's with that Dwayne Parker boy. She said she was staying with a friend of his, but I don't buy that. She also said she wasn't on Twentieth Street yesterday, and she's lying about that."

"Why, the shameless hussy." Fred sat down at the kitchen table with the paper. I stuck my tongue out at him and went to get on my old shorts.

There's something so very nice about bathing a dog— the feel of warm water running over your hand and his fur, the way he looks at you as if to say, *Are you sure this is necessary?*

I squirted Palmolive on Woofer and lathered him. He sat in the wading pool, compliant, sweet, looking half the size he does when he's not wet.

"We had a visitor at three o'clock this morning," I told him. "You didn't bark. Are you all right?"

Woofer held up his chin so I could wash his neck. *Three o'clock in the morning? Decent dogs are asleep in their beds then.*

"True. And you are a decent, good dog." I finished lathering him and rinsed him with one of the pitchers of warm water.

"The water in the hose will be warm," Fred said. He had come out on the deck and was watching us. "I'll get it."

"That cat was on the kitchen table again," he said as we finished rinsing Woofer. He picked him up and handed him to me to towel dry. "Is there anything we can do about it? I was reading the damn paper and he jumped up there big as life."

"Not a thing." I rubbed Woofer's head, the gray hair between his ears. "And the cat's a she."

"Well, she needs to learn to behave." Fred dumped over the wading pool, let the water splash out. The August grass would appreciate it, even with the Palmolive. "Mary Alice called."

"Did you tell her about Sunshine?" I gave Woofer a kiss on his nose and let him go to shake little rainbows into the air and to wallow in any dirt he could find.

"Didn't have a chance. She was wound up about Haley going to the cemetery this morning."

"What?"

"I don't know. I told her you'd call her."

"And you didn't ask her what she was talking about?"

"Honey, you know I don't get much sense out of your sister."

"Lord, Fred, she's not *that* bad." I dried my hands down the side of my shorts and headed for the phone. Haley going to the cemetery?

"God's truth," Sister said when I got her. "She and Nephew are going out to Tom's grave before they come to the church. They're taking flowers, and they're going to have a conversation with him." Sister paused. "A real one-

175

sided one if you ask me."

"A conversation?"

"I don't know, Mouse. That's just what Nephew said. I guess he's going to tell Tom he'll take good care of Haley or something like that. You really need to call her, and tell her not to do it."

"But I think its sort of sweet. Letting Tom know he's not left out."

"Listen, Mouse. Tom *is* left out. The minute that eighteen-wheeler hit him, he was left out."

"No, he wasn't. He'll never be left out of Haley's heart. Or ours either."

"Well, be that as it may, I'm telling you you ought to call and tell her not to go."

"Why? Just because you don't go out and visit your dead husbands doesn't mean Haley shouldn't."

"I visit them on all of their birthdays, Miss Smartypants. Take flowers to every one of them. That's not the point. What time is the wedding?"

I was slightly confused. "Eleven."

"And how hot is it?"

"Very hot."

"And they're going to the cemetery before the wedding? They'll be sweaty and wilted. Haley's hair will be frizzed to hell and back in the wedding pictures. Incidentally, I hired a photographer. And what's more, she'll probably cry and her face will be all red and puffy." Sister paused for breath. "You really ought to call them, Patricia Anne."

"I'll think about it." I knew I wouldn't. If Haley wanted to visit Tom one last time as his wife, that was her business. I changed the subject. "Sunshine was here at three o'clock this morning."

"You're kidding. Where is she now?"

"I have no idea."

"Well, what did she want?"

"She wanted to know how Meemaw was. I told her what I knew. Have you heard anything else about her condition?"

"Haven't heard this morning. And that's another thing. What if Nephew and Haley have a heatstroke out there at Elmwood?"

No way I was going to get back on that subject.

"She said she saw the murderer and he saw her and that's why she's hiding."

"Well, my Lord."

"She also said she climbed out of the trailer window when he tried to come in the bedroom door."

There was a long pause on Sister's end of the line. I could see her picturing Meemaw's trailer. I waited.

"That's interesting," she said, finally.

"Yes, it is."

"Call Haley. I'll see you at the wedding."

A dial tone. Sister drives me nuts doing this, hanging up without so much as a goodbye.

I went to get Woofer's diamond necklace. Muffin was sitting on the kitchen table looking at me as I came back through. "You're not allowed up there," I told her. Muffin yawned.

❀❀❀

Haley and Philip got married. There was music, something classical that I didn't recognize. The girls at the florist had come through with a large elegant arrangement of white flowers. Haley and Philip walked down the aisle together while the photographer crawled across our feet to get a good shot. When they reached the altar, a young man and woman who had been sitting across from us got up to stand with them. Philip's children.

Haley looked beautiful; Philip looked handsome.

Neither looked sweaty or red in the face. They said their vows clearly while I snuffled all my green makeup off onto tissues.

Mary Alice sat across from us on the groom's side. "Well, he *is* my nephew by marriage," she explained at lunch. "And it looked bare over there. It's tacky to take sides at such a small wedding anyhow."

We had a private dining room at the Merritt House, a beautiful Victorian home on Birmingham's Southside, just a few blocks from where Debbie and Henry live. Debbie had made it to the wedding, but Henry showed up for the lunch by himself explaining she couldn't face food.

We met Philip's daughter Jenny, and his son, Matthew. I reminded Fred they were now our step-grandchildren so he should be especially nice to them.

"Which is which?" he asked.

"Matthew is the one with the long blond hair."

Fred squinted at Matthew. "Tell me he's not wearing makeup."

"Neither one of them is," I assured him.

Fred rolled his eyes, but he went over to introduce himself.

Haley and Philip floated into the room. Hugs. Kisses. Champagne toasts. Beautiful and delicious food. Lisa, my daughter-in-law, leaned around Fred and informed me it was the best salmon she had ever put in her mouth, and weren't Philip's children precious?

"Precious," Fred said. I gave him a slight kick and he grinned. "And to think they're our step-grandchildren now."

"You deserve it," Lisa said.

I gave him another kick, this one a little harder. He yelped which startled Lisa.

"Fish bone." Fred pointed in the general direction of

his mouth.

"Well, be careful, Pop. I haven't seen a single bone."

"I will," Fred assured her, touching his thumb and forefinger delicately to his lips to extract the nonexistent bone. "Got it."

"Good." Lisa turned back to Alan. I turned to my right and talked to Ray.

Yes, indeed, Sunshine was fine. Three o'clock in the morning. She said to tell him she loved him.

Had she? I didn't remember. But Ray looked pleased.

"She'll be back probably tonight. She's going to go talk to the sheriff this afternoon."

Well, it *was* a wedding. A little lying is necessary.

Then the cake. The waiters cleared the table and we could hear them conversing in the hall. Then the door opened and two of them wheeled in the wedding cake, the most unusual wedding cake I have ever seen. Instead of a two- or three-tier cake with a bride and groom on the top, this seemed to be a huge mushroom.

Mary Alice stood up and saw that the waiters placed the cake just right, the more sloping side of the mushroom toward the wedding couple.

"Voilà," she said to Haley and Philip. "You'll never guess what it is!"

Haley and Philip looked at each other. "A mushroom?" Philip guessed.

"Close. I'll tell you because you'll never get it. You know what today is?"

"August sixth," Haley said. "It's Philip's birthday."

None of us had known this. There were calls of "Happy birthday" and a few claps. Haley leaned over and kissed him.

"But," Sister said, holding up her hands to hush us, "on the day Philip was born, there was another earthshaking event. It was a big day all around."

Fred and I looked at each other. We had both realized at the same time. "It's an atom bomb cake," he murmured.

"It's an atom bomb cake," Mary Alice announced. "Fireworks for your wedding day."

"It explodes?" Haley asked, moving back slightly.

"Of course not. That was a metaphor."

A metaphor? Sister was getting a lot out of her writing classes at UAB. I was downright proud of her.

Everyone, including the two waiters, crowded around to see the atom bomb cake.

"Who made it?" Henry wanted to know. He was looking at the cake with a chef's eye.

"Some lady in Homewood. She does all kinds of specialty items."

"Somebody get a picture before we cut it," Haley said.

"How are we going to cut it?" Philip asked.

Sister handed him a cake knife. "It doesn't matter. Just dive in. One side doesn't have coconut because not everybody likes coconut. I, for one, hate coconut. It keeps getting bigger the more I chew it."

Fred was laughing so hard he had to sit down. Pretty soon he had his face in his napkin, his elbows propped on the table.

"Is he all right?" Sister asked me as she began to pass out cake. "Fred, you want some atom bomb wedding cake?"

Fred looked up, tears streaming. "I love you, Mary Alice."

"I love you, too, Fred." She pulled me aside. "Do you think we ought to call 911?"

❀ ❀ ❀

Fred giggled all the way home. "An atom bomb

wedding cake. Do you know, honey, I think that's top on my list of Mary Alice stunts."

"Just because it's the most recent." I was thinking about the happy look on Haley's face as she and Philip got in his car.

"But think about it, honey. The ultimate weapon of destruction with coconut on half of it." He wiped his eyes.

"She meant well."

"And the look on Philip's face. And them trying to cut it."

"You didn't have to tell them you wanted half coconut."

"I couldn't resist."

"Well, we'll always remember Philip's birthday. And their wedding cake."

Fred laughed harder. Usually I'm the one who cracks up over black humor, but I was still too distracted by the wedding.

Arthur Phizer was out in his yard picking up a can some litterer had tossed. He had on a white undershirt, plaid shorts, dark socks, and wing-tip shoes. Arthur, Mitzi says, isn't quite ready for the millennium.

"Hey," he called. "How did it go?"

Fred went to tell him about the atom bomb wedding cake. I walked into a house that seemed strangely empty. I went back to the kitchen to get a drink of water, and Muffin looked up from the table and meowed.

I pulled out a chair, sat down, and stroked her. I told her about the wedding, about the atomic bomb cake, how happy her mama had seemed. She purred. As I heard the back door open, I whispered to her that she didn't have to get down unless she wanted to, that she was to pay no attention to that cross old man because she was a good pussycat, yes she was.

181

"Aunt Pat?"

I jumped.

"Sorry." Ray pulled out a chair and sat down across from me. "Uncle Fred said you were in here."

"I thought you were him—he—*whatever* coming in." Sometimes English grammar gets the best of all of us.

"Nope. It's me. I came by to find out some more about Sunshine."

"You want a big glass of icewater?"

"That would be great."

I fixed us both one and sat back down at the kitchen table, pulling off my shoes. "You want me to start at the beginning?"

"Please."

I started with the doorbell ringing at three o'clock in the morning and didn't spare any details this time except my suspicion that Sunshine was staying with Dwayne. I told Ray a friend. I also told him about the windows and doors, or lack of them, in the trailer.

"What do you think?" he asked.

I shrugged. I heard the front door open and Fred head for the bedroom. I drank my water and idly rolled the small pebble that had never gotten thrown away toward Muffin. She slapped it onto the floor and Ray reached down and picked it up.

"My Lord, Aunt Pat."

"I'm sorry, Ray. I know I ought to be able to tell you more, but I just don't know her that well."

Ray looked at me strangely. "Do you know anything about black pearls, Aunt Pat?"

The shift in conversation confused me for a moment. "It's one of Elizabeth Taylor's perfumes. Pretty exotic. I tried it down at Rich's one day, and I really prefer one more citrusy."

182

"This, Aunt Pat. You don't know what this is, do you?"

I leaned over and looked at the rock in the palm of his hand. It had a greenish hue but I guessed, "Black pearl?"

"A beautiful one. Where did it come from?"

"Meemaw and Sunshine were playing Chinese checkers with them." I took what I had thought was a pretty rock from Ray. "They're expensive, aren't they?"

"You better believe it. That baby you're holding would run at least ten thousand dollars and up."

And I had almost thrown it away. I had been rolling it around for the cat to play with. "Fred!" I screeched. "Get in here!"

He came to the door zipping his shorts. "What?"

I held up the stone. "This is a black pearl. Ray says it's worth maybe ten thousand dollars."

"Are you serious?"

"God's truth. Ask him."

"It's true, Uncle Fred. Black pearls are a big business in Bora Bora. The biggest next to tourism." Ray took the pearl back. "This is a beautiful one. A touch of polishing and the green color will really show."

Fred took the pearl from Ray. "And they're expensive?"

"You better believe it. The whole process takes forever. They grow the oysters for a couple of years, seed them, and then harvest them three years later. That's five years, and then only a few of the oysters will have made pearls. Especially this size."

"There were a bunch of them on Meemaw's table."

Ray's face darkened. "I think we've just found out what's caused all the trouble out at the Turketts'."

"Is it illegal to bring them in?" Fred asked.

"No. They can be shipped in legally. There are a couple of companies that grow most of them and ship them around the world. It's like farming, Uncle Fred. There are a few small operations, but if they don't have a good harvest, they can't weather it. And believe me, the Turketts' couldn't have afforded to buy any or pay the import on them."

"Maybe they didn't know what they were," I said. "They were out on the table like they were nothing."

"I hope so." Ray got up and went to the phone.

"Who are you calling?" I asked.

"The sheriff. Whether she knew about them or not, Sunshine's in big trouble."

There was a knock on the kitchen door. Fred went to open it.

"I knocked, Fred. Remember that. You're always fussing when I don't." Sister sailed in. "I saw Ray's car was here, and I came to have a good postmortem on the wedding."

"Bad choice of words," Ray said. Then into the phone, "Yes, I'd like the number of the Blount County sheriff's office, please."

Sister clunked her purse down on the counter with such a noise that Muffin ran from the room. "What's he calling the sheriff for?"

"This." I held up the stone.

"A rock?"

"It's a black pearl. It's the one I picked up in Meemaw's trailer. Remember? She and Sunshine were playing Chinese checkers with them."

Mary Alice sat down in the chair Ray had vacated and took the pearl. "It's green," she said.

"Ray says it's a black pearl, though, and worth a lot of money," Fred said.

"Then what were Meemaw and Sunshine doing with them?"

I shrugged. "I don't know, but they obviously didn't

184

know what they were or they wouldn't have been playing with them."

Sister turned the pearl, looking at it from all angles. "Maybe this is what the Indian was after."

"That's why Ray's calling the sheriff."

"Well, I'll be damned. Black pearls."

"Let me see it again," Fred said.

Ray came back to the table. "He's out fishing or something. They said they'd try to get hold of him and have him call me. I gave him this number and my number at home."

"How do you know this is a black pearl, Ray?" his mother asked.

"They sell them in all the stores in Bora Bora, Mama. You can buy an imperfect one on a tiny chain for maybe two thousand dollars. The large, perfect ones are sent to Saudi Arabia and Kuwait and sell for God knows how much. But there's a sizable market for them here in the U.S., too. Anyway, I've seen a lot of them." He sat down and reached for the pearl. "This one is a honey."

"Then how"—Mary Alice spoke the question that was on all our minds—"did they end up in a trailer in Locust Fork, Alabama?"

"Because someone there had just gotten back from Bora Bora."

This had to be painful for Ray to say. Fred, Mary Alice, and I looked at each other.

"But maybe she didn't know what she had. Maybe someone stuck them in her suitcase and she didn't know anything about it. And that's what that Dudley Indian guy was doing there. He knew the pearls had come in and he came to get them." Mary Alice was talking so fast she was almost out of breath.

"I suppose it's possible," Ray admitted.

"Of course it's possible," I agreed.

"What I want to know is how someone would get them," Fred said. "You say they're farmed? I know this is a simplification, but couldn't you buy some from the farmers?"

"Not as an individual. It's pretty much a cartel." Ray rubbed the pearl against his sleeve. "And that suits the French government fine. Bora Bora's one of the few Polynesian islands that's paying its way."

"I keep forgetting Bora Bora is French," Mary Alice said.

Ray smiled. "Mama, you keep thinking I'm in Pago Pago."

"Is that French?"

"That's American."

"Well, Lord. Those islands are so messed up. Do they have black pearls in Pago Pago?"

Fred tapped his fingernails on the table. We all looked at him. "Ray, how would one go about getting black pearls then?"

"Pay a mint for them or steal them." Ray looked at the pearl. "And I don't know anybody who could buy a bunch of these."

"How would you go about stealing them?" Fred wanted to know.

"The only way I know you could get away with it would be to rob the oyster beds." He pointed to the three-tiered wire basket I keep potatoes and onions hanging in. "You see Aunt Pat's basket there? That's sort of like the contraption they put the oysters in. They seed them and put them in the baskets and lower them into the lagoons. I suppose a diver could snip off a basket, but he'd sure be taking a hell of a chance." Ray thought for a moment. "Let's put it this way. He wouldn't be treated with much compassion by the authorities if he were caught."

"But if he weren't caught," I said, "he'd be sitting on a gold mine."

"If he were lucky enough to get some good oysters." Ray thought for a moment. "And then he'd have to smuggle them off the island and into another country."

Which would be where a cute blonde in a pink sundress would come in handy.

"You say they're seeded," Fred said. "What do they seed them with?"

"You're not going to believe this. They use freshwater mussels from right here in the Tennessee River. Use a little bead of the shell as a nucleus. Practically every pearl you see a woman wearing had its start right here in Alabama or Tennessee."

I ran the string of pearls I was wearing through my fingers. From the Tennessee River. "Do you think a person living in Muscle Shoals would know this?"

"They might. It's a big business. Mostly one big company."

The telephone rang and all of us jumped.

"I'll get it," Fred said. He talked quietly for a moment, then hung up and said, "That was Henry. He's taking Debbie to the emergency room at University. She's bleeding."

Chapter 17

"THINGS COME IN THREES," SISTER SAID AS WE WERE on our way to the hospital. "First there was the Indian's murder, then Sunshine's kidnapping, then Meemaw's sunstroke, then Haley's wedding, and now this."

"That's five."

"I know. That's what's worrying me." She made an

illegal U-turn on Nineteenth Street and whirled into the valet parking. A different guy, young, probably a student at UAB, stepped out of the booth to greet us.

"Hot today, ladies," he said pleasantly.

Mary Alice hopped out of the car, as much as two hundred and fifty pounds can hop, and said, "Put a scratch on my Jaguar and curses will rain on you and your progeny."

The boy jumped back. "Ma'am?"

"Into perpetuity." She started across the street.

"What's that lady talking about?" the boy asked, handing me the parking ticket but keeping a wary eye on the figure dodging traffic.

"She just wants you to be careful with her car."

"That's not what she said."

"It's what she meant." I gave him what I hoped was a reassuring smile and hurried after Mary Alice. Déjà vu all over again, I thought, jaywalking just as I had done the day before. She had already disappeared into the hospital as I started up the steps and nearly ran into a man who was coming out. "Sorry," I said. And then we went through that embarrassing thing where each of you steps to the same side several times. The man looked familiar, but in a place as small as Birmingham you're always running into people you've met.

"Sorry," I said again, and this time we got by each other. Mary Alice was at the information desk and the lady there was confirming that Debbie was already in the emergency room.

"Down that long hall over yonder." She pointed.

"We know," we both said.

"She's going to be all right, Sister," I said as we hurried down the long hall. "Remember I did that with Freddie? The doctor put me to bed for a few days and I was fine.

And now they've got all sorts of things to keep them from going into labor."

"I hope so, Mouse."

So did I. With all my heart.

Henry was sitting in the waiting room. He jumped up when he saw us. "They've taken her for a sonogram. She said she knew you'd be coming so I should wait for you." Tears flooded his eyes. "She's taking it real good. She'd already called the doctor when I got home, and he said it wasn't all that unusual. She's not bleeding much."

"I did the same thing with Freddie, didn't I, Sister? And he was a week late and weighed over eight pounds. Debbie's going to be fine, Henry."

Henry sat down and we sat on either side of him.

"You know," he said, "all the way down here I kept thinking about how complicated women's reproductive organs are. So easy for things to go awry it's a wonder anybody gets born."

Sister patted his hand, comforting him. "Men's organs are complicated, too." She paused. "All my husbands' went awry at times. And you're right. It doesn't take much for it to happen."

I hoped Henry would forget this conversation.

"How long has she been gone, honey?" I asked him.

"Just a few minutes. They said it would take about a half hour."

"Then you know what I think I'll do? I think I'll go check on Meemaw Turkett."

"If you see her, maybe you can bring up the subject of Chinese checkers," Sister said.

"Those Chinese checkers are none of my business."

"Of course they are. Especially now that we know Elizabeth Taylor is involved."

Henry was so sunk in his worries, he didn't seem to

think this was a strange conversation. Or, truth to tell, he'd heard stranger from us.

"I'll see what the checkerboard looks like." This was as much promise as I was going to make.

Back to the information desk where I found out that Meemaw had been moved to a private room on the sixth floor. And sure, she could have visitors. Up to 611 where the door was slightly ajar. I knocked and opened it cautiously.

"Come in," Meemaw said. "I'm awake." She was propped up in bed watching an old movie on TV. She was still attached to an IV, but her color was good and she smiled when she saw me. "Sit down," she said, pointing to the brown reclining chair by the window. "Howard just left."

"You look like you're feeling much better."

"Honey, a dead dog would feel better than I felt yesterday. I almost cashed it in."

"I'm sorry. I shouldn't have let you go out in the heat."

"I should have had more sense. It's not your fault."

"Thanks. I want you to know Sunshine came by my house early this morning, actually in the middle of the night. She heard you were sick and wanted to know how you were."

Meemaw looked pleased. "Tell me about her. Is my baby all right?"

"She's fine. Said she was staying with a friend of Dwayne Parker's."

"That Dwayne. She hasn't got a bit of business messing around with him."

I didn't have a reply for that so I told her about Haley's wedding and about the lunch. What I really wanted to do was what Sister had suggested, ask her if she knew what those pebbles were that she and Sunshine had been

190

playing Chinese checkers with. And I was about to get up the nerve to do it when Kerrigan walked in, beautiful in pale lavender walking shorts and a white sleeveless shirt.

"Guess what, Kerrigan," Meemaw said. "Sunshine was at Patricia Anne's house during the night."

"You're kidding. Tell me about it," Kerrigan said.

Which I did, and which is why Henry and Mary Alice were gone from the emergency room when I got back.

"They're up on fifth in maternity," the nurse told me.

"Oh, God, she's not—"

"She's fine. They're just monitoring her. Got her wired up to see if she has any contractions."

I rushed back up to the fifth floor. Henry and Mary Alice were standing out in the hall.

"They ran us out," she said when she saw me. "They're hooking her up to all sorts of things."

"Just precautionary," Henry assured me. "The doctor says everything looks fine. He asked me if I wanted to know if it's a boy or a girl."

"Which is it?" Sister asked.

"I told him I didn't want to know."

"Are you crazy? Of course you do."

"No, I don't, Mary Alice."

"Yes, you do. Where's that doctor?" sister stomped toward the nurses' station.

Henry grinned at me. "It's a boy. I bet Debbie her mother could find out in under two minutes."

I looked at the nurse who seemed to be in charge, a Nurse Ratched lookalike who was already eyeing Sister coldly. "You may lose that bet."

He didn't, of course. Sister was back immediately.

"It's a boy. I hope you don't name him Philip. We've already got so many Philips, it's confusing."

Henry clasped his hands to his heart. "A boy!"

Sister looked pleased. "I knew you wanted to know."

A nurse stuck her head out of Debbie's door. "Mr. Lamont, you can come in now. Ladies, if you could wait for just a few minutes—"

"Why?" Mary Alice asked.

The nurse shut the door in her face.

"Come on," I said. "Let's go sit at the end of the hall."

Mary Alice surprised me by following without complaint. "A boy," she said. "A grandson." We sat down. "You know, Mouse, I think being a man is so much easier than being a woman. Think of the decisions you don't have to make."

I could have asked what, but I didn't. Instead, I told her that Meemaw seemed to be doing fine and that I had told her about Sunshine's visit.

"The twins are going to be thrilled to have a little brother," Sister said.

This woman had just learned she was going to have her first grandson. I might as well forget conversation. While she talked ("Boys' clothes are cuter than they used to be, Mouse"), I gazed down at the traffic on Nineteenth. A dark-haired woman wearing lavender shorts and a white shirt crossed the street and got into a white van that pulled up beside her.

"I think I just saw Kerrigan leaving," I said. "A white delivery van with writing on the side."

"Even smocking," Sister said. "They smock little boats and ducks on them."

A tall, skinny young man came down the hall and introduced himself as Dr. Lanagan. "Everything looks good," he explained. "We're going to keep her here tonight and she may have to stay in bed for a few days, but I think that baby's going to hang on just fine."

"Can we go see her now?" Sister asked.

"Sure." He patted each of us on the shoulder and loped off down the hall. Medical schools, I decided right then, should teach more patting. I felt better.

Henry was sitting by Debbie's bed holding her hand. She saw us and began to cry.

"You see," Sister told me. "I told you it's easier being a man."

Maybe so.

We didn't stay long. Debbie and Henry needed to be alone. Even Sister realized that.

❋ ❋ ❋

The boy at the valet parking booth rushed out to assure Mary Alice that her car was fine. Good as new. Right as rain. Slick as a whistle.

"My God," she said as he ran to get it. "That boy needs to be on Ritalin." When he drove up, she gave him a generous tip "to help with his medical expenses."

"You know what?" I said as we pulled into the traffic. "When we went in the hospital, I almost bumped into a man who looked familiar. I just remembered who he is."

"Who?" Sister turned the air conditioner on high. "Lord, this car's hot."

"That guy from the antique shop."

"What guy ?"

"When you were trying on dresses and I saw Sunshine. Remember I went in the stores up to the corner to see where she had been? One of them was the antique store. That's the guy."

"So?"

I hate it when people say "So?" like that.

"So, nothing, I reckon. Only maybe he was driving a white van and picked up Kerrigan."

"Maybe he was just visiting a sick relative."

"I guess so."

"Or he could even be one of Kerrigan's boyfriends, for all we know. Hand me the phone. I'm going to call Ray."

I handed her the phone reluctantly. To me, driving and talking on the phone are things that are best not done together. Mary Alice disagrees.

"Hey, honey," she said, almost running a red light, would have if I hadn't screamed. "Your sister's going to be okay. They're keeping her overnight, but she's not showing signs of going into labor." A pause. "He is?" She looked at me. "He does?" She held the phone against her chest and said, "The sheriff's at my house. He wants to talk to us."

"To me?"

"Ray says both of us."

I looked at my watch.

"Oh, for Pete's sake, Patricia Anne. Fred's still stuffed with salmon. Probably asleep or watching a ball game."

I knew she was right.

"Okay," I agreed.

"It'll take your mind off Haley. You need to get the wedding cake to put in your freezer, too."

Actually my mind hadn't been on Haley until she reminded me.

Some of the sprinklers had already come on as we drove through Mary Alice's neighborhood. From the top of the mountain we could see thunderclouds pushing in from the west, though. That was what was needed to break the heat.

Sheriff Reuse was standing on the porch at Sister's house as we drove up.

"Been out to let up my windows," he said. "It's gonna storm in a little while."

He looked nice today. He was wearing light gray chinos, a faded blue chambray shirt, and Docksiders without socks. He looked like he'd stepped straight from a Lands' End catalog. Not bad. Not bad at all.

"You look spiffy," Mary Alice acknowledged.

"I've got a date. When Ray told me what had happened, I figured I'd better come by here first, though."

"Is Ray in the sunroom?"

The sheriff nodded and held the door open for us.

"He told you about the pearls?" I asked.

"He sure did. Smuggling's a federal offense, of course, but I want to get all the facts straight before I notify the authorities. Make sure that's what we're dealing with."

We walked down the hall toward the sunroom. Ray stuck his head out of the kitchen and asked if we wanted something to drink. Both of us wanted a big glass of water.

"Okay," Sheriff Reuse said, "let's sit at the game table. I can write better there."

Ray brought us our water and we sat down. I was in the chair facing west. The storm clouds suddenly blocked out the sun.

The sheriff got out his notepad and pen. "How many pearls would you ladies say you saw?"

"I didn't see any," Mary Alice said.

I tried to picture the Chinese checker board. "Eight. Maybe nine."

"On the table in Meemaw's trailer."

"Yes. In the commotion, one ended up in my pocket. I thought it was just a pebble."

"They had to come back from Bora Bora with Sunshine," Ray said. "But they could have been planted on her."

"I'll bet Buck Owens did it," Mary Alice said. "What do you know about him, Ray?"

"I don't think Buck would have done it, Mama."

"Wait a minute," I said. "Sunshine supposedly won this trip on *Wheel of Fortune*. I've never seen them give away a trip to Bora Bora."

"And Patricia Anne and Fred watch *Wheel of Fortune* every night," Sister said.

The sheriff made a note. "That'll be easy to check."

"And if she didn't," I continued, "then whoever sent her is in on the caper."

"The caper?" Sister murmured.

"Well, you know what I mean."

"All right." The sheriff seemed surprisingly agreeable. "Who could have sent her?"

"Eddie? Howard? Kerrigan? The man in the antique store?"

"What man in the antique store?" he asked.

I explained; the sheriff took notes.

"They all did it," Sister said.

Lord, we were back to that again.

"Did you find any connection between Dudley Cross and the Turketts?" Ray asked.

"Not so far. It would help if Sunshine would show up."

"She's scared," Sister said.

"She shouldn't be scared to come to me." Ray's voice was slightly bitter for the first time.

Thunder rumbled. We all looked up. Rain was advancing down the valley.

The sheriff turned back to his notepad. "About your fall, Mrs. Hollowell."

"I think I know who put the turkey there. I think it was Dwayne Parker. It was a childish warning, and Sunshine seemed startled when I told her about it. So did Meemaw."

"Maybe it wasn't a warning," Ray said. "Maybe somebody, maybe Dwayne, was trying to tell us

196

something."

The rain suddenly lashed against the window. Sister, who had been more subdued than usual, put her hands palms-down on the table. "Jed Reuse," she said to the sheriff, "you want to sit around here on your butt and have us solve your crimes? Okay, I'll solve this one for you.

"Kerrigan Dabbs and Buck Owens have got a pearl smuggling ring going. They're using my baby boy's boat to get the pearls which may get him in a lot of trouble, and they're using my baby boy's wife to bring them back into this country."

The sheriff smiled. "You just may be right." He put his notepad back in his pocket. "Guess I'd better make some phone calls." He paused. "Okay, Ray? You want to add anything else?"

"I've got nothing else to tell you, Sheriff. Call."

The sheriff went into the kitchen.

"What authorities is he talking about?" Sister asked.

"The FBI, I guess," Ray said. He drummed his fingers against the table.

His mother reached over and stopped him. "That's a terrible habit. Makes people think you're nervous."

"I *am* nervous," Ray admitted. But he stopped the drumming.

I was thinking about what Ray had said about Buck Owens. "What makes you think Buck didn't have anything to do with the pearls?" I asked him.

"He's too nice a guy. I bought his boat in a fair transaction, and he's been my dive master for three years with no complaints. He's just a good old country boy, Aunt Pat."

"Who happens to dive a lot in Bora Bora."

"It's his job." But Ray began to drum his fingers again.

From the kitchen we could hear the sheriff talking. In a

197

few minutes he came back into the sunroom.

"Did you call the FBI?" Mary Alice asked.

"I got their office. Somebody's supposed to call me in a little while. I gave them my page number because I've got a lady waiting on me to take her to the movies."

"The FBI," Mary Alice mused. "Do you know when I was married to Will Alec—or Philip"—she stopped to think and then shrugged—"anyway, we went to an inaugural ball and I danced with J. Edgar Hoover in an orange dress."

"J. Edgar Hoover was wearing an orange dress?" Ray asked.

"Not at an inaugural ball, son. I was. Orange knit. Looked good, too." She frowned. "I remember I thought he was Broderick Crawford at the time, and that he wasn't much of a dancer. Will Alec told me later it was J. Edgar Hoover."

"I read in his biography that he was a wonderful dancer," I said.

Sister thought about this. "Well, maybe it *was* Broderick Crawford. Couldn't even two-step. Just sort of shifted from one foot to the other."

"I hate it when men dance like that," I said. "Lazy dancing."

The sheriff cleared his throat. "I'd appreciate it if y'all would stick around. Somebody may call you in a little while."

I looked at my watch. "I've got to get home, but I'll stick around there."

"Fine. You need a ride? I'm going right by your house."

"I remember Edward G. Robinson was at the same party, but it couldn't have been him," Sister mused. "He was too short. Even in those elevator shoes."

"Thanks," I told the sheriff. "I'd love a ride."

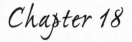

Chapter 18

THE STREETS HAD BEEN SO HOT THEY STEAMED AS the rain hit them. We drove through little pockets of fog on the way to my house. By the time the sheriff dropped me off, the heaviest rain was over. A typical Birmingham summer thunderstorm. But it had cooled everything down, washed the pollution from the air, and given the trees a good drink of water.

I let myself into the kitchen and found a note from Fred on the counter. He had gone to help Haley and Philip lift weights? That couldn't be right. Leap heights? After all those years of teaching school, I can read almost anything. But Fred's handwriting defies translation at times. At any rate, he was helping the newlyweds, which was nice.

There were two bills, an advertisement, a small manila envelope, and a *Time* magazine in the mailbox. The manila envelope was from our cousin Luke in Mississippi, Pukey Lukey, Mary Alice's nemesis. In it were a bumper sticker and a note. Luke, Jr., who was in the House of Representatives, was going to run for the Senate this fall. Would I please put this on my car. Name recognition, etc. Bumper stickers are not high on my list of favorite things, but hey, Luke was family. And who knows. Mary Alice might get to dance at another inaugural ball, this time with Pukey Lukey, Jr.

I put the bumper sticker on the coffee table, pulled off my shoes, and settled down on the sofa to read the *Time*. It was a special issue on the frontiers of medicine, and I made it through the first paragraph on how to keep senility at bay when the last twenty-four hours caught up with me, and I was sound asleep. No afternoon doze, but a middle-of-the-night zonk-out.

The doorbell must have rung several times before I came awake enough to know what it was.

"Damn," I grumbled, and turned over. Maybe whoever it was would go away.

But several rings later, when Muffin jumped up on me demanding that I do something, I got up and staggered to the door. I ached all over, still stiff from the fall over the damn turkey. My head ached from crying at the wedding; my feet ached from wearing heels. I was a mess when I opened the door and saw a smiling Kerrigan and Pawpaw. For a second I didn't recognize Pawpaw. It was the first time I had ever seen him wearing anything but overalls. In khaki pants and a knit shirt, he was much thinner than I had thought. His old shapeless felt hat was clutched in his hand.

"Hey, pretty lady," he said.

My face was black, blue, and green. My eyes were almost swollen shut, and my hair hadn't seen a comb since morning. I had to smile. "Hey, Pawpaw. Kerrigan."

"You were asleep, weren't you, Mrs. Hollowell. I'm sorry." Kerrigan, bright-eyed and bushy-tailed, looked anything but sorry. In fact, she was more glowing than ever. I could learn to hate this woman.

I nodded. "Is Meemaw all right?"

"She's fine." Kerrigan turned and looked at Pawpaw.

"My granddaughter was here early this morning and left something we need to get," he said.

"Sunshine left something?"

"A package, I suppose," Kerrigan said.

I shook my head. Granted, I'm not the best housekeeper in the world and the morning had been hectic, but I would have noticed a strange package.

"It's a little one," Kerrigan assured me.

"Haven't seen anything," I said.

"Then you wouldn't mind if we came in and looked." Kerrigan pushed right by me, followed by Pawpaw. I was so startled by their nerve that by the time I could have said, "Yes, I do mind," which I probably wouldn't have, they were halfway down the hall.

"She said she left it in the den," Pawpaw said. "She didn't say exactly where."

"You mean she wouldn't say," Kerrigan added.

"True. You should have done a better job, Kerrigan."

"There's nothing in the den," I said.

Pawpaw turned to me. "Sunshine said there was."

It suddenly dawned on me that he was hearing everything that was being said. "He can hear," I said to Kerrigan. Smart.

"He's got on those big hearing aids. Show her, Papa."

He turned obligingly. The hearing aids were made like a Walkman radio, but instead of ending in the little earplugs, these ended in brown plastic disks, the size of pocket calculators, behind and slightly above each ear.

"They work pretty good," he said. "I can still wear my hat, too."

"They make them smaller all the time," Kerrigan added.

"The sound's still tinny, though." Pawpaw tapped a fingernail against one of the disks for verification and nodded. "Tinny."

By this time we were in the den. "Listen, y'all," I said. "I haven't seen any kind of a package here."

"It isn't necessarily a package," Kerrigan stated, running her hand along the mantel. If she looked at her fingers to see if they were dusty, I was going to belt her one. What the hell were they doing, anyway?

And then I realized. Sunshine had told them she had left some pearls here. That had to be it. Some pearls that they didn't know I knew about. Some pearls that I'd better not know about from the intense looks on Kerrigan and Pawpaw's faces.

But that didn't make sense. Why would Sunshine have stashed pearls in my den? In fact, none of it made sense. How on God's earth had I, Patricia Anne Hollowell, a retired schoolteacher living a quiet life in Birmingham, Alabama, managed to find a body in a trailer at Locust Fork, fall over a turkey and nearly kill myself, and get mixed up with a bunch of folks who were smuggling black pearls in from Bora Bora?

The answer came in the back door—my sister Mary Alice carrying a large freezer bag. "I tried to catch you but you were already out of the driveway. Here's the cake. You forgot it and I don't have room in my freezer." She saw me standing in the doorway between the kitchen and the den, saw what must have been a strange expression on my face.

"What's going on?" she asked, putting the cake on the counter.

I shrugged. "Kerrigan and Pawpaw are here."

"Oh?" She walked to the door. "Well, hey, you two. What are you up to?"

"Sunshine told them she left a package here last night." I gave her what I hoped was a sufficiently warning glance. Subtlety is lost on Sister, though.

"What kind of package?" she asked.

"A small one," Kerrigan said.

"You mean she might have left some of the pearls here?" Sister asked.

Kerrigan and Pawpaw both paused. I closed my eyes and heard the sound of silence. Simon and Garfunkel had known what they were talking about.

"Could be, little lady," Pawpaw said.

"But why would she do that?" Sister was digging the

hole deeper. Didn't she realize that Kerrigan and Pawpaw were in on the smuggling or they wouldn't be here looking for the pearls?

"Shut up," I muttered to no avail.

"I mean Patricia Anne's bound to find them eventually and turn them over to the FBI."

I have an iron skillet I use for making corn bread. It was on the stove. I could get it and hit Sister over the head with it. That might shut her up.

Kerrigan was pulling the sofa cushions off. Good Lord, the junk. Change. A squashed magazine. How long since I'd dust-busted back there? "Here, Papa," she said, holding up a little drawstring bag. "Here they are."

Mary Alice turned and looked at me as the light dawned.

I nodded. "Deep doo-doo."

Pawpaw took the bag, loosened the drawstring, and shook the contents onto the coffee table. About a dozen black pearls rolled out. "Think that's it?" he asked Kerrigan.

"It better be."

"Well," Mary Alice said, "how nice. I'm glad you found them. Would you like a Coke or something before you go? Maybe a beer?"

"Pawpaw can hear you," I said just as enthusiastically. "Show her your hearing aid, Pawpaw."

He turned and showed her the plastic disks. Sister was thrilled, just thrilled.

"We have wedding cake, too," I said, starting into the kitchen. "Atomic bomb wedding cake." How to reach the phone and dial 911 without them hearing?

Kerrigan never gave me a chance. She was on her knees examining the pearls one by one, but she looked up and said quietly, "Sit down, Mrs. Hollowell. You, too, Mrs.

203

Crane. Papa and I'll decide about you in a few minutes."

"I think I'll get a Coke," Mary Alice said.

But Pawpaw was behind her. "I think you'll sit down. And your sister, too." The two of us obeyed immediately.

Kerrigan raked the pearls back into the sack, stuck them in her purse, and stood up.

"What do you think, Kerrigan?" Pawpaw asked.

"Don't know, Papa. I guess they'll have to go with us while we decide."

"I'm sorry but I have a dinner date tonight," Mary Alice said.

Pawpaw grinned. "Well, pretty lady, I guess some man's just gonna be stood up. We got some planning to do."

"I can't go anywhere," I said. "My husband will be back any minute."

"Then we'd better hurry. I guess you'd better show them some encouragement, Kerrigan."

"Let's go," Kerrigan said, pulling what looked like the biggest pistol in the world from her purse.

"Is that a real gun or a play gun?" Mary Alice asked.

Pawpaw came over and took her gently by the hand. "You know, pretty lady, you hadn't got biddy brains. Now get up off your fat ass before you find out whether that pistol's real or not."

Sister turned around, looked at me, and actually said, "Now look what you've done, Patricia Anne."

The old Chevy Bel Air was sitting on the street. We marched toward it in single file, Pawpaw leading and Kerrigan following with her purse. If I broke and ran, would she shoot?

"Don't be a fool and try anything," she cautioned, reading my thoughts.

"You're not going to get away with this," Sister said. "Tell them, Mouse. Tell them the FBI already knows about them."

"The FBI already knows about you."

Pawpaw and Kerrigan both laughed. "Don't be ridiculous," Kerrigan said. "It's Saturday. You couldn't get hold of an FBI agent if your life depended on it." She paused. "Which it does." They seemed to find this amusing and laughed some more.

Pawpaw opened the back door of the car. "You ladies get in. Kerrigan'll drive and I'll ride shotgun." They found this amusing, too.

"There's dog hair back here," Mary Alice said. "Bunches of it. And I've got on a new dress."

"Slip me the encouragement, Kerrigan."

Kerrigan handed Pawpaw the pistol. I looked toward Mitzi's house, praying that she might glance out of her window and somehow notice. The whole street seemed deserted, though. The thunderstorm had driven everyone in to TV screens.

"Just get in," Pawpaw said.

We did. Kerrigan got in the driver's seat and Pawpaw got in the front seat beside her. But he turned, facing us.

"There aren't any seat belts," Sister said, feeling around behind her, scattering dog hair.

"I wouldn't worry about it if I were you," Pawpaw said.

"Well, where are you taking us?" she asked.

Pawpaw turned slightly toward Kerrigan. "Where are we taking them, Kerrigan?"

"We'd better decide."

"How much time do we need?"

"Not much. I'm ready. If the fools have really called the FBI, I guess we'd better hurry."

"Take your time," I said. Pawpaw grinned at me. He looked like nothing so much as a friendly, pleasant fellow.

"Tell you what," he said to Kerrigan. "Let's go on out

to Locust Fork. Buck can collect Meemaw for us."

"So you *are* all in on it, stealing the pearls," I said.

"Mama doesn't know a thing about any pearls." Kerrigan turned onto the interstate ramp. "And Sunshine didn't until that damn fool broke into the trailer."

"Damn fool in there after our pearls," Pawpaw said.

"And you stabbed him?" I asked.

"Now, missy, there's no way I'm going to tell you I did or I didn't. Somebody sure did, though."

"How did he know about the pearls?" Mary Alice asked.

Kerrigan swung the car skillfully into the traffic. "What are we going to do with them, Papa?"

"Get rid of them, I reckon. It won't hurt to go on and tell them."

"Well, it's kind of a long story." Kerrigan passed an eighteen-wheeler and waved; the driver blew his horn happily. "Pawpaw and Buck worked this thing up years ago. When Pawpaw lost his hearing, he worked for a while for a company in Muscle Shoals that ships the nacre to the South Pacific. That's what they call the stuff they seed the pearls with, nacre. Buck worked for them, too."

"We decided to go into business for ourselves," Pawpaw added.

"Buck had made a couple of trips to Bora Bora by that time," Kerrigan said.

Mary Alice poked me and whispered, "I told you it was Buck and Kerrigan."

I poked her back. Hard. Here we were, kidnapped and being taken God knows where, and all she could think about was being right.

"We even bought a boat," Pawpaw said. "We were going to grow the things. But we found out how long it took."

"And anyway, there were thousands of them already

there just waiting to be harvested. That's why Buck sold Ray the boat, so he'd have more time." Kerrigan changed lanes and turned to Pawpaw. "I'm going up Old Highway 31, okay? These old fools just might have somebody looking for them."

Old fool was right.

"Listen, Kerrigan," I said. "Sheriff Reuse knows about the pearls and he's called the FBI. Why don't you let us out? You're just asking for more trouble."

"Because you're lying. Jed Reuse wouldn't know a black pearl from a sheep pill. And we're not going to hurt you, for goodness sakes. We just need some time."

"Where are you going?" Sister asked.

Pawpaw shook his head. "Hadn't got biddy brains."

Sister's eyes narrowed. "I do so have biddy brains."

"Just shut up," I whispered. And to Kerrigan, "How did you get the pearls back here?"

"You mean into the United States? I made a couple of trips to Bora Bora, and Buck came home a couple of times. I swear you can just walk in with them in your purse."

You probably could if you looked like Kerrigan, I thought.

"But what about when you got them here? What did you do with them?"

"Simple. Toddy Monroe handled them for us. He's Buck's half-brother."

The guy in the antique store. I knew it before she said, "He runs an antique store. That damn fool Dudley Cross worked for him part-time. The only thing we can figure is he heard Toddy and me talking about Sunshine bringing some pearls back."

"Or that Toddy Monroe fellow sent him out," Pawpaw said. "Squinty eyes." He looked disgusted. "Never have trusted that guy."

"Don't say that in front of Buck, Papa," Kerrigan warned.

"Is this Toddy Monroe taking off tonight, too?" I asked.

"I guess he'll have to now." Kerrigan turned onto an exit ramp.

Mary Alice grabbed my arm and motioned toward the traffic light at the top of the ramp. "If it's red, jump," she mouthed.

Jump? Ignore old bones, traffic, and a gun aimed at us?

But Pawpaw had also noticed the light. He turned and said, "Kerrigan was lying when she said we wouldn't hurt you. Try anything and you're dead meat."

Neither of us had a hankering to be dead meat.

At some point on the trip to the Turkett Compound, I realized why Dudley Cross had been so well dressed. He'd worked next door to a consignment shop. I don't know why that struck me as being very sad.

Chapter 19

AS WE PULLED INTO THE CIRCLE OF TRAILERS, the dogs came up, wagging their tails at the sight of the familiar car.

"I swear I hate to leave the dogs," Pawpaw said.

"Shoot them," Kerrigan said. What a doll she was.

"No way. I'll leave them some extra food and water. Eddie'll be out here looking for us. He'll see about them."

"Probably shoot them," Kerrigan said, getting out of the car.

Pawpaw opened the back door for us. "Y'all come on in my trailer. Kerrigan, come help me put some duct tape around their hands and feet. I don't want to be worrying about these two for a while."

"I have to go to the bathroom," I said.

"Well, I've got one right in my trailer you're welcome to use."

"And I'm thirsty, too."

"Well, missy, we're not mean folks. We'll give you a glass of water, too."

A light fog had crept up from the river. The sun was low in the sky, a murky glow. Because of the thunderstorm, it would be cooler tonight, but as those of us who have lived here all our lives know, when the sky looks like this, the heat will build up again the next day. This had been an afternoon-heat type storm, not a front moving in.

Mary Alice was being very calm. She stepped from the car and walked into Pawpaw's trailer without protest. Like me, she took advantage of Pawpaw's bathroom, drank the glass of water he offered, held out her wrists for the duct tape. Her only comment when I asked her if she was all right was a whispered "I'm thinking."

"What are you thinking about?" I asked her as soon as Pawpaw and Kerrigan left. For some reason, I thought she might have figured out a way for us to get out of this mess.

"I'm thinking about having a child."

"What?" I practically screeched it. "Listen, Sister, you've lost your mind. They did all kinds of things to that sixty-two-year-old woman who had a baby, all sorts of hormones and stuff. And I know good and well she had to lose weight and quit eating things like boiled peanuts that would make her blood pressure go up. And now she's got to go to the PTA all over again."

Sister was looking at me as if I were crazy. "I didn't

mean give birth to a baby, Mouse. Lord! How could you even think that? Been there, done that, thank you, ma'am. Three times."

"Well, that's what you said."

"I meant I was thinking about the last few days. Who have we been worried about?"

"Ray, Debbie, Haley."

"Our very grown children."

I nodded; she was right.

"And who," she continued, "got us into this predicament?"

"Ray?"

"No, Mouse. We got ourselves into this. We're still trying to mother our children too much. We need to let go more."

I looked down at my bound wrists and ankles. This was because we were mothers? "Listen," I said. "We may not have to worry about letting go. But if we live, we'll all go for family counseling."

"Even Fred."

I didn't answer that. Instead I asked, "What do you think the Turketts are going to do to us?"

"Well, they're not the most polite people in the world."

A slight understatement. I wondered what Pawpaw and Kerrigan were doing. I couldn't hear any noises from outside, but the air conditioner was groaning so loudly, it would have to have been a loud noise.

It was growing dark. There were no lights on in the trailer, but a mercury vapor light high on a pole lighted the whole compound and cast enough light through the windows for us to see. We couldn't see outside because of the high windows, but we could see inside the trailer well enough to walk around. If we could have walked around. Fred would be wondering where I was. He would have called Mary Alice's house. He wouldn't be alarmed yet.

"I'm hungry," Mary Alice said.

Somewhere along here, I lost track of time. I may have dozed some. So I have no idea what time it was when we heard the car drive in, heard voices outside.

"Must be Buck and Meemaw," Sister said. "I'm glad Pawpaw made him get Meemaw. She'd have been so hurt if her stud muffin had gone off without her."

"Hmmm," I agreed. But I was thinking of the two couples, Kerrigan and Buck, and Meemaw and Pawpaw. If they were going off together to start a new life somewhere, wouldn't the older couple be excess baggage for Kerrigan and Buck? Wouldn't it be simpler for them to go it alone? Especially if the FBI was after them?

I shivered, remembering how calm Kerrigan's voice had been when she said, *"Shoot them,"* about the dogs. But surely she wouldn't do Meemaw and Pawpaw any harm. They were her parents.

"Don't bet on it." It was a man's voice speaking right into my ear. I jumped so, I almost toppled over.

"What?" Sister asked. "What?"

"I think I just heard Gabriel."

"Don't be ridiculous. You're dreaming. You've been snoring for I don't know how long."

I hoped she was right.

The trailer door opened and Meemaw stepped in and turned on an overhead light. "Well now," she said. "Look who's here."

"Kerrigan and Pawpaw kidnapped us," Sister said.

"So I understand. They said you'd found out too much about their business."

"If that's what you want to call it," I said. "What do you know about their 'business'?"

"Know it's best to let sleeping dogs lie."

211

"God's truth," Sister muttered.

Meemaw sat down abruptly on the sofa.

"Are you all right?" I asked.

"Still a little weak-kneed." She ran the back of her hand across her forehead.

"Shouldn't have left the hospital," Sister stated.

"I'll be okay. Pawpaw needed me."

"Listen, Meemaw," I said. "I don't think you and Pawpaw should leave with Kerrigan and Buck." I hesitated and then said, "Gabriel told me."

"Bless his heart. I wondered where he'd been." She stood and steadied herself against the door. "You tell him I'll be fine and to stay in touch."

"No, I'm serious. Let Kerrigan and Buck go on. You and Pawpaw stay here. I'm sure you can work things out."

"Not hardly." Meemaw opened the door. "I just wanted to ask you to look after Sunshine for me. Tell her I'll be in touch when I can. Tell her I said 'A bushel and a peck.' She'll know what I mean."

I knew, too. That's how much I had told my own children and grandchildren I loved them.

"Wait a minute, Meemaw," Mary Alice said. "We're hungry."

"I'll send Pawpaw in," she said. And she was gone.

"Are you nuts?" I asked. "We're kidnapped, bound up with duct tape, God knows what's going to happen to us, and you're hungry?"

"Well, everyone isn't anorexic like you. I was just thinking while you were snoring that I'd like to be at the Redneck in Destin having boiled shrimp and slaw. And then a big piece of their key lime pie."

I had to admit it didn't sound bad.

The door opened and the light came on again. This time it was Buck Owens who stood there grinning. "Well,

well," he said. "You've stepped in a whole pile of it this time, haven't you, ladies?"

"Not as much as you have," Sister said.

"Hah. Tomorrow Kerrigan and I will be sleeping like babies in Toronto."

"Any particular hotel?" Sister asked. "We want to be sure and tell the FBI right."

"Sarcasm," Buck said. "I declare."

Pawpaw came into the trailer behind Buck and announced that everything was ready.

"Come on then, ladies," Buck said.

"Where are we going?" Sister asked.

"Not far."

"Because I have to go to the bathroom."

Buck looked at Pawpaw.

"I think they've got bladder problems," Pawpaw said. "But let them both go. Give them some water, too."

Buck laughed, but he took the tape off first Mary Alice and then me. My hands tingled as I held the glass of water; my legs shook as I walked to the bathroom.

"Okay, potty break's over," he announced as I came back.

"I'm hungry," Sister said.

"Dear Jesus," Buck said. "Ray always said you were a pain in the butt. He just didn't say how much."

Sister bristled. "Ray never said that."

"If he didn't, he should've." Buck took the tape from Pawpaw and secured our wrists again. But he left our ankles free.

"Let's go," he said.

Mary Alice and I didn't move.

"Want me to encourage them?" Pawpaw asked.

"No. They're going to cooperate." Buck leaned over and grasped my right shoulder and Mary Alice's left with his huge hands. "I said, let's go." We could smell butterscotch on his breath, so unexpected that we each hesitated, but only for a moment. The fingers clamped into our shoulders. We got up and walked out of the trailer.

Kerrigan and Meemaw were nowhere in sight. A white delivery truck with TODDY'S ANTIQUES painted on the side was backed in between Pawpaw's and Meemaw's trailers, though. This was where Buck led us.

"Get in," he said, opening the back door.

"Where are you taking us?" I asked.

"I told you. Nowhere much. Just a couple of cotton fields over."

"But why?"

"Neither one of them's got biddy brains," Pawpaw told Buck.

"Call the dogs," Buck said.

Pawpaw whistled, and Mary Alice and I made a dive for the truck. The double doors slammed shut behind us, and we could hear the men laughing and the dogs yelping.

"Mouse." Sister's voice was shaking. "They're going to take us out and shoot us, aren't they?"

"I'm not talking to you," I said. "I've let you push me around for sixty-one years, you hear me? Sixty-one years. And where do I end up? Dying in my bed like a nice decent person? Of course not. I end up on the floor of Toddy's Antiques delivery truck in some cotton field out in the middle of nowhere. And of course they're going to shoot us over some black pearls that when they first talked about them I thought was that perfume they sprayed on me out of the testing bottle at Rich's. Damn it to hell! And the skin's off both my elbows to boot."

"Lord, you don't have to be so snippy."

Someone, probably Buck, opened the front door of the

truck and got in. We couldn't tell who it was because the body of the truck was enclosed. If someone had broken into the cab, they still couldn't have gotten to the antiques. Smart for Toddy; not smart for us.

We heard gravel hitting as we went down the compound road. Then there was the smoothness of the highway, a left turn, and what could only be the rows of a cotton field. The bouncing and rocking brought us the knowledge that Toddy had been preparing a delivery when Buck took the truck. He also had not tied the delivery down well.

"Cover your head," Sister said, unnecessarily. My behind was already in the air, and my head covered with my still-taped arms.

Finally the truck stopped. Now, I thought, Buck will open the back door and take us out one at a time like that guy in the Tombstone Pizza commercials.

"I forgive you, Sister," I said. My last words on earth.

"I forgive you, too, Mouse."

We waited. Buck banged on the side of the truck, making us both jump. "Enjoy yourself, ladies."

And then there was silence.

After a few minutes, Sister whispered, "You think he's gone?"

"I don't know."

A few more minutes passed.

"I guess he is," I said.

"You think he really did what he said he was going to? Leave us in a cotton patch?"

"Buying time." I felt around. "Where are you?"

"Here. I think I'm under some kind of little table."

"I'm coming over there."

"Be careful."

"Keep talking," I said. "I think we can get this tape off

215

of each other's wrists."

"I'm over here. And what did you mean by you forgive me? I haven't done anything."

"Well, you forgave me back. What for?"

"Just in general."

"Me, too." My outstretched arms hit something soft and squishy. "What's that?"

"My stomach, you fool."

"Hold your arms out, then. If I can find the end of the tape, I think I can get it off."

It took me about fifteen minutes since I was working with taped wrists. Sister had me loose in about five.

"Now we need to get out," I said. I crawled toward what I thought was the back door, lucked out, and touched the handles. They wouldn't budge. I rattled and shook them. Nothing.

"They won't open," I said.

I heard Sister crawling toward me. *Whump*. Right into me.

"Sorry," she said. "Let me try it. There should be a button you push."

I moved to the side.

"Here it is," she said.

I could hear her pushing the button, jabbing at the button. Nothing. We both knew the truth before Sister voiced it. "We're locked in. They've fixed the door so we can't get out."

The rest of the truth hit us about the same time. We were locked in an enclosed truck parked in a cotton field, therefore in the full sun, during an August heat wave. How diabolical. By ten o'clock the next morning, we would be dead.

"Someone will find us soon as it gets light," I said. But I knew better. No one would be looking for a white delivery truck. And even if they got a helicopter out to search, and they spotted the truck and sent someone to look into it, by that time it would be too late.

✿ ✿ ✿

We talked about a lot of things that night, my sister and I. We talked about Mama and Papa and Grandmama Alice. We talked about old loves, old grievances, childhood trips and traumas. We didn't talk about Fred or Haley, or Ray, or Debbie. We couldn't. We didn't talk about tomorrow, or about how we had ended up in this truck. We simply talked about a shared lifetime, swimming at Blue Sink, how I got caught on a tree root while I was sliding down the clay slide and ripped off my bathing suit. Trips with Pukey Lukey. Aunt Lottie's peach cobbler.

And sometime during the night, we went to sleep and slept deeply on the hard floor of the truck. There was nothing else we could do.

I was dreaming I was jitterbugging with my high school friend Cynthia Collins. I could hear "In the Mood" plainly. "My turn to lead," I said. Cynthia grabbed my shoulder. "Mouse, wake up. We can see."

"I'm not asleep," I said.

"Then open your eyes. We can see."

For a second I was confused, still dancing to "In the Mood," and then I was back in the truck rubbing sleep out of my eyes and trying to sit up. Every bone in my body ached. "I don't think I can move," I groaned. "I need aspirin quick."

But Sister was poking me. "Look, there's a skylight."

I looked up very carefully, having to move my whole body since my neck seemed frozen in place. She was right. Light was pouring through a small skylight toward the cab end of the truck. "How come we didn't see that last night?" I asked.

"We were under a ton of furniture."

I looked around. Tables, chairs, hat racks. Toddy's business must be doing well.

"You can climb through it and get us out," Sister said.

"No, I can't. I told you I can't move. Try the door again."

Mary Alice crawled by me. "We don't have much time, Mouse. It's already hot as a firecracker in here."

She was right. The back of my neck was wet with sweat. I watched her jiggle the door handle, push against it, even kick it. She must be in better shape this morning than I was.

I looked back at the skylight. It wasn't very large, but there was a possibility. "Didn't some UPS guy win an award for coming up with the idea of skylights in their trucks?"

"What?" Mary Alice gave the door a final vicious kick.

"UPS or somebody had a contest to make delivery more efficient, and this guy came up with skylights so they could see what they were doing. They also have the locks fixed so you can't be locked in."

Sister was rubbing her foot. "Then tell me the secret, Miss Jeopardy."

"Buck and Pawpaw rigged the lock. They've got it plugged up or something."

"I figured that out."

We sat on the floor and looked at each other. Then we looked at the skylight.

"I don't have a choice, do I?" I asked.

"Not much time, either. It's hot in here."

"Well, let me study it a minute. I'm not even good and awake yet."

"You can stand up on that table"—Sister pointed in the

general direction of some jumbled antiques—"put a chair on top of it and go right out."

"That skylight doesn't let up and down. Besides, you broke my arm last year. I don't think I can pull myself up."

"We'll bust the glass out."

"Burst, not bust."

"Like I said, we'll bust the glass out and I'll get up on the table and shove you. And how the hell was it I broke your arm? I wasn't even there."

"It was your fault."

Mary Alice grabbed the arm I had broken and snatched me up off the floor. "Crybaby. Mama always said you were the crybaby. Now get up off your crybaby butt and let's get out of here."

"I'm up."

We extricated the table from the pile of antiques and cleared a place for it under the skylight. It looked like a sturdy table. It would have to be. Mary Alice's two hundred fifty pounds and my hundred six was a considerable amount of weight.

I climbed up on it and felt the skylight. "I think it's that Plexiglas stuff. We'll still have to hit it with something hard, though. And it's going to fall back in here and cut us."

"Wait a minute. I'll find something." In a moment Sister was back with a tin tray and a hat rack. "Hold this over your head and hit it with this."

"Damn it, Mary Alice. This is a two-woman job."

She climbed up on the table with an agility that surprised me. The table wobbled but held. "Okay," she said, "I'll hold the tray over us. You jab the skylight."

"I can't see with the tray over me."

"Dammit, Mouse. Just aim." Which I did. The end of

the hat rack went through the skylight with a loud popping sound. No Plexiglas rained down on us.

I looked up. There was, indeed, a hole in the skylight. The plastic had been pushed upward and out around the hole the hat rack had made. It took a lot more work and a lot of sweat to clear the whole opening.

We sat down on the table and rested a few minutes, but we knew we didn't have much time to waste. I got a straight chair, placed it on the table, and put my hands on either side of the skylight. It should be big enough, I figured. But the metal was too hot for me to hold.

"Hand me your slip or something," I said. "This is burning me."

"It's a new one. All silk. I paid a fortune for it."

"Dammit."

"Well, I did." In a moment Sister handed me her panty hose. "These'll work better, anyway. They've got two sides."

I grasped the sides of the opening and pushed my head out. My shoulders made it okay. "Shove!" I told Sister.

I came out of that truck like a jack-in-the-box, slid down the windshield, bounced off the hood, and landed on a couple of cotton bushes which sound soft, but which are nothing but sticks and sharp bolls.

Dear Lord, I might never move again. I lay there with the bright Alabama sun shining down on me from the deep blue Alabama sky and thought, There it is, Patricia Anne. You didn't think you'd see it again.

"Mouse!" Sister beat on the side of the truck. "Are you okay? Come let me out!"

"I'm okay," I yelled. I wasn't, of course. I was burned, cut, bruised, dehydrated. You name it. But I was looking at the blue, blue sky.

❋ ❋ ❋

Getting Sister out turned out to be a problem. I finally found a couple of rocks and was beating on the locks when I heard something click.

"It's the safety button," she yelled. "Move. I think I can open it now."

And she did, crawling out into the cotton field. Hugging me. Wanting to know what I'd done with her good panty hose.

We stood in the shade of the truck for a few minutes, trying to decide which way to go.

"Maybe Buck left the keys in the truck," Sister said. It was a great idea, but, of course, he hadn't.

"Let's follow the truck tracks," I suggested. "He turned off a road not too far back."

So that's what we did. It hadn't seemed far the night before in the truck. Walking in the sun was an all-new ball game. The field seemed to stretch forever.

"We'd have died just as well close to the road," Sister grumbled.

But eventually we did come to a road, one of the farm-to-market roads that Alabama politicians are so fond of building. And whoever they are, they have my vote. I have never been so glad to see a strip of asphalt.

"Now what?" Sister asked as we sank down beneath an oak tree. An acorn landed in my lap. The first sign that summer was ending.

"Wait, I reckon."

"I'll bet a car doesn't come by here once a day. Maybe there's a house nearby. I've just got to have a drink of water."

"I'm going to wait," I said. "Fred and the FBI will find us here."

"Fred?"

"Fred." Tears filled my eyes and rolled down my

sunburned cheeks. "Fred will find me."

"I'll bet he *is* worried," Sister said. "I'll bet they all are."

This just made me cry harder.

I was wiping my nose on the hem of my skirt when an old pickup came around the curve. A man and woman were in the front, the back was loaded with turnip greens. We waved frantically and they stopped.

"What are y'all doing out here?" the woman asked. "Did you have a wreck?"

"We got kidnapped," Sister said. "And we need some help. Have y'all got any water?"

The woman looked sympathetic. "You poor things. There's a watermelon or two in the back. If y'all don't mind riding back there, you can bust one of them."

"Who kidnapped you?" the man asked.

But we were already heading for the back of the truck. And that's how we arrived at the nearest gas station, surrounded by turnip greens, watermelon all over us.

Chapter 20

"I CAN'T BELIEVE IT, I JUST CAN'T BELIEVE IT," Haley said.

I was lying on my den sofa with the heating pad on my back, an ice cap on my head, and various and sundry ointments smeared on my cuts and burns. Fred had pulled a kitchen chair in and was sitting beside me feeding me Jell-O which I was perfectly capable of feeding myself, but, hey, don't knock a good thing. And it *was* a good thing.

Mary Alice and I had been checked out at the emergency room, declared fit but slightly dehydrated, and sent home to rest and drink fluids. She was getting the same attention I was; I had just talked to her.

"They won't get far," Fred said.

"But smuggling black pearls. That's wild." Haley held out a glass of iced tea. "Here, Mama. Take another sip of this."

I sipped.

"Actually," I said, "it all fit together. Pawpaw's a scientist, albeit a rocket scientist, and when he went to work for the company that furnishes the seed material, he saw an opportunity."

"Probably didn't have any trouble talking Buck and Kerrigan into going along with him."

"Probably not."

Fred held out another spoonful of Jell-O. Bless his heart. I had slept some the night before; he hadn't. And he looked it.

"I want you to go take a nap," I said.

"I'll sleep tonight."

Stubborn man. Lovely man.

"And it was Kerrigan who murdered the Indian guy," Haley said.

"Yes. Other than chiefing, Dudley Cross worked at Toddy's Antiques. Which is how he learned about the pearls and decided to help himself."

"But what about Sunshine? Was she involved?"

"Not with the murder. I don't know about the pearls. I think the sheriff and the FBI will have some questions about that." I looked over at Haley. She looked tired, too. Not surprising considering the last few days. "I'm sorry about your flight," I said.

Haley shrugged. "Don't worry about that one minute, Mama. We can go tomorrow just as well. We kept thinking of things we hadn't done, anyway."

Fred yawned.

"Sweetheart," I said. "Why don't you and I go lie down on the bed for a while. Haley needs to go see about Philip."

"Do that, Papa. I'll check on you later this afternoon."

He agreed so quickly, Haley and I smiled at each other. And he was hardly on the bed before he was asleep.

I had thought I would sleep, too, but I lay there with a "busy mind" as Mama always said. I finally sneaked out of bed, got the phone, and went into the bathroom so I wouldn't wake Fred up. I sat on the toilet, feet propped on the tub, and dialed Mary Alice.

"You okay?" I asked when she answered.

"Feeling pretty good. I'm surprised. How about you?"

"Not too bad. How's Debbie?"

"She's okay. She spent the night in the hospital, so she didn't know about our disappearing act."

"Just as well. How about Ray?"

"He and Sunshine are closeted in his room. They've been there about an hour. The sheriff was here questioning her for a long time."

"I figured as much. Did she have any interesting answers?"

"I don't know. They were in the living room with the doors closed. Tacky." The call-waiting beep sounded. "Wait a minute, Mouse," Sister said.

The minute turned into five, but the bathroom was cool, and an emery board was on the counter. My fingernails needed work, Lord knows, from that Plexiglas skylight. So when Mary Alice said, "Mouse?" I jumped.

"That was Sheriff Reuse. Buck and Kerrigan were arrested while ago in Kentucky. Kerrigan's being charged with murder."

"And Meemaw and Pawpaw?"

"Weren't with them."

"Dear God," I said and hung up. I shuffled over to the kitchen, got out a quart of Baskin-Robbins pralines and cream from the freezer, and tried to straighten things out in my mind. Ate almost the whole damned thing and still felt like I'd been hit over the head with a two-by-four.

❁ ❁ ❁

"Sunshine came in that?" I pointed toward the old green car parked in Sister's circular driveway. "That's Dwayne's car, isn't it?"

Sister nodded. "She and Ray are still talking. Come on back to the sunroom."

I followed her down the hall. "I'm stiff as a board. How about you?"

"I'm feeling pretty good. I'm surprised Fred let you out, though."

"He doesn't know I'm gone," I admitted. "He had to go over to the plant to check on some things and I took off." I sat down in a wicker chair. "Actually, I don't feel as bad as I took."

"Good," Sister said, looking me over.

"And no Meemaw and Pawpaw?"

"That's what the sheriff said."

"I was afraid of something like that."

Mary Alice stood up. "You want some Coke?"

I followed her into the kitchen and patted Bubba Cat, who was asleep on his heating pad. He stretched and yawned. "What about the pearls?" I asked.

"I didn't know what they were," Sunshine said. She and Ray had walked into the kitchen so quietly we hadn't heard them. Sunshine looked as if she had been crying. "Dwayne had to tell me. He'd just seen an article about black pearls in *National Geographic* while he was waiting for the dentist."

Sister handed me my Coke and offered one to Sunshine

225

and Ray. They both said no.

"Here, Aunt Pat." Ray pulled out a chair for me. "You look like you need to sit down."

"I feel better than I look," I said again. But I sat down at the kitchen table. Sunshine and Ray pulled out chairs and sat, too.

"Sunny's been telling me what happened," Ray said. "How she got involved in the murder."

"I wasn't involved in the murder, Ray." Sunshine frowned at him. "I told you that."

"Well, I'd like to hear about it." Mary Alice sat down with a Coke. "The whole time we were locked up in that truck I kept telling myself there was a logical explanation for how I got there. But I couldn't figure out what the hell it was. One minute I was delivering an atomic bomb wedding cake and the next minute I was halfway through the pearly gates."

"I'm sorry." Sunshine took a paper napkin from a holder and began to pleat it like a fan. "I'm sorry about hiding the pearls at your house, Mrs. Hollowell. It just suddenly seemed like a good safe place for them while we tried to figure things out."

"Not safe for us," I said.

"I'm sorry," she said again, wiping her eyes with the corner of the napkin.

I wasn't letting her off that easy. "Kerrigan and Pawpaw said you told them where you'd hidden them."

"I had to. They found me at Dwayne's and said they would do something to Ray if I didn't." Tears overflowed Sunshine's eyes.

"What I want to know," Mary Alice said, "is how long this pearl thing's been going on."

"I don't know." Sunshine began to cry in earnest. Ray, who hadn't said a word, handed her another paper

226

napkin. "I should have known I hadn't won a free trip to Bora Bora, though. And now everything's all messed up."

I looked over at Ray. There was a deep sadness in his face I had never seen before. Whether his golden girl was telling the truth or not, and I seriously doubted it, things would never be the same.

"Start at the beginning, Sunny," he said.

"You mean winning the trip?"

Ray nodded.

"Well, I got this letter from the *Wheel of Fortune* people that I'd won a trip to Bora Bora. Meemaw and I had entered one of their viewer games and I just thought now that's good luck, things evening out because I'd just lost the Miss Alabama contest and was down in the dumps." She glanced at Ray. "And I really believed it. The letter was registered and everything. I had to sign for it, and it said *Wheel of Fortune.*" Sunshine took another napkin and began pleating it. "It was the grand prize and all I had to do was call a 1-800 number and claim it. So I did, and the tickets and all came in the mail with a certified check for $2,500 for expenses."

"And you didn't question any of this?" Sister asked.

"No, ma'am. Everything was registered and certified so I just went on the trip. I had a great time and I met Ray and fell in love, hook, line, and sinker." Again she looked at Ray, but he was picking at some invisible spot on the table.

"Anyway, after we'd been out a couple of days, Buck came up and asked if by any chance I was kin to Kerrigan Dabbs. He said he saw on the roster that I was from Locust Fork and he used to be in love with a girl from there named Kerrigan Turkett and he thought she was married to a man named Dabbs for a while.

"Well, of course, I was tickled to think what a small

world it was, and when I left, after the wedding, Buck gave me a present to take to Mama, a box about the size that thank-you notes come in, all wrapped up pretty. He said it was a necklace for her to remember him and the good times. And he said it was right nice, so I should put it in my carry-on bag."

I looked over at Ray to see how he was taking this story; he had his arms folded and was drumming the fingers of each hand on the opposite arm.

"Is that what you did?" Sister asked.

"Yes, ma'am. It was wrapped like a present. Had a pink ribbon on it."

"Which you unwrapped," I guessed. Actually, it wasn't much of a guess.

"I did. When I got home." Sunshine fanned herself with the pleated napkin. "I just wanted to see the necklace and, instead, it was all these old pebbles. I thought Buck was being ugly to Mama because maybe she'd ditched him. I showed them to Meemaw and she thought so, too. So I just put them back in the box, most of them. Meemaw kept several of them to glue on a lamp. She makes real pretty lamps, you know. Gets them at garage sales and dresses them up."

Ray got up and got a can of beer out of the refrigerator. "Tell them about the murder, Sunny."

"I was there." Sunshine pulled her hair back as if she were going to put it in a ponytail. "Dwayne and I was there."

For a moment there was silence. Then, "Dwayne? Is that why you sent Meemaw for the soup? Because Dwayne was coming?" Mary Alice asked.

Sunshine's grip tightened on her hair. It gave her a defiant look. "Well, he called that morning so sad about the party the night before and me marrying Ray and I said

228

come over and we'd talk. But I knew Meemaw wouldn't like it. So Dwayne parked in the woods and came in as soon as Meemaw left." Sunshine let go of her hair. It fell around her shoulders as blonde and shiny as a Nice 'n' Easy ad. I wondered what color it was.

"And there we were just talking when we heard a car drive up. I thought it was Meemaw, that she'd forgotten something, but it was Mama's car. She and a man got out and went to her trailer. Dwayne said he'd better go, but I said she didn't know we were there and wouldn't come in Meemaw's trailer anyway. So we kept on talking." Sunshine paused. "He was real upset."

Ray turned up his beer and drained it. "I think they can figure out the rest, Sunny."

"I can't." Mary Alice leaned forward. "How did the man get killed in Meemaw's trailer instead of Kerrigan's? And what were they doing there together?"

"Well, Dwayne and I were in the bedroom because I wasn't feeling well, you know. And I was showing him the pebbles and he was saying 'God, Sunny, these are black pearls!' when we heard Mama and the man coming across the yard and up the steps. The man was yelling that Mama was holding out on him and she was yelling that she was sick and tired of being blackmailed by a pissant fake Indian."

Sunshine paused. "And then we heard a whump and someone running down the steps and Mama's car starting. When we looked around the curtain, we saw the man. That Dudley Cross."

"And you ran," I added.

"We didn't know what else to do. We were so shocked, we couldn't think."

"And you took the pearls."

"Well, the box was still in my purse."

229

"And, of course, you remembered to get your purse," I wanted to say. "And did Dwayne know you borrowed someone's pickup to come see what Toddy would give you for them?" But the look on Ray's face stopped me. Right now he didn't need anything else. It would all come out in time. Instead I asked, "And the dead turkey and the note threatening Ray?"

"Dwayne's idea. We were hoping y'all would be scared away while we were trying to decide what to do." Sunshine wiped her eyes again. "We didn't want anything else to happen."

A call to the sheriff would have sufficed, I thought. I also thought, very generously, that those two kids in that trailer would have been scared to death , and that, given the circumstances, running like hell must have seemed the only thing to do.

The kitchen was quiet. Bubba Cat hopped down from his heating pad and got in Sister's lap, purring loudly. Down the valley we heard the first rumble of late afternoon thunder. The four of us were caught in a moment of waiting.

And then Sister said, "Sunshine, Meemaw said to tell you 'a bushel and a peck.' "

Sunshine held out her hands, looked at them, and then brought them to her face.

Chapter 21

"YOU LET ME KNOW EVERYTHING THAT HAPPENS, now, as soon as it happens," Haley said the next morning as we were waiting for their plane to be called. "And how Ray's doing. We've got a phone in the apartment. I'll call you as soon as we get there and give you the number, and

Philip's got e-mail at the university. Or you can fax us. I'll give you that number, too, when I call."

"Ray's going to be okay," Sister said. "I think he's feeling right now like he stepped in a bed of fire ants, but he's going to be fine. He says he's going back to Bora Bora soon as he can. Without Sunshine, of course."

"Think she's in much trouble?" Philip asked.

Sister shook her head. "Nothing she won't slide right out of."

"I'm just glad Meemaw and Pawpaw are okay," I said. "I was so relieved when the sheriff called and said they were in Muscle Shoals."

"Pawpaw'll probably slide right out, too," Sister said. "You watch."

The man was a smuggler, had kidnapped us and left us to die. But, for Meemaw's sake, I was hoping her old stud muffin did get off light. He had refused to leave without Meemaw and, in my book, that earned him a lot of points. As for Kerrigan and Buck, I hoped they threw the book at them. And they probably would. And Toddy? I thought of the pleasant, handsome young man in the antique store. I hoped he sang like a bird for the authorities. Toddy in prison was not something one wanted to picture.

"If you've forgotten anything, I'll mail it," I promised. "And Muffin will be fine."

Philip shook hands with Fred. "I'll take good care of Haley."

"Your uncle took good care of me," Sister said. "Of course he died real early. He had a mint of insurance, though. A mint. It never hurts to have a lot of insurance. You know?"

Philip laughed. "I'll take care of it, Aunt Sister."

"Where's Ray this morning?" Haley asked. "I was

hoping he'd be here."

"I didn't wake him up. At three o'clock, he was still in the den watching TV."

"Well, I'm so sorry about Sunshine and the whole mess," Haley said.

"I wish we'd gotten the chance to see her fly-fishing and dancing," Fred said. I looked to see if he was serious; he was.

The plane was announced, and there were the last hugs, the last kisses, the last promises to take care of Muffin. And then our Haley was gone with her new husband to a foreign country.

We walked back through the airport slowly. "Let's stop and get something to drink," Sister said. "There's something I want to show you."

We sat in an Orange Julius booth. Fred held my hand.

"Here," Sister said, handing us an envelope.

"What's this?" Fred asked, taking it.

"Your Christmas present. Open it."

He handed it to me.

But Sister was telling us what it was before I could get it open. "We're going to spend Christmas in Warsaw. It's tickets on the Concorde, three seats together. They're little, but, Mouse, you're little, and, Fred, you and I can scrunch up. We'll be over the Atlantic in nothing flat. And then we've got two whole weeks in Warsaw, the three of us. I've got all sorts of stuff planned for us to do besides seeing Haley and Nephew. We'll go to museums and concerts and on day tours. Won't it be wonderful? Can you think of anything more exciting?"

"It's wonderful," I agreed. "Thank you, Sister." I kicked Fred, who was thinking.

Over the noise of the Orange Julius, we could hear the roar of a plane taking off. Haley.

Fred rubbed his leg and smiled. "I can't wait."

Vulcan's Buns

Henry wishes to thank
Mary Jo Deaver for this recipe.

1 package active dry yeast
¼ cup warm water
½ cup butter
2 T. sugar
2 eggs, plus 1 yolk, beaten (preserve extra white and set aside)
1 t. oregano
1 t. basil
1½ cups shredded cheddar cheese
½ cup chopped dried tomatoes
1 cup milk
5 cups all-purpose flour, sifted 3 times
1 t. salt
olives or feta cheese

Dissolve yeast in water. Cream butter and sugar. Add yeast, eggs, oregano, basil, cheddar cheese, dried tomatoes, and milk to the butter and sugar mixture. Add flour and salt. Knead 5 to 8 minutes on floured board; place dough in a greased bowl, covered; put in warm place and allow to rise one hour or until doubled.

Stir down risen dough, turn onto a lightly floured surface, and form into smooth loaf. Divide into about 36 balls, each the size of a large walnut.

With a finger, punch a hole in the center of each ball and put either one pimento-stuffed olive or a chunk of feta cheese in each hole; pinch closed. Place 2 balls, pinched side down, in each cup of a greased muffin tin. Mix the extra egg white with 1 T. water and brush it on the tops of the buns. Allow to rise 45 minutes to an hour until almost doubled.

Preheat oven to 375 degrees. Bake 7 minutes; brush again with egg-white mixture and bake another 7-8 minutes, or until golden brown.

Yield: 18 buns